Seven Houses

♒

Other Books by Alev Lytle Croutier

Seven Houses

A Novel

ALEV LYTLE CROUTIER

ATRIA BOOKS

New York   London   Toronto   Sydney   Singapore

This book is a work of fiction. Names, characters, places and incidents are products of the author's imagination or are used fictitiously. Any resemblance to actual events or locales or persons, living or dead is entirely coincidental.

ATRIA BOOKS
1230 Avenue of the Americas
New York, NY 10020

Copyright © 2002 by Alev Lytle Croutier

Photo credits: Cem Ener; author photo—Jerry Bauer

Library of Congress Control Number: 2002104587

ISBN: 0-7434-4413-2

First Atria Books hardcover printing September 2002

10 9 8 7 6 5 4 3 2 1

ATRIA BOOKS is a trademark of Simon & Schuster, Inc.

For information regarding special discounts for bulk purchases,
please contact Simon & Schuster Special Sales at 1-800-456-6798
or business@simonandschuster.com

Designed by Jaime Putorti

Printed in the U.S.A.

For Sadri and Yümniye,
my parents

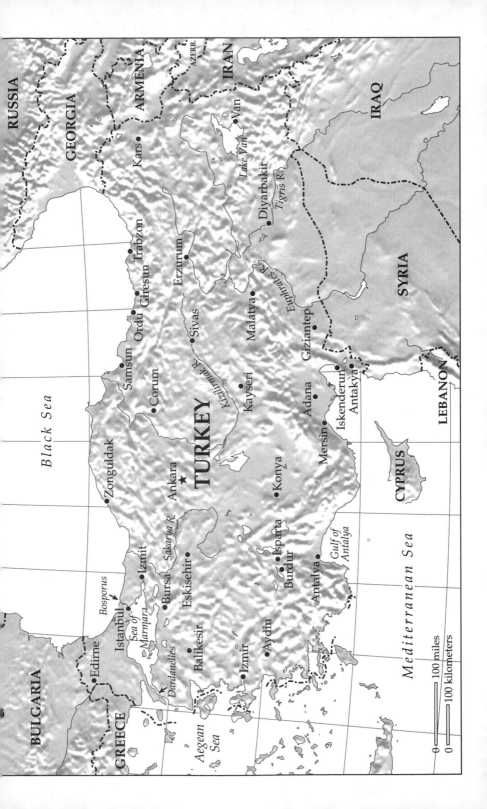

The Ipekçi Family Tree

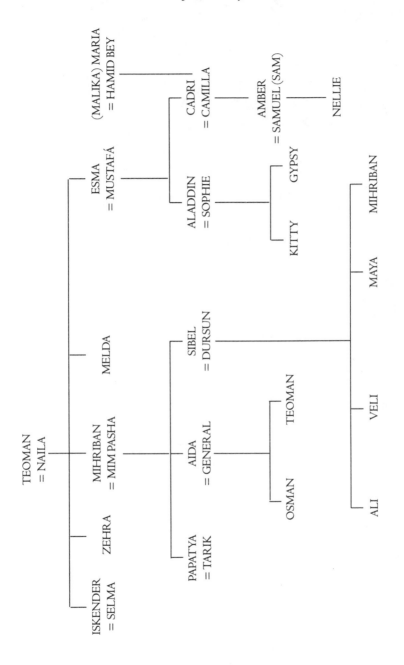

I

The Delicate
State of Silk

֍

And one should know beforehand that there will be in
this book no terrible adventures, no extraordinary
hunts, no discoveries, no dangers; nothing but the
fancy of a slow walk, at the pace of a rocking camel,
in the infinite bliss of the pink desert.

PIERRE LOTI, *The Desert*

The House in Smyrna

❧

(1918–1952)

A hundred secrets will be known
When that unveiled face is shown.

FARID UD-DIN ATTAR, *The Conference of the Birds*

࿔

Once upon a time here in Smyrna, a city as ancient, as
infamous as the Olympians, the gods had changed a
king's daughter into a myrrh tree for incest. The love
child of the trespass, Adonis, was born from her split trunk.
Adonis was so handsome that Aphrodite, the goddess of beauty
herself, coveted him as a lover. Her only true love—really. Fruit
of a tree.

Since then, a deep, palpable humming pervades this town of
rumors. Maybe even before; surely even before. All you have to
do is listen; you can hear so much—the birth cry of St. Paul,
the scratching of St. John's quill as he labors over his Gospel.
Through the fog, you can see Anthony and Cleopatra, lost in
horrid ecstasy, floating on a golden barge. Or a vision of
Mother Mary deep in meditation, mourning for her dead son.
It all happened here. They all occupied this same land, along the
same sea. The Aegean. The mirror of mirrors.

On the Bay of Smyrna, the air always smells of rotten

plankton and salt. Clusters of debris lap ashore, gathering into sculptures of melon skins, cardboard, and kelp. Across the Bay, one can imagine Homer gleefully watching Odysseus' ship gliding across and composing the *Odyssey*. Four thousand years later, in retaliation, the defeated Greek army burns all memories, at least so they say—all in this lifetime. But the smell of ancient ashes never subsides. The embers from time immemorial still smolder beneath the Bay (some say, the lava of Hades' breath), long before the great fire almost consumed all. Here, it's unavoidable. To go back in time. Live past lives. Be other people. Some places store memory. This is one.

ᘒ

I was built in Smyrna in 1890, the year of Esma's birth. A slender, many-roomed Victorian dwelling of wormwood, snuggling against an unworldly, umbrageous rock—obsidian, rumored to have been lowered down from the sky, the rock that gave the district its name: Karatash, or Black Stone.

My balcony and the windows are covered with trellised fenestration that conceal the harem apartments, where jasmine and pomegranate vines cling to the facade, and linden and horse chestnut provide shade from the intense Aegean sun reflecting off the most saline, the most turquoise water. A *cayique* perpetually bangs against a hollowed marble dock, remnant of an ancient Lydian water temple. (The outbuildings were built much later to house the servants and also served as kitchen and laundry rooms.) The stained glass dome of the *hamam*, vapored from the steam of the baths below, against the skyline stands like the silhouette of a forlorn Mughal villa. Different than the rest.

Some believed that the myrrh tree in the garden was the actual Adonis tree. They believed it was sacred and left votives and humble offerings on the double altars of its fracture. Others took it to be an ordinary myrrh cracked by natural forces. Over the years, its persistent branches stretched into Esma's room and, later Amber's, becoming the center of mysterious incidents. Like the time a hand burst out holding an amber egg with a frozen moth inside; or when a triple lightning burned it to the ground, only to be reborn the following night.

For the first twenty-eight years of my life, a Pasha lived here with his harem—three wives, servants, and various offspring. The Pasha himself stayed in the boathouse annex, conducting otherworldly business—an unscrupulous and selfish rich man concerned only with his vanities—cultivating the white opium poppy and belittling the unfortunate. After the exile of the Sultan, the Young Turks, declaring him guilty of unspeakable crimes, exiled him to the purgatorial ice lands of Kars where, they say, he committed even worse things. They say, old dust never settles. That's another story.

But the women in his harem, suddenly finding themselves with no sustenance and nowhere to go, and no resources to keep me, had to flee in a terrible hurry, abandoning their splendid clothes, fine china, and priceless furniture. It was at this juncture that Esma arrived, just at this instant of their imminent departure as if on a theatrical cue.

A hazy winter afternoon. Shrouded and veiled in black, she arrived with a go-between, walking three steps behind her older brother Iskender, her identical sons—Cadri and Aladdin—clinging to her skirt. (You can always tell orphans.) And three paces behind followed her two maids, Gonca and Ayşe, heads down, furtive steps.

Like an apparition, Esma shuffled from room to room, as if talking to the invisible faces on the walls, touching and smelling objects that caught her eye, chanting prayers. She opened the doors to every room cramped with dusty episodes, the basement resonating with the constant sound of dripping water from the *hamam*. *Tip, tip, tip.* How to fill the emptiness, revitalize the neglect. Yes.

Out the back window of the third story, she saw the black rock, the cracked tree. Felt the tremor from the lapping of the waves against the stilts. Her eyes watered. She had come home. Love at first sight.

"The house could be yours for nothing," whispered the go-between, who followed her into the attic strewn with the indulgences of women from a distant era—balloon pants, satin slippers, gauzy veils. "Number One Wife desperate to get rid of it all. They have nowhere to go. They must leave the house by dawn."

Esma ignored her and returned to the harem where the women offered her coffee and confections. They watched intently as she removed her kid gloves, squeezed a sapphire ring the size of a hazelnut—a last vestige of her dwindling jewels— and slid it on the Number One Wife's finger.

It fit perfectly.

"Payment for the house," Esma told her.

The older woman began to weep, tried kissing her hand in gratitude, which Esma would not allow. Esma put her arms around her until she stopped sobbing.

From that moment, we were inseparable. Even after death.

❧

Each time she heard the story, "What happened to the harem ladies?" the child Amber would ask.

"A sad story. Their eunuchs took them from village to village in distant lands of Europe and displayed them as curiosities. Sort of like dancing bears."

"Why?"

"Because they were nameless and had no other place to go. No one to claim them. They were stolen from their homes so long ago that no one remembered them anymore."

ॐ

"I can't allow you to live in a strange city all alone! In a big house like this! Who is to protect you? What will the people think?" her brother Iskender paced, exasperated . "Stop being so stubborn and come to the plantation. The boys must have other men around! A woman shouldn't stray from her family."

"This is my home," Esma was firm. "I must stay in Smyrna. Where my husband brought me as a bride. I have the girls to help me. We'll find our way somehow. God is on our side."

"The girls" were the two Kurdish odalisques, the servants— Gonca and Ayşe they were called—gifts from Esma's brother-in-law, the kind-hearted Mim Pasha. I heard their story repeated many times over and over again. How four little girls, sisters, lay half dead among the debris of a massacred village in the region of Mount Ararat. With admirable heroism, Mim Pasha had saved their lives and brought them back as gifts for his wife, Mihriban, and for Esma. Now they belonged to the family.

"It breaks my heart to see you like this. But you've been stubborn since you were born. Remember, though, no one knows what fate brings. If you ever change your mind, you always have a place with me," Iskender told Esma before returning to the silk plantation in Bursa. "Rain or shine. Don't forget to remember."

"I'll remember."

Could they have known as he rode away? Could they have known how fate would soon pull them apart?

꿍

The picture of the stern gentleman in the white turban, old enough to be her father, instead belonged to Esma's husband, recently deceased. Forced to sell her finest jewelry in order to survive after his death, except a precious stone or two and a few yards of sumptuous *crepe d'amour,* crepe of love. Genuine silk. The finest of all for a wedding gown. But never to be her own. Nor her daughter's—at least on her wedding.

How do I know these things, these inconspicuous things that fill the space between the walls? I listen. I listen to everything, their synchronous breathing at night, the whispers hissing like snakes on all floors, the sounds of their dreams, the impact of cat paws against the cool cellar leading to the subterranean catacombs under the city. I listen to the children's voices echoing and expanding in the tunnel beneath; as if the Minotaur of the cave is blasting fire out of its nostrils. Or the streetcar tooting its horn like a capricious siren each siesta afternoon; and at midnight, the night watchman's stick striking the cobblestones. *Tap, tap, tap. Rap, slap, clap.*

Every night, when the town sank deep into slumber, the distant voice of a woman's singing seemed to be rising from the depths of the Aegean. *"Dandini, dandini, danali bebek. Elleri kollari, kinali bebek."* My little babe, whose arms and hands are hennaed, oh my little babe. She was singing a lullaby to an infant resting in a secret place nearby. Gone mad when her baby died, she'd buried it in a golden cradle, then offered herself to the waves.

Esma always lay in bed listening to this lullaby, muffled from having to pass through a curtain of fog—itself an apparition. The lullaby stole quietly into her room, wrapping her entirely in its fluid warmth, whispering, *"Dandini, dandini, danali bebek."*

When the boys asked if it was the sirens singing, she told them, "There's no such thing. I once thought I heard the sirens, too, when I was a child but later, later they disappear. Ignore them; they're nothing but the spit on the devil's tongue. Their songs wreck ships and those they lure meet unspeakable deaths. Once, a man named Odysseus tied his men to the mast so the sirens' voices could not entice them. It was the only way."

I listen and peer into their lives—the most private moments when they close their doors and retreat into their private dreams. I even see those dreams. I read their thoughts. Make judgments. Even manipulate situations when I can. I, too, have frailties.

I look in on the boys asleep in the room they share. And just outside, Gonca, the ageless odalisque with the mustache whose eyebrows meet in the center, the one who dries bat wings for good luck and pulverizes sea horses, sleeps mattressless on the floor—the only way she knows to sleep—and breathes in harmony with the children. After a while, their exhalation takes on colors, continuously dissolving into new shapes and spiraling into a common dreamworld and fall, fall and fly, fly and float.

Before retiring, Gonca always locks up her sister Ayşe. The moon makes the young girl wild and frenzied. As if in heat, Ayşe stirs like a boa, aroused by her own writhing. Her bed in the night, always drenched, her jasmine vapor always steaming.

On the third floor, Esma untangles her waist-long hair, her sunken eyes flashing like jewels in the dark, her heart flying, and her mind alert. She parts the curtain, seeing no one. Suddenly, the muezzin's voice rises like a raptured bird as he begins the midnight prayer. Esma covers her hair, rolls out her prayer rug from Ushak. Stands facing the East, joins her fingertips, and mumbles incomprehensible incantations. She rubs her face slowly, her willowy figure crumbles, her forehead kisses the floor.

The curtains billow in the wind, the balcony door parts, and wearing a fez and a pelerine, Süleyman arrives like a Valentino sheik. His hawk nose bespeaks of his wild nomadic ancestors who once crossed the Urals and the Altays. He is like a lean mountain gazelle, open chested, his heart pulsing with his smile. Pearl white teeth, searching eyes.

Quickly, Esma rolls the prayer rug under her bed. Adjusts her hair. Süleyman's the only man to see her without her veil outside of her family. He removes his fez and bows to her. Then, they sit on the heirloom Louis Quinze couch, to watch the moon, if there is one in the sky. If not, the stars, if it's a clear night. Their heartbeats harmonize. And their breath.

Now and then, distracted, they glance at each other instead of the sky. They peer with burning eyes, but hands, hands they restrain. Never to touch, the vow they made, the vow that allows them to come together like this every night. For years. To love like this. Without a blemish.

He asks her, "Esma, Esma, why won't you become my wife?"

Esma casts down her eyes. Still in widow's black.

"Once there was, once there wasn't," she begins with the words that begin all stories. "Once, a nightingale loved a rose. And the rose, aroused by his beautiful song, woke trembling on her stem. She was white, as all roses were in those days. But she had tears of dew."

"The nightingale came ever so close and whispered, "I love you, rose," Süleyman continues where Esma left off, "which made her blush, and instantly pink roses burst out of their buds.

Then, the nightingale came closer. Allah meant the rose never to know earthly love but she opened her petals and the nightingale stole the nectar. In the morning, the rose, in her shame, turned red, birthing red roses."

"Ever since then, the nightingale visits her nightly to sing of divine love, but the rose refuses, for Allah never meant a flower and a bird to mate. Although she trembles at the song of the nightingale, her petals always remain closed," she terminates.

A moment of silence.

"Three apples have fallen from the sky," they then recite in unison. "One belongs to the storyteller, one to you, and one to me."

And one to the walls that can hear and see all.

They laugh. This is how all the stories end. Until the dawn prayer, they recite poems and stories to each other like this, to compensate for all they cannot fulfill. No one else will know of their secret world in which love is transcendent and suffering a joy.

Each time they part Esma gives Süleyman a handkerchief full of something, like the most delectable Turkish delight from Hadji Bekir. Süleyman bows, puts on his fez, and blends into the dusk. Esma unrolls her prayer rug, joins the tips of her fingers together, falls prostrate, an enigmatic smile on her face. In that position she stays, curled like a fava bean, on her prayer pod.

This happens every night. Well, almost . . .

In the morning, Gonca, finding her mistress like this, covers her with the silk blanket woven of millions of cocoons, her brother Iskender's gift—the finest silkmaker in Bursa, they say. The one who will arrive that day and will change their lives.

Gonca can smell man in the room. She knows. Like me, she knows but will not talk. She knows, if others were to know, they might stone her mistress. Or cause other unspeakable torments.

Esma could be defaced, and the man, exiled. She can't forget the image of the woman she once saw in the desert, buried up to her neck in the sand and her accomplice up to his waist, left to the vultures of kismet.

As the night predators flee the sun, a new cast of characters, the yogurt-man, the rag-seller, the bundle-ladies pass by, staring at me. I could sense they are imagining a procession of ghostly images, as if a veil has been drawn over this timeless face. House of dreams, they whisper to each other.

In daylight, legitimate this time, Süleyman arrives again rowing his *cayique*. Şükrü, the running boy, greets him at the dock and leads him to the Learning Room—piled with old maps, peculiar medical instruments that once belonged to the boys' father—a great scholar, everyone says—the serried, dusty volumes, almost murmurous with accumulated meaning, arranged meticulously along the high walls.

But the most compelling object for the boys is a skeleton for their anatomy lessons. It's of a very short person they have endearingly named "Yusuf." They tell stories of him before he became a skeleton.

Dressed in their black suits, they approach Süleyman and kiss his hand. He pulls their ears affectionately; then, all of them sink down at a low table with intense male seriousness. Süleyman knows how to draw them to himself.

The boys wait silently as their teacher slowly stirs his tea. *Clink, clink, clink. Slurp.* Cadri always dreamy, Aladdin restless twirling his pencil.

They recite verbatim the previous day's history lesson. The conquest of Constantinople. How their Great Sultan, Mehmed the Conqueror, stretched oiled sleds across the Galata and slid his ships into the Golden Horn, vanquishing the ancient city of the Byzantine Empire.

"And when did this occur?" Süleyman asks.

"1453," Cadri effortlessly replies before the question mark. "When the crescent broke the cross."

"Does anything make that date special?"

"Yes, that was the event that ended the Middle Ages. The Islamic people overpowered the Christians. They turned the churches into mosques."

Or they recite how their great admiral Barbarossa was losing his fleet in the Mediterranean until a crescent and a bright star, Venus really, formed in the sky, a divine omen that changed the course of history. It takes a heavenly incident like this to change fate. Any fate. Anywhere.

Or the story of the *croissant*. How the Turkish invaders were advancing toward the gates of Vienna with their crescent and star banners and how the bakers of the city concocted crescent-shaped rolls to warn their people to mobilize. Odd, how this common breakfast pastry once saved Europe from the sons of Allah. If the Turks had succeeded in passing through those gates, imagine what could have happened to the Western civilization!

Süleyman makes them repeat: *Calligraphy is a spiritual geometry manifested by a physical instrument or device, strengthened by constant practice and weakened by neglect.*

Cadri copies the words slowly in ornate calligraphy—from the back of his notebook, to the front—and from right to left, the way his mind moves, from right to left. The way it would be the rest of his life even when everything changes. From right to left.

But Aladdin's eyes, they wander far, counting every ship leaving the harbor. Forty-seven. Forty-eight. Forty-nine. Words don't interest the boy. The magic of numbers forming and re-forming themselves. He is already far into his calculus. Eyes drifting across continents, across constellations.

"Where do your eyes wander, my son?" Süleyman asks.

"What is beyond the Aegean?"

"The Mediterranean."

"And beyond that?"

"The Atlantic Ocean."

"And beyond that?"

"America. The unknown continent Cristophe Colombe discovered."

"What about the Red Skins?"

"They were already there."

"So, how could he discover a place if people were already living in it? It would be theirs."

"You see the truth, my boy."

A pandemonium outside. Veiled women arrive in their *cayiques* paddled by their eunuchs or in *phaeton* carriages. They can hear the voices from the learning room.

"*Yo-ho.*"

"*Yo-ho, yo-ho,* Esma. Are you home?

The girls take the guests' bundles up to the *hamam* and the food they brought to the kitchen. The women remove their veils. Esma kisses each on both cheeks and, sitting at the edge of her seat, serves them freshly ground Turkish coffee in thimble-sized cups.

"How are you?"

"Fine. And yourself?"

"*Maşallah.* No complaint."

"And the boys?"

"They, too. Just fine. And your household?"

"Not so fine. That spoiled new wife throws jealous tantrums."

"Pray tell."

"Oh, she's a young blossom, you know. Not keen on men's nocturnal wanderings. She will soon compromise."

An older woman weeps. "My sons joined the army."

"*Vah, vah!*"

"But the war is over."

"They say there will be another one."

And so on. And so on.

They scurry up the stairs into the *tepidarium*, remove their clothes—everything—put on high wooden clogs, wrap themselves in soft Bursa towels before entering the vaporous sanctuary. There, they stay all day, camouflaged in the silver mist, all breasts and hips, ladling water out of marble basins, rivulets of henna running through the small gutters, scent of lilac and muguet mingling with the foul odor of muddy depilatories, their hollow voices bouncing off the walls muffled by the steam to the skylight as pink as Turkish delight. They wash, they scrub each other, buffing the skin with pumice and loofah, extracting noodles of dirt that swim in the rainbow-colored water, running under their feet like freshly hatched tadpoles.

In a private corner, the old women pour blue powder into copper pots and rinse their white hair with indigo to achieve a fluorescent sheen. Afterward, they wash their underwear with small cakes of the same in marble sinks.

They watch each other. The older women watch the bodies of the young girls; it gives them pleasure. Yet, they are jealous of the luminescent skin, the unnursed breasts, the unspoiled vaginas. The young girls wear evil-eye charms on their ankles or wrists to protect themselves from bad spells. Transfixed on clusters of cellulite, the infinite forms of breasts, the w-shapes where the legs meet, the children gape at everyone.

These women, chefs of depilatory, masters of lemon paste, slap patches on their pubis, arms, legs, even the crevices inside nostrils, inside ears. Yank out all hair, whimpering in pain. God created woman without hair. Only after the great sin her hair grew like other animals. It's the memory of her shame. Any sign of it must be obliterated.

ॐ

So, this is the daily life here, more or less, day after day, but today things are slightly different because Iskender is visiting from Bursa. He has come to persuade his sister to take her boys and come back to the silk plantation in Bursa where he is convinced they would be safer since there are rumors that the allied forces intend to occupy Smyrna.

Meanwhile, he is doing a bit of business. Ferret, an associate who comes to call on him, steals into the washroom on his way up the stairs, peeks into the *hamam* through a hole on the wall that he himself has pried. His arteries burst as if filled with noxious gas. Watching the women's private nudity, his breath grows leaden, his hands slide into his trousers—shaking with grotesque contortions.

For months, he's been pursuing Esma's scent through the corridors, inhaling the rooms she had recently walked through, licking the walls, fondling the drapes. A man of such lickerous and unsavory intentions.

Around noon, steaming bodies sprawled out on the cool tiles. The beautiful male voice of the muezzin resonates outside—way outside, in a world unkind to them. It rises into the heaven as if he is drinking the song of its deity. In unison, the women raise their palms, standing in a circle, mumbling mysterious prayers.

Meanwhile, in the enormous cellar, the girls work, their hands deep in flour and eggs. They roll huge circles of dough, paper thin, stack the circles on big trays, layering with eggplant, pistachio, figs. The running boy, Şükrü, rushing to the brick furnace down the street, a tray in each hand held above his head like some Corinthian caryatid, his perfect balance, his golden sinewy arms, his blond mustache making the girls giggle and blush.

Gonca flushes at the sight of him but he's got the hots for her curvaceous sister Ayşe. He sneaks through the watchman's path and comes to Ayşe's window each dawn, on his way to the bakery. Bars separate them but only at arm's length. She bares her breasts for him, one at a time. Sometimes he brings her grape molasses and she lets him touch her nipples and tweak them. Sometimes tahini. They coo and gurgle unimaginable ecstasies that awaken the roosting doves.

Iskender has invited the Ferret for *mezes* and *raki*—the transparent liquid that the dervishes call "white writing," or invisible ink. The Ferret, squishing the seeds out of a plateful of olives with his fat fingers, watches out the window, the boys waving at Süleyman's disappearing *cayique.*

"The boys need a better education," the Ferret tells Iskender. "Why don't you send them to the Sultaniye school?"

"My sister prefers a private tutor. Süleyman is a clever lad. Educated. Inventive. The boys like him."

"But an empty pocket," Ferret says. "With holes in it. Hair down to his shoulders, clothes like those degenerate Frenchmen. Libertine ideas admittedly borrowed from the Young Turks. Bad example for the boys whom I myself hope someday to parent."

"Ah!" Iskender takes a long sip of his *raki*, avoids the insinuation. He won't disclose to this impudent his plans of taking his sister back. "Süleyman is a fine lad. Sincere. Honest. Well mannered. Nice."

"Only if one is blind to vice."

"Meaning?"

"Well, there's talk . . ." A wry smile. The Ferret whispers something in Iskender's ear.

Iskender's eyebrows meet in a frown. He asks the Ferret to leave.

⁂

That night, Iskender reclined in front of a blazing brazier, smoking his secret affliction while he watched a ghostly procession parade endlessly across an invisible screen. His pain stopped, all edges dissolving into a continuous flow. Whispers throughout the city stretched like taffy. Strains of music in distant rooms, runaway phrases. Deep bass of the fog horns. The lamenting woman's lullaby as she rocked her golden cradle. Invisible hands reached out of the walls and caressed him. Everything he touched became an extension of his own extremities.

All night long, as he swam through a corridor of silk, as the children and the servant girls slept. Süleyman arrived at the usual hour at Esma's room. They sat across from each other whispering because they knew of Iskender's sentience, that he could sense things in other rooms.

Iskender indeed heard them although he could not make out the words. Their poetry sounded to him like the seventeen-year locust falling from the sky he had heard in the Far East. He had journeyed to Isphahan from where he joined camel caravans to the distant reaches of the Silk Road, Samarkand, Tashkent, and Bohara, carrying *The Travels of Marco Polo* under his arm, searching for clues on the origins of the Turkish civilizations. He had even dared cross the Takla Makan, the desert of irrevocable death dreaded by all travelers, journeying to Uygur—thanks to his camels, possessing a secret knowledge of springs, who led him to mysterious sources of life-giving waters and eventually to the great wall of China. There he had been stricken by an ailment that made him delirious and he was treated with strange needles they stuck into his body, as well as opium, an affliction that accompanied him through the rest of his life.

At dawn, still awake, Iskender rose absently to the sound of prayer and looked out the window. Against the cool darkness of the obsidian, he saw the silhouette of a man gingerly ascending the invisible steps. So much poetry in that vision, but as a patriarch he had obligations. He could not allow the family to lose face.

Esma was kneeling down in prayer when she heard the firing—three shots. She ran to the balcony. The smell was familiar to her, the smell of burning gunpowder seasoning the night. The smell of her father's factories. The smell of her childhood. Saltpeter and sulfur.

Who? Who? Who? She heard the golden owl. Her beloved's totem. A rifled silhouette barely discernible stood above the obsidian. *No, dear God, no!* Then, she saw Iskender descending. Pain filled her chest. All the doors to the outside closed. All expressions locked inside her. She passed out.

༃

As the new day began, everything seemed normal on the surface. The peddlers barking, the girls waking up, the running boy Şükrü shoving coal into the furnace, Iskender at breakfast, feta and olives. A *cayique* arriving. But instead of Süleyman, as it had been until that morning, Iskender ushered the young Doctor Eliksir into Esma's room. Somber.

A sheet was stretched across her bed to prevent the doctor from seeing her face. Through a hole in the sheet, he examined, his scythe-like fingers groping for her privates. A pelvic exploration by feel. Gonca's hand guiding to lessen the pain, he slid inside Esma, digging for evidence.

Esma wept and Gonca did, too, on the other side of the curtain.

The doctor shook his head. "You're misinformed," he told Iskender as he walked out the door. "There is no evidence of any misdeed. Your sister is a virtuous woman. Always has been."

The boys wanted to know why their teacher did not come. And why their mother remained in her room and why they would not be allowed to see her. Although Esma silenced her tears in her pillows in order to protect her sons, they could sense something pitiful.

Gonca fed them copious amounts of Turkish delight to lessen their loneliness. She cut their hair. Showed them how to fold paper boats, float them in the water, then set them on fire. Aladdin drew maps. Cadri wrote poems in careful calligraphy. Each sank into his own desert.

Iskender retreated to his room, closed off the curtains to sunlight, fed the coals until the embers whispered through an iridescent glow. Esma had buried her face in the pillows when he had tried to apologize. He knew she would refuse to come with him. He might never see her again. He squeezed into his amber pipe a black paste smelling like manure. He swallowed the smoke, sank deep into the velvet oblivion. In his hand, he clutched the handkerchief that Süleyman had dropped. Inside was an egg-shaped piece of amber. He held it to candlelight and saw a moth escaping its cocoon. The eye of the insect was still open, although the wings were folded back inside. How incredible to see something that existed so long ago arrested in the midst of metamorphosis!

Soon, he drifted off into a dream that even the quiet sobbing of his sister, directly above, could not disturb. It sounded like another siren's song, Esma's cries and whimpers. As if the *imbat* wind was filtering the voices of the lamenting Trojan women from the Dardanelles. The women who had lost their men. No song more beautiful than grief.

At dawn, Iskender left. He'd never smile again until a very old man.

❧

Esma wept in her room for months. She wanted to die but could not endure the thought of abandoning her sons. Every soul must confront the lament of loss. This life is but the curse of our desires.

Gonca read spiderwebs; she read pebbles and coffee grains. "So much darkness in your heart," she told Esma, peering deep into her cup. "Azrael, the angel of death, is perched on your left shoulder like a vulture. You're trying to reach someone on the other side but it's not possible because that someone has not yet crossed to the other side. I see him walking on a bridge. I see an unexpected reunion. But I see worse things before that. Dark clouds over a burning sky. Oh, mistress, pray for the winds to stop. Pray."

The Ottoman Empire and Germany were defeated at the end of the Great War and with the signing of the Moudros armistice in 1918, the Allied forces began the occupation of Anatolia. They parceled off the glorious Empire—the great lands stretching from the Caucasus to the Persian Gulf, from the Danube to the Nile. They invaded Istanbul. The British occupied Urfa and Antep and the East. The French claimed the province of Adana and the South. Italian units quartered the interior province of Konya and all the way down to Antalia. All that was left was an interior terrain.

On a gloomy day in May of 1919, Greece invaded Smyrna. A cyclone appeared in the sky, twisting the city's fate.

At this juncture, as the Ottoman parliament dissolved and the Sultan yielded to the wishes of the Allied forces, a voice resonated all across the nation, campaigning along the Black Sea, shouting, *"Independence or Death,"* a phrase which became an infectious slogan on everyone's lips. The people put all their hope in their new hero, the commander of the Lightning Army, the hero of Gallipoli. His name was Mustafa Kemal.

So came the Independence war. Everyone took to arms, even children and grandmothers. People who had lived together for hundreds of years, who had mingled so many seeds that it was impossible to tell them apart, suddenly turned mean. Turks, Armenians, Greeks, Albanians, Kurds, Jews, Rums. Foreseeing the future, many old and wealthy Levantine families left, taking their wealth. Whole armies were maddened by contaminated grain. Families were broken; brothers killed brothers (how could it be!); friends betrayed one another while Greek soldiers cruised the streets, deafened by the wailing of spirit voices.

꒦

The men were gone from Smyrna. Even the running boy Şükrü was no longer around to watch over the family. One day, shaving his head, he slung a sack across his broad shoulders, stopped for good-byes before going off to the front. Gonca and Ayşe each wept privately. One for love, the other for lust.

With no one watching over them now, the women boarded me up from the inside. The girls kept vigil behind tightly closed lattices for bread and yogurt from black marketers, as the opportunists gnawed their way around town like hungry rodents, taking advantage of misfortune.

When a neighbor's maid was shot while hanging the laundry, Esma prohibited the boys from going on the roof terrace. They sneaked up anyway, to watch the ships with different flags in the harbor—how could a boy resist such? A great orgy of colors splashed across the sky, crimson and black, like Gonca's paper ships they used to set aflame. Smell of gunpowder suffused the air, lingering, potent like the smell of skunk. Cannon shots in the distance. Shrapnel. Dead horses. Screams.

On one occasion, lowering a basket from the third-floor window to receive some provisions from a street peddler, Gonca was astonished to pull in a stewing chicken. She excitedly presented this rare commodity to her mistress.

They did not know who had sent it but since it was the boys' seventh birthday, Esma decided to make Circassian chicken to celebrate. They still had the last season's walnuts in the deep cellar. As she reached inside the thin carcass to pull out the entrails, her hands felt something hard and metallic. It was a key. How absurd. Why would someone put a key inside an emaciated chicken?

She washed the key and polished it. It was a well-crafted key.

"What will you do with it, Mistress?" Ayşe asked Esma.

"I don't know." Yet a strange instinct made Esma keep the key though she did not know why. She put it in a mother-of-pearl box where she kept her hairpins on her dressing table.

The children were restless. They had now taken to playing underground where subterranean arteries, from the times the Greeks pirated the Aegean, meandered across the entire city. This humid darkness now belonged to the children of Smyrna. They hid inside the enormous cisterns, where once sacrifices had occurred, that had doubled as sewers since the Roman days. Rumors of hidden treasures enticed them immensely. But rumors of slimy prehistoric animals that lived in those oily waters kept them from wandering too far into those forbidden passages.

It was dark and damp and scary down there but secret and they could pull their pants down, show their "organs" to one another and sometimes even be daring enough to touch because it felt good to touch things in the dark.

They waited for the streetcars that made the walls shake as if suffering a seismic tremor and the sounds of the tracks groaned like a trapped Minotaur. Convinced that a giant beast was pursuing them, the children managed to work up hysteria, and with rampant adrenaline, plunged upstairs to find refuge under their mother's satin arms.

Two men arrived carrying a lovely walnut wardrobe that had miraculously survived the danger outside.

"But who has sent me this wardrobe?"

They told Esma that it was from her brother Iskender. They said he had found it in the city of Saffron where craftsmen excelled. Esma refused to believe them at first; it seemed incongruous that at such time of war and famine her brother would bother sending her a gift like this, even if it was to ask her forgiveness. People did not even have enough bread or coal.

But Gonca read their coffee grains and persuaded Esma to accept the enigmatic wardrobe. One should never turn down a gift. From the way they labored up the steps, it was obviously heavy. Esma asked them to open it but they said it was locked.

"What good is a locked wardrobe?" Ayşe complained. "We can use it for firewood, I guess."

"We can't even find a locksmith at a time such as this."

But that became unnecessary. That night, as Esma kneeled on her rug praying for her dead lover, only one thought invaded her mind. She felt him so close that it was as though he was in the room, near her. She felt his presence. She could almost hear him whispering her name.

"Esma, Esma."

It was something between thrill and fear. The euphoria of incertitude.

"Esma, Esma," the voice repeated, erasing any doubt in her mind as to the identity of its owner. She had never seen a ghost but her mind was open.

"Süleyman!"

At first, it seemed to be coming from inside the walls or from the rustling of leaves outside but as her ears became attuned, she heard the tapping inside the wardrobe.

"The key," the voice whispered. "Please, hurry!"

"The key!" Trembling, Esma searched for the box. The key. There.

The key fit perfectly into the lock. She opened the wardrobe.

Instead of a transparent ectoplasm, Süleyman stepped out flesh and blood, dressed in a khaki uniform with brass buttons that glistened in the dark. He gasped for air.

"I've been in there for days, it seems, but I've lost all track of time. My senses are dulled."

Despite the fatigue that painted dark circles under his eyes, despite the gauntness from undernourishment, despite arthritic joints from the dampness of war, he exuded an unworldly radiance. Something had hardened his jaw, saddened his features, bridled his tongue but he was no ghost. He reached out and touched Esma's face.

"I thought my brother . . ."

"Only to warn me he would, if I showed my face to you again."

"I'd given you up to the holy martyrs," she began to cry.

"Thank heaven you've appeared to me like one of the seven sleepers of Ephesus."

He removed his high-collared tunic, his astrakhan hat. His hair shaved like a *Mehmetcik*, a Johnny Turk, a soldier of the armed forces, bitter fate for a pacifist. For anyone, really. Especially for Süleyman.

"I'll sacrifice the fattest sheep in Anatolia," she told him. "I'll protect you."

"No fat sheep left in Anatolia," he laughed ironically. "You don't know what a miracle it was to find even a chicken. But, please, give me something to eat, dear heart. My soul is about to leave my mouth."

The cellar smelled of warm milk and cinnamon. Gonca was stirring *salep*, a warm pudding made from the *Orchis mascula* root. When she saw Esma breeze into the kitchen, she sensed that something unusual ailed her mistress but kept quiet, fearing the words might spoil the spell. She watched Esma hastily gather things on a tray and run upstairs.

Süleyman voraciously gulped down the fermented root, devoured the dark bread. Later, she poured water from the copper pitcher for his ablutions. Starting from the right, working to the left, she washed his hands, his feet. He wiped her tears.

Blessed heaven. Oh, yes. That night, Süleyman was emanating a fervor as in the paintings of the Divine; flames poured out of his body, invigorating everything around him. The tingling in the air, the song of silence was even more alluring than the singing of the sirens. Contagious, it washed her all over. He reached out to Esma, consumed her with his gaze.

Esma and Süleyman forced themselves to sit down on the Louis Quinze couch like the old times, with distance between them. They were not to touch. They stared at the sky to calm themselves. This privileged them to witness a miracle. They saw something that night no one else had ever seen. They saw, instead of one, double moons in the sky. So it seemed. Saw them approach each other weaving through the fast moving clouds. Closer and closer they came, like the moons, their radiance increasing as they were enraptured in a constellation of unconsummated passions.

In her room, Gonca also saw the double moons. She knew it was an eclipse—for her, an ominous sign. She smudged the boys' bedroom with juniper branches. To protect them from the evil eye, she lit a candle to Aesculapius, the heathen healing god, and let it burn till it expired.

Down on earth, Esma unrolled her prayer rug, though it was past the prayer time; she peeled off her clothes just like in the *hamam* and concealed her nakedness with a piano shawl before lying down on the rug and opening her legs away from the obsidian rock.

Süleyman bent his knees and touched his forehead to hers. Mutable like ever-changing colors of the sky, the patterns and colors of the shawl, the rug, the floor tiles inextricably blended, free of contours. They began moving at the speed of dark.

For hours and hours.

Never a greater blessing.

Never a more ardent prayer.

Knowing it was the last.

Before sunrise, Süleyman vanished.

❧

From that day on, Esma surrendered herself to prayer. It was like she'd gone mad. Like other women who go crazy over war. All day long, bending her frail body up and down so much that she shrank into a skeleton, then began swelling like a starving child. In the mornings, she threw up. At night, out of exhaustion, she collapsed.

At dusk, when Gonca came to cover her, she felt her mistress's forehead for fever, counted her pulse, and thought to herself. "Oh, great Goddess. What shall we do?" She knew Esma was with child. She was certain, having midwifed the *Imam's* daughter and other girls before. And, I knew as well, maintaining all pretense of peace while the war ravaged my skin. I tried to spare the ones inside me. I was well built, resilient.

Nightly, the Ferret, that old creep who had brought so much misery to Esma, prowled outside, milky eyes protruding from his fecent face like a predator circling his prey. He strained to hear the murmurs inside, contracted his nostrils, his eyes leaped out of their sockets into private interiors. He was like a disease, chrome yellow and mephitic. One time, he urinated on the outer walls, marking his territory. If I had tears, I'd cry. If I had a voice, I'd swear. If I had hands, I'd slay. As providence would have it though, the nightman caught him in the act and kicked him away from the wall with his staff. Beat him to the ground. *Tap, tap. Slap, whap.*

"Son of a whore. Shove off. Go piss on your mother, will you?"

It must have been around the same time when a soldier delivered a letter through the kissing window, a small opening for the delivery of messages. Scribbled on tar paper. "Promise, you won't utter a word to anyone, the apple of my eye," she told Cadri as she handed him the letter. "Read this to me. Read"

The boy read with easy fluency:

In the mountains, I carry orders. The earth, my bed. My roof the sky. You and the boys, my stars. Why must we? I ask each time I take a breath. Why must we? But when I return and we transcend all this, I know, and I know we'll find some bliss. My thoughts, my dreams are always with you, my love. You are my soul."

No signature. No need for one. The boy recognized the writing. "Why must we?" he asked, comprehending the gravity but unprepared for its consequences. "What happened to the egg with the cocoon inside?"

Cadri saw, for the first time, the tear-shaped diamonds falling off his mother's eyes and gathering into a pile on her lap, the diamonds that would save the family from being destitute, in the next few years when things became much worse.

But with all the devastation around her and the stirring in her belly, Esma knew she had to find a place of silence where the rumors of this damaged city could not harm her. Where she could be near her sister Mihriban. Where her sons and the girls could find some calm. Where she could give birth in the solitude of silk.

So, one day, they abandoned me.

ぺ

What lonely moments followed! Abandoned. Boarded up to prevent pillage, to listen to the silent moaning of the burnt houses surrounding me. Yes, houses hurt, too, with each fire, flood, and frost. Grateful to be spared. Darkness outside, no life inside. I slept a great deal, letting myself disengage from the influence of the elements.

We each desire a lovely setting. Good design. Solid construction. Harmony with our surroundings. Kind inhabitants. Constant maintenance. Long life. Tender love and care. All this, all this gives us life. And, in turn, we do the same. Determine the inner landscape of those who occupy us.

I must have slept for months, uncertain of my fate, gather-

ing dust, uncertain whether I'd be left forever to he throes of
kismet or someone else's whims, especially someone whose only
purpose was to profit. How I began falling part! I abandoned
my will.

Just as I'd forsaken the thought of ever seeing them again,
they returned one day. Esma with an empty womb but no infant
in her arms. Her eyes sadder. Her lips tighter. The boys taller.
The girls older and gnarlier. Ripened fruit now.

But things got worse. On a dark September day, the Turkish
armies entered Smyrna forcing the Greeks to leave, forcing their
fleet to sail back, taking with them a shipful of immigrants. A
terrible anger, stifled in black smoke, splashed across the sky.
When the *imbat* wind began to sway, the tongues of flames
spread rapidly while the sirens whined ominously to warn the
people of the city. The fire quickly moved from the Armenian
quarters to Alsancak to Konak, meandering its way toward the
neighborhoods of Karantina and Güzel Yali.

As the hordes rampaged through the city looting everything
in sight, the rage, the hatred trailed in their wake, spreading like
a contagious disease. Little fires broke out in houses and shops
between St. Stephan's church and the fruit bazaar. The flames
took the palm trees. Took the intricately latticed mansions that
gave the sections their names. Took the great gardens of paradise. Temples, marble statues of great deities, gymnasiums,
dream centers. Domes, cupolas, minarets. In a day, four thousand years of human expression was wiped out. Just like that.
Who can forgive such madness! The firemen clamped around
on horses, unboarding houses, drilling cisterns in search of
water sources. Water pumps broke down. Hoses caught on fire.
Men rushed around filling buckets of salt water from the Bay.
Esma and the boys watched the flames swallow their landscape
out of existence, their noses pressed against the window, as if

staring at the other side of reality from which there is no return. They watched until the window shattered from the heat, their faces subdivided in each piece of broken glass, their hearts irreparably broken.

⌃⌃

The wind seemed to be dying down at first but suddenly, unexpectedly changed direction, heading toward us. The shutters were already bolted. The servants scurried down to the garden, frantically pumping from the well, filling pots and pans, setting them along the boundaries.

Out of the sea of flames, the Ferret materialized; crimson and horned, "Leave with me," he begged Esma.

"How could you imagine that I'd ever abandon my house at a time like this?" she told him, holding the edges of her scarf across her mouth. "If its kismet is to burn, so is mine. So be it."

She prayed for ice not knowing what else.

The flames were now devouring the little shops farther down the street, the creamery, the butcher, the grocery. Globes of flames billowed, bursting apart and fading into a whirling smoke. Terrified of looters, some neighbors hid inside their houses, letting themselves be devoured by flames instead. Some leaped out of windows to their death. Others ran the streets carrying pieces of furniture, lithographs, candelabras, anything they could salvage. Cinders, ashes rained on everyone like the spitting of a volcano while a muffled mass of figures approached the waterfront and threw themselves into the sea. Others walked in hypnotic ecstasy into the fire, imagining themselves indestructible like salamanders.

The beauty of flames carried contempt in them. Stationary, immobile, helplessly delicate against the intensity of heat I stood my predicament. No choice but to suffer the voraciousness of burning death. At that moment, I realized that I, too, had a soul. My body may be consumed by flames but something else would live on. That we do not exist only in space but in the silence of time.

Esma watched the Adonis tree go up in flames. She felt the end was approaching. Cuddling her boys to her bosom, she kept praying. She raised her hands, she wept her tears to the great male God.

Occasionally, the Ferret's face kept appearing over the brazier like Satan. The girls refused to flee, out of loyalty, or maybe lack of choice. Where else could they go? Who would care for them?

Gonca made a magical charm to protect them from enemies, devils, thieves, lizards, scorpions, magic, and fear. She ran down to the cellar; sacrificed their last rooster to Yadaji, the rain goddess. She carefully removed the bezoar stone from inside the bird, rubbed it over her face, and prayed for water.

"Yadaji, send us rain. Let the heavens pour their great tears. Let the thighs of the Goddess giggle with joy. Send us heavenly waters to wash away this infernal curse, Yadaji. Bring on the rain. Bring on the rain. Bring on the rain."

Cadri, curled in a ball, cried silently. Peed in his pants. Aladdin continued staring at the flames. Mesmerized.

"Why does the heat make the glass shatter?" he asked, watching the explosions across the way. The neighbors' houses, on the right and on the left, now blazing up while the paint blistered; windows shattered to particles of crystal.

"Because he is angry," Esma replied, holding the boy on her lap. Not the answer Aladdin was looking for but he put his arms around his mother's neck and kissed her cheek.

"Are we going to die?" he asked. "Are we?"

Then, it happened. A great thunder overwhelmed the crackling of the fire. An aggressive outpouring of tiny shards of hail countered. Ice curses fell from the sky with deliberate fierceness, sharp and determined, melting like a salve over our burning flesh. Spitting into the fire, sizzling into steam, sizzling until the embers weakened and lost their determinate glow.

Within an hour, the fire had subsided, leaving us, the inhabitants of Smyrna shrouded in black mud and mourning. The white city buried in a shroud of black mist. Like its women. The whole city weeping for human stupidity. As the world wept for the city.

Esma thought it was her prayers that brought on the miracle, that made ice pour from the sky. She felt optimism about the future. Yes. She was convinced her lover would return now before long. He would marry her and they would become a family. Yes, she would finally consent. To insure this, she offered a sacrifice.

Gonca, on the other hand, attributed the ice magic to the power of the bezoar stone. She saw Yadaji's dark, luminous eyes in the sky. She saw her tears. She saw her enigmatic smile.

The next morning, although the whole city still suffered the chaos, Iskender broke through the crowds.

"You are leaving this wasteland and coming up to the plantation with me," he pleaded. Esma did not respond. She still was not on talking terms with her brother. How could she since that horrible night—even though her lover was still alive! Iskender had defiled her, taken the amber egg.

So, she refused to follow him.

ॐ

On a gentle day in early spring, the cannons exploded announcing the end of Liberation War. Overnight, Smyrna became

Izmir, a statement of the Turkish victory and claim. Some men returned home. But some did not.

The treaty of Lausanne settled oppositions with a population exchange. The Rums, the Turkish Greeks, as well as other Christians, were deported to Greece, a land foreign to them, among people who were strangers. In exchange, the Greeks expelled their Turks from Lesbos and Crete to the mainland Turkey, these people who had known no other land.

As the Rums left, they offered their homes for a few piastres to their friends—a few friendships still survived the war—with the uncertainty of ever coming back. Arriving in a hostile new land with a few coins would be infinitely preferable to arriving with empty hands.

Just before their departure, they frantically buried treasures in their gardens, inside rafters, everywhere, in hopes of returning someday to reclaim their past. (Some did manage to find their way back years later after the peace was made, only to discover that their precious and exaggerated treasures had become worthless—except for gold, of course.)

It was a time of need and of greed. Everything went on ration. Outside, treasure hunters projecting Y-shaped doodlebugs—dingus, doohickeys, thingamabobs—dowsing interminably for metal. They sauntered like blind people, or ones risen from graves, floating in the mists of the flame-lit mysterious world outside.

Others dug graves. The locals called the diggers "crows" because they resembled the quick-billed scavengers searching recently plowed soil for worms. After each rain, carrying pickax and shovel, they traveled to abandoned excavations, poking for undiscovered treasures. Not just a passing fancy. Nor for the love of art. These ignorant locals had cultivated better knowledge of appraising antiquities than the experts. Some had the nerve to establish a network of connections stretching from Istanbul to Frankfurt, the British Museum to the Metropolitan. The world was growing fast.

Finally, Esma decided it was safe to unboard me but I had suffered so many scars.

"This poor house," Esma said. "We must again infuse it with life."

"Where to begin?"

"Touch the walls. Touch the walls, children. Give them your breath. Bring the spirits back."

They opened all the doors and the windows, airing out the aftermath of fire and war. Gonca stole from room to room, burning juniper, and chanting pagan prayers. *"Hosh! Hosh! Hosh! Hosh! Hosh!"* For forty days and forty nights. The center of interest. The object of desire. Washed and scrubbed. Sang and smudged. New curtains. New kilims. New paint. New hope.

In the days that followed, Esma watched the street day and night, her heart agitated at the sight of each passing uniform until they turned around. None was the face she had hoped to see. She listened to every whisper in the air, trying to identify the voices, rushing to the balcony at the slightest provocation, the faintest hiss of the wind, only to be repeatedly disillusioned.

For the boys, too, a new teacher came. They called him Agop the Four Fingers because the man's thumbs were missing.

"What happened to your thumbs?" Aladdin asked.

"The war took them."

"How?" the child wondered. The image of war as a raging maniac chopping people's fingers.

"They were amputated."

"How come?"

What interested the boys were the nuts and bolts and body parts, not the ethics of disaster. Nor the ethos.

Holding a pen between his toes, Agop the Four Fingers taught them to write from left to right. And front to back. In Latin roman alphabet. The new way. Unlike the Arabic letters they had learned. Things were changing rapidly. Europe was taking revenge by imposing its own image. The country was now leaning to the West.

Moving the centers of his brain, a struggle for Cadri at first. But Aladdin adjusted instantly, impressing Agop the Four Fingers with the way he conceived symbols and abstractions. But he was testy with the boy who craved the challenge.

"Aladdin should be sent away to a school in the West," Agop the Four Fingers told Iskender as they sat in a seaside tavern nearby, a liaison Esma was unaware of. Over mussels and calamari, they sipped the municipal brew. "The numbers here are not big enough for the boy's mind. Maybe Germany. Maybe even America. He'll someday be someone. Mark my words."

Cadri heard them, eavesdropping outside the door to the men's quarters. Cadri heard everything. He had sensitive ears. Ears that would make him a poet in the years to come.

Above the picture of her deceased husband Esma put the picture of another, a dashing blond man with an iron face, a strong jaw, and penetrating blue eyes—eyes capable of the greatest hatred and of the greatest love. Who was he? A new prospect? Would there be a new master? What had happened to Süleyman?

Süleyman's picture remained in Esma's precious wardrobe, inside a medallion. Everyday, she put it to her lips. Forty days and forty nights had long come and gone. There was not a sign of him. Not even a letter.

For days, parades floated down the streets; young girls with laurel and white flowers crowning their freshly cropped hair, displaying larger-than-life pictures of the blue-eyed man. The same as the one on Esma's dresser. Men paraded in *borsalinos* instead of the fez; the Great Leader himself had appeared in Kastamonu wearing one. Women burned their veils, revealed their faces, at long last allowed in male company, allowed a social life. Slogans read, "Can one half of the population rise to the skies while the other is chained to the ground?" promoting women's rights. And, "Turkey can no longer be the stage of religious fundamentalism and *sharia* schemes." People hung from the balconies around the quay chanting and cheering:

> *Where shall we find the skies and seas?*
> *And where are the rocky mountaintops?*
> *Where are the singing birds and trees?*
> *Comrades, come, march along with me.*

The convertible Daimler passed in front of the mansions near Alsancak, penetrated the hearts with his eyes. His name printed in Roman script appeared everywhere, his picture larger than the city: Mustafa Kemal Atatürk. The ancestor of the Turks. (*Ata* meant ancestor.) The savior from the tyranny of the Sultans, the greed of the Allies. The hero of Gallipoli. The new God. The blond savior. The man of great reforms. Atatürk. Amen.

 كي

She had become mindless with her sons and although she held them close to her, they sensed her absence. Nothing seemed to console her, not until the day a letter arrived from her sister, Mihriban. Esma read the letter and folded up her sleeves.

For forty days and forty nights the girls slaved, rolling a thousand and one sheets of filo, pickling bushels of eggplant, churning tahini with grape molasses for halvah. Esma herself resurrected precious fabrics out of her old dowry trunk. She cut them into a little girl's clothes—aprons and pinafores and frilly, lacy, ribbony, embroidered, gauzy delightful gowns. Who were they for? What child stirred her so?

On the last day of Ramadan, at an ungodly hour, the mysterious guests arrived—Mim Pasha and his wife Mihriban, Esma's sister, their three daughters and two maids. Mihriban had the same paisley eyes as Esma but lacked the ethereal delicacy of her sister's features. She had her feet on the ground and her head in the soup. But from a distance, they looked almost identical. The Pasha, a dark man born in India, solid as granite. The two older daughters, Papatya and Sibel, had his eggplant skin, curly hair, and full lips but the youngest girl's blond ringlets and paisley eyes set her apart from the rest. Her name was Aida. The lady of the Moon.

Aida was the most beautiful child in the world, with a celadon glow, translucent and radiant. Gazing at her face, it made one cry and smile at the same time, always wrought in some sort of deep revelation.

When Esma saw the child she began to weep and disappeared into her room. Aida instinctively followed her, wobbling her plump little body like a penguin. Esma embraced the child in her arms, rocked her to the sound of the waves, yielding to the trance of the old lullaby. *Dandini, dandini, danali bebek.*

Aida followed Esma everywhere, sneaking into her bed in the night, following her precise gestures in prayer, sitting across the loom, and imitating Esma's expressions. She wanted Esma to bathe her in the *hamam*. To scratch her back. She wanted Esma to curl her hair. She wanted to dress in her clothes. She wanted Esma's stories. She wanted to eat out of Esma's mouth.

"What should we do?" Mihriban asked the Pasha, as she washed his feet in the *hamam*.

"She is ours now," Pasha responded. "That's all there is to it. The child shouldn't be confused about who to call mother. You should not encourage her either."

"But she is such a comfort to my poor sister. They belong together. I feel as if we should . . ."

"Your poor sister should have thought twice before having a child out of wedlock. She should be grateful we were able to shield her from dishonor. From all of us losing face. Besides, with two boys to bring up, she shouldn't be afflicted with another burden. This way, she can have the best of all worlds. So could Aida."

It was to Esma's arms that the child ran, the night of that intense snowstorm, even on the night that a fateful incident changed the course of Esma's life when Lady Luck became cross. What occurred on that evening deflated her dreams, took away her sweetness.

It happened that Ferret came to call on Mim Pasha, bringing a bucket of warm *boza* for the family. On that chilly evening, the taste of warm fermented millet with a sprinkling of cinnamon would be welcome in any household. As his hand groped for the knocker, a dark figure appeared out of the shadows.

"*Selam Aleyküm,*" he greeted.

The Ferret shrank as if he had seen a jinn, then gathered his wits. A parody of himself.

"Süleyman! We had given you up for dead!"

Süleyman nodded. "I was." His skin leathery from the elements. His eyes dim. He looked anxious. He limped and shuffled one leg as he walked.

The two men stood across from each other, rubbing their hands to keep warm. The blizzard slapped their faces, urging for combat.

"I'm bringing *boza* for them," Ferret explained, pointing at me. "The boys needed a father. A young woman cannot live alone forever, you know?"

Süleyman had seen the like of this happen to other men who went to war, men whose women could not endure loneliness. Uncertainty was part of survival, but Esma? The love of his life. The fire of his groins. She would never. Unless, unless her conniving brother Iskender urged her into an undesirable and forced union.

"I don't believe it," he said. "I don't believe a word you say."

"See for yourself," the Ferret gestured the way. "Come, then."

Through, an opening in the curtain, Süleyman looked inside. There was Esma, the love of his life, so thin and gaunt. Then, a little girl ran into her arms and her face lightened up and she covered the child with kisses. That moment would never leave him.

"You can't let her see you like this, like a cripple," Ferret told him.

A murderous impulse was rising in Süleyman's veins faster than mercury. But he only raised his hand and slapped his opponent, slapped him hard, so hard that the Ferret lost his balance, tumbled down. Then without a word, Süleyman walked away. His walk turned into a trot. He galloped to the end of the street without stopping, his arms lifted up to the sky. Once, he looked back. He saw the Ferret knock on the door. He saw a woman open the door and let him in. He heard a child's cry. He saw the door close.

He limped his way to the obsidian, sat on a step, strange sounds escaping from his throat, sounds that exploded into a sad *gazel*, a ballad in the minor key. But it was so cold that long before reaching the air, the notes turned into snowflakes.

It snowed that night in Izmir for the first time in its history, the white blessing burying wounds while preserving the color of blood. Flakes piled, entombing Süleyman. He became a snowman. Had the night watchman not stumbled on him, thawed him with his stick, he would have been frozen to death. *Slap, slap, slap, slap.*

"Wake up, poor slob! Here, drink down some *raki.* Come on."

He blew his whistle, to which a retinue of other night watchmen responded within seconds. They bundled Süleyman in their coats, carried him into an *araba,* and drove away from Karatash.

Oblivious to all this, Mim Pasha and the Ferret warmed themselves around the stove, drinking *boza* in stern silence. Ferret was restless. Every few minutes, he went to the window and looked out as if he were anticipating something.

"Are you expecting someone?" Mim Pasha questioned him.

"Just checking how deep the snow . . ."

The children slept, the girls in one room, the boys in the other. Gonca, Ayşe, and their two sisters, huddled around the boiling kettle in the kitchen. In the old harem, Esma and her sister sat across from each other now over the loom that had once belonged to their mother, and that Mihriban had transported from the plantation to distract her sister.

"Don't worry," Mihriban told Esma, as they collaborated weaving an old pattern. "I know Süleyman will soon return. He's an honorable man." But inside, she feared the opposite.

Despite the multiplying tension caused by their complicity, Mim Pasha's family remained for the full cycle of the moon. The children protected themselves by playing together; Papatya, Sibel, and Aida bonded with the boys. From then on, they were brothers and sisters.

Süleyman did not return. Everyone assumed he had been a

war casualty. But the night watchman, who made love to Ayşe across the bars, told her about the night he had discovered the man under a mound of snow and how he and the other watchmen had revived the poor devil. The next day, Süleyman had wandered off to the docks, without a possession, looking for a ship to sail on.

Ayşe was afraid to tell this to her mistress, not wanting to incriminate her source of information. Besides, Süleyman was gone now anyway. She did not wish for Esma to stop hoping for his return. Her mistress had nothing else left to hope for.

But something inside Esma told her he was still alive. Every morning as soon as she woke up, she would tap the wardrobe, as if sending someone a Morse signal. She then closed her eyes and fell into a trance, her last hours with Süleyman repeating themselves in her mind's eye. She talked to him endlessly and answered questions that no one else could hear. She told him stories, recited poetry. She told him about their little Aida. Like that, she carried on a dialogue by herself. Even in her dreams, she kept him captive in a continuous narrative, as though they had contacted each other on some other dimension of existence that was only theirs.

She had retreated into a netherworld no one else could fathom. Her eyes no longer looked outward, her hands perpetually occupied with trifles to conceal her resignation. She was running out of precious stones and she had stopped crying diamond tears. Too proud to ask her family for sustenance, she faced the challenge of feeding her own children. Prayers had gone feeble during the war.

Suddenly it came to her. She sat on her knees, her hands plucking the strings of her loom, as if playing the harp and then casting a fly in the air. She made music of colors, plant juices that tinted the wool in rich autumnal hues. Her prayer rugs, the same design as the one she had learned from her mother in Macedonia, who had learned from hers, an inheritance from their nomadic ancestry. Wild intoxication of shapes and colors, animated, hypnotic trances opened doorways into imaginary worlds, just as in fairy tales.

They were so whimsical that everyone wanted one. So, she was occupied. When people bought Esma's magic carpets, they dreamed sweet dreams, escaping into realms free of hate or pain.

Esma slowly reached an inner peace never granted her before. Like Penelope, she focused on weaving her patterns to perfection. She knew them so intimately that she could compose with closed eyes, her attention elsewhere. Her weft and warp, her plucking and pulling made melodies for sensitive ears. So much so that *Jinns* and *peris* crawled out of their crevices to dance.

Cadri, transported by his mother's weaving music, the mystery of symbols—chevrons, diamonds, trees of life, birth-giving goddesses—sat on the other side of the loom, watching Esma through the crossing threads of yarn, as if through the lattices of a harem window.

My mother weaves her pain
entangling the threads,
so they will not break
their tension.
My mother weaves her sacred self.

ॐ

The days passed. The boys grew. Cadri lost in books and Aladdin in the stars. Cadri turned an empty room into his *pensatorio*, his thinking room, to retreat for contemplation. Or to pin his butterflies and spell their Latin names. Or to practice calligraphy and read archaic texts, while Aladdin constructed telescopes, and made model airplanes.

But Cadri's temple was elsewhere. Ever since Iskender had taken him to his first Nickelodeon in the alley across from the Clock Tower, the boy had fallen into a trance. He cut school—out of character—he spent his pennies in the arcades; he swore to himself he'd see everything that lived in that shadowbox during his lifetime. He fashioned an altar with the photographs of his love goddesses. He managed to teach himself enough English to write rudimentary fan letters to his favorites. All identical. In return, he received their glamour photos signed to "Dear Cadri, best wishes, Theda Bara." "To Cadri, yours always, Billie Dove." "To Cadri, affectionately, Marion Davies." Lillian and Dorothy Gish. Louise Brooks. Gloria Swanson. The silent ones. The vamps, the ingenues, the "It" girl, Clara Bow. The flappers. Then, the talking ones. And last but not least, the queen of queens herself, Dolores. Dolores Del Rio.

The boys' imagination was so rich and peopled that neither felt the urge to seek other company. An invisible umbilicus still united them, sealing their sufficiency. Even when their sexual urges came, they just went inside Ayşe in the cellar or the broom closet. Ayşe willing, of course; in fact she'd lure her lovely boys into the dank corners of the cellar, seeking their lips, guiding their hands to her full breasts and other succulent crevices. The boys could never be certain to whom the breasts belonged but no matter. Because the cellar was so dark, Cadri and Aladdin had the fortune of being initiated into lovemaking by touch rather than visual stimulation. Their sensualness increased, making them good lovers of other women in years to come.

Ayşe did not mind at all the touch of young sinew, fleshy palpitations, the steam of warm breath. Ah, Heaven! Drowned out every prayer time by the muezzin's song, she made sounds of such pleasure that the blue wisteria clung itself deep into the outside walls and produced a profusion of dangling blossoms that chimed like tiny bells. Although she was getting on in years, her body never changed, which everyone attributed to her insatiable carnal appetite.

Aida came to visit frequently, enslaving the family with her blossoming beauty. Esma indulged herself playing with Aida's hair—braiding, curling, crimping, weaving. For a while, she forgot her pain.

"What do you want to be when you grow up?" she asked Aida, who at the age of eleven was already deliciously pubescent.

"I'd like to be a beauty queen."

Esma smiled, having herself known impossible dreams of little girls.

When the boys turned eighteen and graduated from the Lycée, the inevitable happened. Aladdin received a scholarship to a faraway place called Boston. Esma wanted to keep him, sensing the loss would not simply be a temporary one.

"The boy's eyes always wandered away from home, almost since he was born," Mihriban reminded her. "You gave him wings to fly. You cannot clip them now."

Esma wept as Aladdin's ship left the harbor, waving at the disappearing face, sensing it might be the last vision of him, her hands digging into Cadri's and grafting themselves.

Aladdin sent her postcards from the world's most famous edifices—the Eiffel Tower, the London Bridge, the Empire State Building, the Golden Gate. To Cadri only, he sent more provocative ones, of bare-breasted women, extolling their smells and erotic nights in strange houses, in strange cities. Mysterious lust. Unfamiliar tongues. Unspeakable delights.

Cadri stayed home, faithful and devoted to his mother whom he attended with deified reverence, swearing always to kiss her feet. An anemic young man from having been weaned in a library and drawn to artificially lit rooms, Cadri perceived the world through thick glasses that made his face appear cyclopean and he concentrated intensely when he looked at things. The sun disturbed him, freckling his prematurely balding pate, protected only by a crescent patch of hair below his ears. He was always seen wearing a hat (fedora in the winter and Panama in the summer) to conceal his baldness, which he said made his head vulnerable to the attack of the mind predators. Even in his sleep, he wore a night cap.

Cadri had become the center of the three women's affection, the master of his harem, the perpetual boy. All the women were convinced that this was how it would always be, to compensate for the loss of Aladdin, silently claiming their special place in his heart.

Gonca sank deeper into her world of the intangibles. Cadri sometimes noticed how things moved of their own accord and levitated when she was around: He would move through the rooms feeling a sense of something breathing that often startled him. Struggling with his thoughts, he'd try to understand just what Gonca was seeing and clean his lenses to improve his own vision.

Ayşe, at long last, realizing that the night watchman had no intention of ever leaving his wives and his many children, not to mention his adventurous night life, one day stopped baring her breasts. With this withholding, a certain kind of moisture left her, she became fat, and her sister Gonca was no longer compelled to lock her up at night.

When the muezzin sang at midnight, Cadri stole out for his nocturnal stroll, waiting for the moon to taste the licorice night air while the rest of the town slumbered. The women would call out after him or stand at the threshold until he disappeared into darkness through an avenue of gaslight, like a somnambulist, seeking worlds beyond physical reach.

One such night, the cicadas came. The hell chatter lasted all night, driving to madness the inhabitants of the city who could not sleep. In the morning Esma's garden was ravaged, the Adonis tree, which had come back to life with even a greater vengeance than before, stripped of all its bark. The wisteria, jasmine—everything lay in a chaotic heap of limp brownness.

"Bad omen," Gonca told Esma. "Something else will have to replace the vines—which may not be so bad but will change the balance of things."

Esma fell into a deep state of drowsiness. She slept for seven days and seven nights. And Cadri, worried about his mother's condition, went to fetch Doctor Eliksir. On the way, he stopped to buy flowers for Esma. That was the day that kismet knocked at their door again in the form of Camilla. Another gain. Another loss.

❧

Camilla. What can I say about Camilla? From the day she arrived, as stubborn as an Angora goat yet unblemished as an unfolding gardenia. The spitting image of the woman adorning Cadri's walls: Dolores Del Rio—as if she'd dropped from her nose. A hint of Loretta Young, maybe, in the cheeks. Pistachio-skinned and succulent, apple face, chestnut eyes, intense and calculating, and never, never without reason, without assessment. Not even in bed.

The morning after the madness of the cicadas, Cadri stopped at a flower shop near the ferry landing. It was the sweetest scent that had lured him, the scent of orange blossoms. A young woman greeted him. Pearl teeth. Opium eyes. He confessed to her his plight, of his mother's ailment and the Adonis tree. Camilla arranged a bouquet of black tulips and forget-me-nots. She also gave him a bouquet of valerian.

"Make tea out of this. It will make your mother feel better. I promise you. As for the Adonis tree, don't worry. It will sprout again just as it always has. It's an immortal. Don't fret."

When Cadri returned with the doctor, Esma was sitting up in bed, having her afternoon tea. The minute she laid eyes on the bouquet, she broke into uncontrollable shivers as if someone had given her a shock.

"Burn them, burn these wretched flowers so that no other soul can inhale the stink," she wailed. "These flowers are evil."

"I don't smell anything, mother," Cadri told her, "least of all evil. I bought them from a very nice young lady."

He coaxed his mother to drink the valerian tea, covering her under mounds of colorful satin quilts while singing praises of Camilla. She'd spent her childhood in an ancient region of the Aegean where archaeologists and treasure hunters persistently stalk in search of lost cities, of gold, and missing parts of goddesses. Blood memories of primeval dreams, of human sacrifice, fertility rites. "But all that's just below the surface. In truth, she seems to have an iron will."

He said she was different, different from them, weaned on a peculiar diet, which also included consumption of flowers—honeysuckle, gardenia, nasturtium, lavender, calendula. Perhaps, there's a point to it. Perhaps, they themselves should reconsider their diet. Perhaps.

"You've certainly discovered a great deal in such a short time," Esma told him. "Did you find out about her family?"

"Her family has been in deep straits, her father very ill. Her mother grows the flowers she sells to support the family."

Sensing the inevitable threat of a prospective rival, Esma prayed to her God, "Spare me the pain of losing my second son, my favorite, to a nectar-sucking witch. Make him blind to her charms." The girl had charms, no doubt about that, clearly with connections to the plant kingdom and all that. The well had been poisoned already.

But, alas, God paid no attention to Esma's prayers. Nor did the devil mind her spiky-tongued curses. Resignation and loneliness took hold of her as Aladdin's letters became less and less frequent and Cadri ceased kissing her feet. A few weeks later, a priceless fire opal with diamonds graced Camilla's finger. And shortly after that, Camilla herself graced us.

༄

From the beginning, Esma's Macedonian temperament, passive and prone to pining, caused a tug-of-war between the matriarch and the daughter-in-law. Fighting for her status, Esma abandoned her precious weaving, distracted now by the necessity of casting mean spells at Camilla and lying in wait for their repercussions.

Camilla had no suspicion that her terrible mooncycles and frequent falls down the stairs were symptoms of curses. She was resilient and feisty; reflected the evil eye right back at her mother-in-law. The two women mirrored the darkness in each other. Glassy silence erupted with a pandemonium of dubious spirits prancing around night and day.

Loneliness occupied the rooms, especially in the evenings, each of them sitting in separate rooms like solitary inmates of a prison. Persistent, frozen images affixed like perfume, invisible but lasting. Esma slowly combed her wavy white hair now reaching down to her knees. Her hands, gnarly like pruned sycamores, sorting out worry beads. Her back a question mark, still praying. Praying for all the lost ones, their only connection now through pictures—all except Süleyman's. His image as a young man was fixed as was hers in her own mind, with certain relief that he could not see her as she is now and only knew her youthful beauty.

Camilla sat on a window seat, looking across the Bay toward Cordelio, singing an old Rum song:

> Farewell, my dearest father, farewell
> Farewell, my darling mother.
> I'm moving to a stranger's house
> To serve my husband's mother.

Seeking her way to her mother-in-law's heart, she cooked pots and pots of pilaf, burning it each time, stinking the space with a lasting odor that repelled Esma even more. She planted a variety of flowers in the garden that withered before they bloomed. Her green touch, her divine connection to growing things had vanished. She conceived many babies but all were unborn.

Each time she was expecting, a recurrent dream visited her in which an invisible hand reached from an imaginary sky, zipped her open, and removed the baby. After her seventh miscarriage, Gonca, unable to endure burying another embryo, told Camilla about the Red Woman, the ogress that attacked the pregnant, but concealed Esma's role in the curse. First loyalty first.

Unable to detach herself from her disembodied mother-in-law pacing above her room, Camilla escaped into books about tormented heroines. Gone with the Wind. Rebecca. Forever Amber. Anna Karenina. Madame Bovary. Disenchanted. She devoured the words until she could no longer sustain them, until she could no longer keep her eyes open, trapped in the realm of fiction.

Cadri's response to the ancient harem feud—the one between mother and daughters-in-law—was to retreat even deeper. He withdrew once again in his *pensatorio,* composing esoteric verses that he kept locked up in an étagère along with his archives, rosettes, and lepidores. In this sanctuary of collectibles, he constructed a city of the mind, neglecting the desolate emotions that floated like burnt paper in every room. He stayed up, drinking endless cups of coffee that kept mysteriously appearing on his desk, served by invisible hands, while concocting words that inexplicably burst into life. His vastly populated verbal universe shaped itself into volumes. At last, he had become a true poet.

When the streets stopped humming, he pursued the night, leaving Camilla alone in bed, shivering. Sometimes she wanted to go with him but he refused, possessive of his nocturnal peregrinations.

"Do you have another woman?" she asked.

He laughed. And she knew he didn't because when he returned, he didn't smell of one. He was ardent, waking her up with his need. Dark and impersonal, yet slow and sensual. For her, it was just another part of the dream she was in the midst of.

On such a night, Iskender encountered Cadri drifting aimlessly along the Cordone. He appeared to be wandering in a trance. Iskender realized that the silent war between the women must have brought on his nephew's sleep disorders. As a rescue remedy from this magnetic domain, he offered Cadri a job inspecting the family's silk interests in the rural countryside—the beginning of Cadri's political awakening. Another turning point.

So, it all came down on Cadri, early mornings and bright days, exposure to a disturbing solar intrusion. At dawn, Camilla shook him out of sleep; they whispered in the breakfast room trying not to disturb the others. In his impeccable suit carrying a leather suitcase full of papers and shoe trees, his fetish, he kissed his wife as if for the very last time, before jumping into the rattling old Citroën TA (traction avant)—"the Dachshund," as they lovingly called it—to drive off to the provinces while Camilla went back to bed for another hour or two before entering her own day.

Cadri traveled as far as the Citroën could endure, then on mule or on foot, to small worlds of hidden desire. Each time, he sent his women photographs of himself taken in ever-changing landscapes. Always wearing a hat, always the same winning, confident grin, even when caught off guard, the one he reserved for the camera.

In his absence, the two women spoke to each other only through the girls, or sometimes other women guests.

"Gonca, will you tell my daughter-in-law that we don't put pistachios in grape dolmas."

"Gonca, will you tell your mistress that there is more than one way to skin a cat."

Sometimes, Cadri was gone for months, leaving the women in suspense of his whereabouts, except from letters both received on the same day in separate envelopes:

December 5, 1945

My Camilla,

I arrived in Salihli on muleback at 13:00 yesterday in cloudy weather and checked into the Sun Hotel near the train station. In the afternoon, I strolled the streets under the rain you love so much, stopping at the Town Club to visit the mayor whom I had previously met in Soma. He was pleased to see me again and promised his help contacting local employers.

They had just begun rationing bread in Salihli and I obtained a weekly card. I will save it until my return so that you and mother could get more flour and wheat. In the meantime, the delicious boereks mother had baked for me fulfilled my hunger. Tomorrow is market day and if the cherries are not full of worms after the rains, I will bring home a nice basket.

At night, the generator in the hotel was not working; so, no heat or electricity. I was freezing all night and I had difficulty falling asleep. Luckily, I had a flashlight so that I could read. Finally, I must have dozed off thinking of you, for you appeared in my dream. (Hope it is a good omen.) We were in an enchanted place together with lots of other young people. We were feeding each other fruits and cakes, and laughing. Since I'm no psychic oracle I don't have a clue how to interpret this dream but I must confess it made me ecstatic to have you in my bed in Salihli.

I woke up at dawn; and at 9:00 I raided a textile factory and finished my inspection late afternoon. The conditions are much worse than anyone can imagine. The exploitation of the workers is beyond comprehension. I never knew such injustice was possible.

I found this town incredibly unattractive. Even though it's on the main Smyrna line, it's extremely neglected. Blizzard, mud, frost, and desolate as the heart of the ignorant. Dilapidated buildings—not a pleasant sight but it's my duty, my obligation to seek solutions.

How is your cough? Are you getting along better with my mother? You know how important this is to me. Is she still upset about my brother Aladdin's marriage to that Irish-American girl? You must try to console her. Be her friend. You have no one but each other when I'm away.

Tomorrow, another factory. But now, my gastronomical needs beckon. I kiss your beautiful eyes and . . . (I'll tell you the rest on my return.) I love you more when I'm away from you.

So, like this . . .

Your husband,
Cadri Ipekci

When Cadri returned home, he was so preoccupied sorting out his thoughts about his trips and writing reports that he no longer occupied his *pensatorio*. The green door remained locked; everything inside gathered dust, buried in an interminable slumber. Smelling the decaying paper and neglect, the mice made camp, devouring his precious books, fringes of his invaluable rugs, and the gold dust of his prized butterflies and moths. Finally, they devoured his poems.

When he came home, he was exhausted. Cadri and Camilla retired to their bedroom, so as not to stir Esma; made love for hours in total silence. Esma knew anyway, no matter how they concealed their desire. Not difficult to smell those things.

Once again, Doctor Eliksir told Camilla that she was expecting. She already knew from the way her body had become ravenous as if a parasite starved inside her. Gonca found her one night, sitting alone in the kitchen and gorging on a plateful of raw lamb chops. She offered to cook them. Camilla consented. She had become a carnivore.

This time, Doctor Eliksir told her, no more chances. "I'm confining you to bed for the full term. You will not allow yourself to slip this one. You must be still."

Camilla lay mummified in a white bed overlooking the Izmir Bay, reading gothic novels while watching the passing of the ships, the gathering of storms, the setting of the sun and of the moon. She counted flocks of migrating pelicans. She continued dreaming, dreaming of deformed babies with missing parts, Siamese twins, elephant babies, horned babies with webbed feet, furry babies with tails, harelips, dwarves, imbeciles, idiots, and ones with the pink disease. She felt the swimming of life inside her without sex or sin.

"I will keep my baby this time at any cost. It will not leave my body prematurely this time," she repeated like a mantra, oblivious that the baby was full grown, ready to burst out in the seventh month but had not yet found a soul. They were already contesting wills.

The dream returned. The hand came down, reached inside her bandages, but they were tied with the devil's knot that no one, not even the Red Woman, could unravel. Realizing she had been tricked, the Red Woman attacked. In a flash, Camilla realized she was dreaming and, therefore, could stop the dream if she wanted to. She entered her dream, pushed the Red Woman's hand forcefully away from her body, before waking herself up into a starless night all alone in bed, soaked in sweat.

The dream visited again the following night but before the hand could touch her, Camilla let out a savage scream, sending chills to everyone in the neighborhood. But they forgave her trespasses, knowing she was from the opposite shore where many were still the descendants of the Rums, spoke an ancient tongue, and others kept the faith of old slave women out of the Anatolian darkness.

"Go away where you came from, the face of darkness, and never, never never never come back. Go back into the dark distant star, home of your own kin. Go back. Go back."

Startled by such a display of courage and recognizing her own defeat, Esma pilgrimaged to the temple of Su Baba, the great water saint, and prayed for a grandson, a little boy to fill the place in her heart that Aladdin had left empty. Prayed for her daughter-in-law's madness to stop. Prayed for the Red Woman to leave her alone. She promised to love Camilla as her own flesh and blood if her wishes were granted. She promised to sacrifice her soul in return.

After Camilla's waters broke and she transited into labor, the Red Woman pursued again. This time not in her dream but in the same room, hovering over her birth chair.

"Get her out of this room," Camilla begged Gonca.

"There is no one in the room, mistress. Just us."

"She's leaning on the counterpane. Get her out!"

Gonca sought Esma. "Mistress Camilla has puerperal fever," she cried. "The Red Woman's consumed her. I need help. Or we'll lose the baby."

Esma prayed, "Great God. Take my life instead. Let my grandson live. Take my soul. Take what you want from me."

Camilla's body refused to open up and let the infant leave as if she were determined to keep it inside forever. But her pain was so unbearable that it turned on itself, carrying both her and the baby into a jagged twilight. She would have been lost there had Gonca not interfered and slit her belly—just like in the dream—to take the baby out.

The child did not cry when she broke out of Camilla's womb, covered with a silver web of mucus. She was silent. She didn't scream like other babies. She didn't tense her hands and feet. She seemed lifeless but her eyes were wide open.

Esma picked up the tiny little girl in her fragile arms and looked into her eyes—void as if she belonged to the soulless ones. She cut the chord. She licked the vernix. She breathed on the child's face. Within seconds, the baby's eyes became alert and inquisitive like a sea mammal. She stirred like the baby dolphins seen gamboling along the Aegean. Paisley eyes like hers, like Mihriban, like Aida. Esma perceived in her granddaughter the reflection of her own spirit. The tiny creature looked as though she was smiling and then winking. Esma winked back as if she thought they shared a great secret but felt herself swiftly expiring.

Camilla lay quietly as Gonca delivered the afterbirth, watching her mother-in-law claim her baby. Tears were streaming quietly down Esma's cheeks but at the same time, a peaceful smile formed on her face.

"What will we call her?"

"Her name is Amber," Camilla announced.

The baby's skin had a translucent amber glow but it was Camilla's perverse infatuation with *Forever Amber*—the book she had been devouring—that had inspired the name. She had learned to view the world through an amber-colored filter ever since she had come here in order to survive.

Camilla soon returned to her twilight, rid of the Red Woman once and for all but also rid of her womb. Her face a pale glow. A mother now.

"Your name is Süleyman," Esma whispered to the baby. Then, stuck a piece of Turkish delight wrapped in a handkerchief between her lips, so that "She will have a sweet life."

When she returned to her room that night, Esma looked at the picture of Aladdin with his Irish-American wife dressed in winter coats with fur collars, standing in front of a white colonial house somewhere in a snowy New England landscape. Picture of Cadri and Aladdin as boys, in gilded white satin hats during their circumcision ceremony. Her stern old husband— the same old picture. Aida as a beauty queen. And inside the wardrobe, Süleyman wearing a dark fez and *pelerin*.

Too weak to stand up, she lay down to pray. She told God her life had been fulfilled. She no longer feared the breath of Azrael. Death was not the end of life, she knew. Multiple souls went on living eternally. She told everyone in her prayers not to fear for her. Her body may leave, but her soul would always return.

That night, in her sleep, she separated from her body. At dawn, Gonca came running upstairs. The sight of her mistress curled up on her prayer rug like a fava bean as in the old days of her passion. Brought tears to her eyes. She covered Esma. Then, she knew.

A blue spirit floated over Esma's lifeless body; formless at first, it began to change like the clouds until a piece of it broke off and became a nightingale. The bird flew out the window, perched on the Adonis tree. The muezzin chanted the dawn prayer. The nightingale sang. And the baby began to cry.

The Silk Plantation

ᔥ

(1930–1958)

Still round and round the ghosts of beauty glide.
And haunt the places where their honour died.

ALEXANDER POPE

࿊

THE BEAUTY QUEEN

*E*sma's sister *Mihriban* first came to live here in Bursa
pushing her husband's wheelchair, his dark face distorted
from the stroke—one lip facing the sky, the other the
earth. Their three pubescent daughters followed, glued at the
hips like vocalists in some singing group: Papatya, Sibel, and
Aida. The two older girls took after their father, Mim Pasha, a
kind man, people said in his time before he was struck, though
somewhat ornery. But Aida, the youngest, was fair with almond
eyes, cherry lips, and irresistible radiance as if spawned by a
houri.

The family sent Sibel and Papatya to get educated—it was
fashionable now for girls since Atatürk's reforms, but Aida they
groomed only in matters of beauty. Beauty, they believed, held
the reins of power. And Aida was born to be a queen.

They took great pride in cultivating this beauty that God
had clearly sent them as a gift planted by him in Esma's belly.
They spent a fortune on Aida's wardrobe, which contained

Mandarin gowns, saris and sarongs, charshafs and chadors, caftans, kimonos, and kebayas, pallium, peplum, peplos. Not to
mention the accessories to accentuate: tiaras, shawls, stoles,
capotes and capes, bloomers and boleros, petticoats and pinafores, knickers and fans, yashmaks and mantillas, hats, and gam-
bados and gloves.

Her sisters stole books from the library containing illustra-
tions of costumes from different regions of the world and Sibel,
an accomplished artist in her own right, made sketches to conform to her sister's mermaid proportions.

The women residents, skilled with their hands, dexterous in
the art of lacemaking, embroidery, crewel, needlepoint, crochet,
shadow stitch, and appliqué, sat around, making impeccable garments for Aida. And their servants, proficient in silkmaking,
cultivated silk oak trees and raised silkworms. The men built
enormous looms and before long, the family was producing so
much fabric, such amazing textiles that Iskender Bey, the family
patriarch, was driven to travel to the distant provinces of the
Silk Road to market their goods and search the secrets for
higher-quality silk.

Years later, when Iskender Bey returned, he brought back
not only musk, fine fabrics, diamonds, rubies, perfume, rhubarb,
and other assorted objects of desire but the *Bombyx mori*, the
most coveted silk moth, a secret that the Chinese had guarded
viciously for many centuries, its theft considered the greatest
taboo, punishable by violent death.

But Iskender took his chance and smuggled the worm's eggs
and mulberry seeds in his simply crafted ivory cane. No mean
trick this. A turning point in trade history. Just a few insect eggs
and a couple of seeds!

In no time, the mulberry trees replaced the great oaks,
which had until now produced the silk and the silkworm *Bombyx*

mori, and replaced the oakworm *Antherea harti*, whose silk was infinitely inferior.

So, I became a vast plantation above Bursa, in the foothills of Mount Olympus bubbling with sulfur springs—mulberry thrived on thermal soil—quickly becoming populated with mulberry trees. Iskender Bey, then, officially changed the family name from Barutçu, which meant the "gunpowder makers," to İpekçi, the "silkmakers." He'd never felt an affinity to manufacturing the war products that had made the family rich anyway. Iskender Bey was at last following his poetic bliss.

When Aida turned thirteen, she was as lovely as the pale moon—her name meant the lady of the moon—because the family kept her in the shade. Even on the rare occasions when she was exposed to the sun, they made her wear enormous hats with veils or carry parasols so that her skin would retain the priceless ivory color she was born with. Her lustrous chestnut hair, which had never been cut, cascaded all the way down to the ground, folded over and tucked under so she would not step on it and trip. Every day, she brushed it a thousand times with the special boar bristles that Iskender Bey had brought back from Asia.

Aida, of course, was never allowed in any other part of the estate where work occurred, since no one could endure the thought of risking her hands, so smooth, so fine, like the marble hand that Iskender Bey had purchased from a grave digger near Knidos, convinced beyond any doubt that it had belonged to the Aphrodite of Praxiteles, the most beautiful statue ever cast and one of the Seven Wonders of the World. (Mind you, the country possessed four: the Mausoleum of Halicarnassus, the Colossus of Rhodes, the Temple of Artemis in Ephesus, and the renowned Aphrodite.) Iskender Bey had an extraordinary knack for acquiring objects of high resonance.

Aida glowed from the endless hours spent soaking in the

mineral baths, scrubbed, exfoliated, anointed, detoxified by the sulfurous steam. Her muscles were pliant and languid, owing to the massages she received daily. Of course, like the rest of the women, she shied away from any form of physical exertion because, well, Eastern gentlemen like women with flesh (after all what's a body for?), not like those toothpick foreign hussies. So what choice did women have but to aspire to look plump like the figs growing by an emerald sea? (This would not be significant until much later in life when their legs and thighs looked as though they'd been injected with tapioca pudding but even then, they took it as a sign of their kismet, or perhaps the evil eye, most likely an inevitable curse of their heredity, since they had witnessed the same happen to their own mothers and grandmothers on the wheel of fortune.)

But Aida, being only thirteen, was still endowed with God's gifts before He withdrew them, while blessing women with more children and longer life. If anything, she appeared undernourished. So, the family tried fattening her with enormous portions of sugar and lard—*boereks, tatlis,* baklavas, ladyfingers, beauty's navels, Imam fainted, slashed bellies, *dolmas,* tripe soup, and fatty mutton stews—the cuisine of their native Balkan regions that the Ottoman Turks had once annexed. In those days, nobody knew that kind of food was bad for health so they all lavished Aida with sinful delectables, which she continued burning off effortlessly. Alas, nothing, nothing seemed to work.

Out of desperation, poor Mihriban took her to an *evliya,* a seer, named Kum Baba, the *sand master,* who possessed a reputation for having the power to cure every imaginable affliction.

The *evliya* breezed her with prayers and blew on her face, washed her mouth with a sacred spring water, looked into her eyes. "My beauty, I have never seen anyone like you," he told her. "The whole world is right at your fingertips but your vanity, your vanity is your curse. Someday, it might cost you your happiness, even your life. I know because of what I see in your eyes—the smut, the impurities reveal themselves in those brown specks (Aida had paisley eyes like Esma—green with brown specks.) "You have to purify them, dissolve those dirty spots so that your eyes can turn blue—the way they are meant to be, the color of your soul."

He gave her special herbs to brew and Aida promised she would, but in no time became so absorbed with herself that she completely forgot the herbs. Gradually, however, a slight change came over her as a layer of softness padded her bones and a fine cushion of baby fat pampered her fairy tale fineness. Still, she was as slender as a willow but the family had good reason to be ecstatic because she secreted a liquid that smelled like the attar of roses. They celebrated by sacrificing a whole flock of sheep, whose meat they distributed among the poorest of the poor along with five thousand bowls of *bulgur.*

Alas, at last, their Aida had become a woman. Now she had the power.

Aida's scent wafted from street to street all through the city and lo, the *görücü,* those abominable matchmakers, those harpies in never-ending droves trailed to our threshold every hour, every day of the week to negotiate on behalf of their sons and nephews and uncles. But Aida showed not a trace of interest in any of the proposals. She found them so revolting that she decided to revolt herself.

Being the youngest she knew that her sisters had to be married off first before her own turn came. Dressed up in one of her fabulous outfits, curving her hips right and left, she would prance into the living room, carrying a coffee tray, flash a seductive smile as she served the *görücüs* but left the room immediately afterward, refusing to sit in a corner like a closed-up morning glory. Refusing to sit her head bent, eyes downcast, and hands folded on her lap—as the etiquette demanded—retaining this pose for interminable hours while the *görücü* went through their lists of criticisms, appraisals, offering points of negotiation, day after day.

I must say that Aida made it clear to everyone that she was doing this only because she did not wish to embarrass the family, but she was a modern girl, a living emblem of Atatürk's ideal of youth. She'd never, ever allow the *görücü* to dictate her marriage partner.

This was a relief for the household since they themselves had been obligated to spend too much time being hospitable to those leeches, so they put a sign on the gate which read: "*Görücüs* not accepted," a sign that eventually discouraged the suitors—unfortunately including the ones who came for Papatya and Sibel. Those girls required greater effort.

But Aida was still restless. A small passion had wedged itself into her heart of hearts, a passion greater than a wedding ring. But not a word did she whisper even to her sisters, who did not have an inkling of her secret desire. She confided only in her aunt Esma, who never came here but whom Aida visited occasionally. She felt a special affinity with her aunt that chagrined her parents at times, despite their generous, good hearts.

But one day, Iskender Bey found Aida weeping under the lilac gazebo. "What is it that ails you, my child?" he asked. He had great fondness for the girl who clearly had the *mana*, the female power. That's why he had given her the amber egg with the moth, which had once belonged to the girl's real mother, who had never forgiven him. "You can have anything you wish, you know?"

Unable to endure it any longer, Aida announced her dream, "I want to be the queen, dear Uncle."

"I'm sure you can if you wish. I'm sure there must be royalty who would be delighted to have your hand."

"I want to be a beauty queen."

On the one hand, they'd groomed Aida to compete with the most beautiful women in the Empire to become the Sultana. Now challenged to compete with others who lacked her breeding and looks, and rise above all as the beauty queen. This, of course, would bring the family into the public eye who thus far had simply been prospering in vast wealth and fortune, but managed to maintain an illusion of privacy.

Iskender Bey believed that such things as beauty contests were for common people and by participating, Aida would tarnish the family honor, but the women in the family vehemently disagreed with him. Wasn't Aida their collective creation who'd live out the dreams they themselves were not fortunate enough to manifest? In their hearts, all of them secretly desired the same, the triumph of their beauty. And finally, Iskender Bey, being a sensitive man who appreciated the wisdom of women, acquiesced without much issue.

But there was one problem. The contestants had to have short hair in order to set an example and support the modernization. Iskender Bey asked for exemptions and exceptions, even trying bribery and other unsavory methods of persuasion but the rule was unbendable. He asked Aida to change her mind, he offered her and her sisters a trip to Paris but Aida was so persistent, so determined that nothing, nothing would stand in her way even sacrificing her precious hair kissing the floor, which had taken her an entire lifetime to grow.

Since no public hairdressers were here in those days, her sisters, aunts, and great-aunts accompanied Aida to the barber shop on a humid midsummer's day. She was wearing a white straw hat with an enormously wide rim to protect her skin as she left.

I only know what happened from hearsay. This is what I've been able to conjecture, putting all the bits and pieces together:

They said when Aida sat in the barber's chair and took her hat off, the poor man was so moved with such celestial hair that he refused to cut it at first but she begged him.

"Are you certain you won't regret this?" he asked Aida pitifully.

"Absolutely," Aida replied.

So, the barber uttered a short prayer as he reluctantly grabbed his scissors and slashed her hair in one great strike—so as not to prolong the pain—right below her ears.

Then, it happened. Although he had shut the shades and put a "closed" sign to provide the women with full privacy, the door flew open and a young man in a military uniform, decorated with golden tassels and epaulets, walked in. The women gasped.

The barber was standing in the middle of the floor, holding the long beautiful mane in his hand with tears in his eyes. When the young lieutenant noticed the beauty unlike any other he had ever seen sitting in the barber chair, who now looked as vulnerable as the paintings of women martyrs, with an uncontrollable impulse, he got on his knees in front of her, took her hand, and kissed her on the wrist. Then, apologetically, he slipped outside as the barber shouted after him, threatening to yank out his ear and asked the forgiveness of the lady visitors, above all to Aida, for his son's impetuous behavior.

His son? A barber's son? The beginning of the end of it all. Such is fate.

Aida sat there, still feeling the young man's breath on the Y-shaped vein of her wrist, the same sensation she had witnessed being fondled by Azrael, the angel of death, who had stalked her since birth.

"Azrael likes beauty," Mihriban had told her once, "and when he isn't busy inhaling the last breath from old people, he visits pretty young girls and flirts with them, giving them a mysterious shiver all over their body, but especially their nipples and between their legs. If the beauty yields, Azrael keeps his embrace until she becomes weak in the knees, collapses, and begins suffering from consumption. Then, he abandons her, returning a few months later, to claim the beauty as one of his wives."

But later a wise old woman who worked at the silk house had told her that if you felt Azrael fondling you, pushed him away, and told him, "Go away now, and come back in the winter of my life," then swallowed three pomegranate seeds, he'd leave you well alone.

"But I thought pomegranate seeds caused Eve to be expelled from Paradise," Aida had exclaimed.

"Which do you prefer, the apple of my eye, death, or expulsion from paradise?"

So when Aida felt the breath of Azrael from the young man's kiss, she shouted, "Go away now, and come back in the winter of my life." With that, she grabbed the bowl of fruit next to the entrance, pinched three pomegranate seeds, and swallowed them immediately.

The young man returned for a moment and said, "I cannot wait that long. I'm the angel of life," and stormed out, leaving all the women in gasping suspense. He was a handsome youth, the spitting image of Robert Taylor in *Camille*, maybe even more dashing in his lieutenant's uniform. Son of a barber, yes, but fighting for his country and among the young elite. He belonged to the future.

The barber tied Aida's mane with a silk ribbon and gave it

to her. "Save this," he said. "It's priceless. If you like, I can make you a hairpiece." Then, with a smaller pair of shears, he shaped Aida's short hair, starting just where her cervical vertebrae ended in the back, tapering it longer in front, leveling just under her chin. Combing all the hair forward, over her face, he selected a handful and mowed it down, giving her some neatly tapering bangs. Then, he danced, letting the hair sift through his fingers like tiny feathers and catching the wisps in the air with his beak-like scissors. It was done.

"There," he said, and gave Aida a hand mirror so that she could see the back of her head. A perfect bob like Clara Bow's. The perfect "It" girl, but the rest of the women were wiping their tears, sensing something irrevocably lost.

Convinced that Aida was standing at the threshold of change, Mihriban took her to Kum Baba's shrine once again. "You must restrain your vanity," he told her as he read the coffee grains. "Or it's bound to be your doom." Aida laughed at the absurdity of the old man's prediction. She did not then believe in doom or gloom.

~

Besides losing her hair, two other important things happened to Aida in the following weeks. She lost her innocence and she became the queen.

The spinsters pulled out of the hope chest the finest *crepe d'amour* Esma had sent her for the occasion—spared all these years for an epiphany—and busied themselves day and night, imitating a ball gown for Aida they had seen in the movies. It was the loveliest dress in the world, yet the simplest.

The moment of her crowning lingers in everyone's memory, stretching like a flexible piece of gum passed from mouth to mouth. Wearing butter-colored swimming trunks that came to the middle of her thighs, on her shoulders an atlas cape in midnight blue trimmed with ermine, Aida paraded on the municipal stage along with the other beauties, all flashing pearl teeth and ample bosoms.

Just as the jury was getting ready to cast its vote, the door opened, and in he came, dressed in tails, a top hat, and a white pelerin. The great magician. They say he took one look at Aida and became oblivious to everything else around him the rest of the night. She kneeled in front of the Great Atatürk and he placed the golden coronet on her head.

"Like your family, I'm from the Balkans where I have seen many beautiful women," he told her. "Macedonian, Serbian, Wallachian, Romanian women, Bulgarian, Thessalonian, Thracian, Albanian, Slovenian women, Croatian, Transylvanian, Montenegrin, Besarabian, Moldavian, Bosnian women. But none, none of them can hold a candle to you. Never have I encountered a face more angelic, a spirit more radiant. You carry a piece of every one of those women! You carry their voices, their stories, yet unlike them, you're not of the past. You're the symbol of a modern world, a model for all its women. What I've been searching for all these years. The vision of a new nation! As such, I crown thee Miss Turkey."

His eyes rested on the tiny crescent-and-star birthmark on Aida's cleavage, the emblem of the flag. "And I see that I'm confirmed with every sign," as he kissed her hand.

Aida flashed her perfect pearl teeth and blinked coyly under her finely trimmed bangs and suddenly burst into tears. People gasped. Atatürk pulled his neatly folded monogrammed handkerchief and gave it to her. An unforgettable moment.

After the contest all the guests were invited here for an outdoor feast. Once the contestants and the public arrived, men and women separated like oil and water; they were not used to any other way.

An *al'a Turca* quintet consisting of an *ud*, a *ney*, a *tambour*, a *saz*, and a *davul* stirred in their seats. An aide of Atatürk's, a Rum of Italian descent, accompanied with an accordion. Cymbals clashed. The *ney* blew a melancholy breath, the musicians fumbled with their instruments as they slid into "La Cumparsita," the tango of all tangos, in the minor key.

The beat was sluggish at first, like a record playing at the wrong speed, but the momentum gained swiftly, as the music took baroque turns sounding like a circus overture.

Atatürk walked over to the women's side, bowed in front of Aida.

Although an accomplished belly dancer, Aida had never been exposed to the waltz or the tango. But she was the queen and the king himself was inviting her to the dance arena. She flashed her radiant smile and allowed him to put his arm around her waist—ah, the touch of *crepe d'amour*—and lead her to the middle of the floor as if in a trance.

They glided across the parquet like a pair of swans while everyone else watched, holding their breath. He held such dictatorship over this nubile beauty prone to having her way! She yielded to him with no resistance. No one could have guessed it was their first dance. As the accordion quivered, so did Aida, undulating her curvaceous hips, her supple shoulders and Atatürk, wearing an impeccably starched white grosgrain vest and a white papillon, his sun-bleached hair neatly slicked back, led with fluid steps despite his age, fashioning intricate poses and attitude, now bending Aida from the waist, now whirling her around the freshly polished parquet. To all eyes, they had become Fred and Ginger.

Atatürk, mind you, unlike other scruffy politicians and dictators, was a man of extraordinary elegance, extraordinary grace—a narcissist, an exhibitionist of the first degree. They say, as a young man in Paris, he'd made it his business to learn the tango from the famous Argentine Carlos Gardel himself, anticipating the right moment to dazzle his subjects.

The other male guests, trained to mimic their leader, walked one by one to the women's side and steered their wives, sisters, daughters to the dance floor. Ah, what an evening! Tango on a pentatonic scale but soon drowned in the rapture of the dance itself, the bodies were rippling with their own compulsive rhythm to the voluptuous beat. The dancers contorted their bellies and snapped their fingers as if dancing the *zeybek*, a rhythmic pattern of nine beats, rather than a tango of four. But it was so inspired.

The musicians, deciphering from the sheet music of the accordion player, freshly promoted to the position of band leader, expanded their fledgling repertoire to "La Violetera, Vida Mia, El Esquinazo," and "Jalousie," as the older ladies with babushkas watched the dancing couples, not knowing whether to smile or scorn, whispering prayers and rolling their worry beads.

At the end of the night, Atatürk handed Aida over to his first lieutenant, lo and behold none other than the barber's handsome son, which he never should have done but, then again, no one can interfere with the hand of kismet. It's written on one's forehead at birth, they say. Atatürk's kismet was never to make a family—perhaps why, in years to come, he would adopt nineteen children. His skills in patience and strategy, attack and retreat, had made him the finest of military leaders but he had miscalculated the power of youth. What a defeat!

After that night, it was as though Aida had fallen under a mystical spell that suddenly gave her the power to attain *anything*. But still living within her world of carnal limitations, she was oblivious to this endowment. Even though her boundaries were vast, she was trapped in her flesh, bursting with the visceral urge of eros and confronted with the impossibility of going against one's destiny.

What happened that night after the contest? No one knew for sure but most presumed that the lieutenant simply drove Aida to the Palace and delivered her to the Leader. He sat in the silver Daimler the rest of the night, waiting.

Some imagine, however, that he drove silently in Atatürk's silver Daimler until they reached the top of Camlica, the highest hill overlooking the Bosphorus with the most splendid panorama. He stopped the car, raised Aida's *crepe d'amour* skirt, and put it to his lips.

This is one of those secrets we'll never know for sure—except for Aida, Atatürk, and the young lieutenant.

~

No one bothered washing out the rose stain on Aida's dress, accepting it as a badge of honor. Not for a second did they doubt that it belonged to the great man and had to be preserved. They folded it carefully, and kept it in a trunk as though it were a holy relic. (Her niece Amber would inherit it later on.)

The lieutenant now came here every day in Atatürk's Daimler to collect Aida and brought her back at the hour of the wolf. Everyone in the family wishfully assumed, of course, that she was being delivered to the Leader, and although they were dying to know where the "couple" went, what they did, what he said to her, how she responded, no one asked questions and Aida's own lips were sealed.

She began to sleep till noon and in the afternoons stayed in her room, surrounded by exotic plants and birds, eating boxes of chocolate bonbons, *maron glacées*, Turkish delight, and colored marzipan in the shape of animals and fruit that her suitor had sent her.

Before long, her body began to fill, and the family cheered, because although most efforts had been futile in getting her plump, obviously the great man's sweetmeats were doing the magic—or so they thought but the women noticed the vacant gaze, the aloofness surrounding Aida since the beauty contest. She no longer seemed enthusiastic about her fittings, or priceless fabrics or designs from Iskender Bey's travels.

Everyone in the city knew that the Number One Daimler came to the İpekçi house every evening and left with the beauty queen. Droves of distant relatives, forgotten acquaintances appeared at my doorstep, trying to get a glimpse of the goddess—strangers dangling like evil-eye talismans from the tall stone wall surrounding the house. In response, Aida flaunted her own charms, modeling her legendary wardrobe, but in her own eyes she was absent, having dissociated from the needs of others. While she continued her secret outings, her body was also ripening. How women repeat their mothers' sins!

❧

It happened at the end of Ramadan just like this: The family had woken up to a predawn feast. They came to the dining room in their sleeping clothes, huddled together sleepy-eyed around the copper brazier, but none would miss a delicious middle-of-the-night *iftar* feast for the sake of empty dreams.

The servants brought tray after tray of delectables, forty different kinds of olives, *boereks* and *dolmas* stuffed with every possible nut and grain, green, red, purple vegetables and fruits, goat cheeses, Circassian chickens, giant baked mussels, numerous eggplant dishes, marrow and tripe soup with yogurt and peppermint, pita breads, baklavas, *ashures,* puddings, and *helvahs.* Fingers were into everything.

Aida was out as usual. Papatya and Sibel, not really fasting but pretending to in order to feast with the rest of the family—that's why those girls were always so plump.

In the middle of their feast, they heard the engine of the familiar car and soon Aida came in, her hair tussled, her dress creased in her midriff—she was bursting in the middle. In her hand, she held a bowl of cocoons. She sat down next to her uncle Iskender and proceeded to crack the shells and devour the pupa as if eating pistachios.

Everyone was speechless. Had their beauty gone loony?

"*Görücü* will be visiting in the afternoon," she announced casually. "Please, remove the sign from the gate."

Sighs, and squeals of delight rose from the women's sweet throats.

Iskender Bey told Aida he was proud, he knew she'd be a perfect wife for an important man, give him the best of children. She'd be a real queen. "May you and your husband grow old on the same pillow," he blessed her, a father to the young woman since the Pasha's passing.

In her room, Aida cried all night. Normal, they thought for a bride-to-be.

Great preparations took place the next day, the ladies eager to meet the Leader's emissaries. But, alas, it was the barber's wife who arrived with the *görücü*, asking Aida's hand in marriage to her handsome lieutenant son.

That's when Iskender went to Aida's room and took away the amber egg with the frozen cocoon inside.

ॐ

Fate has mysterious ways. Soon after the modest wedding, the lieutenant was sent to Germany as the military attaché and his wife accompanied him.

"Aida," they'd say later, "had the power to change family history but instead she chose an ordinary life and married a barber's son." Even though he'd become a great general later on, in their eyes he remained a flea. Blame it on beauty.

After Aida left, Iskender Bey did not smile for years. Ending his travels in pursuit of the finest threads, he retired here with his consorts, irrevocably lost in a vacuous world of silk dreams.

ॐ

Spinster, *n, 1. a woman who spins, whose occupation is to spin thread.*

ॐ

ISKENDER AND AMBER

The first time Iskender saw Amber was the end of silk harvest, a sultry June day—the end of Ramadan. Ever since Esma's death, he had not returned to Izmir. In fact, he hadn't gone anywhere for ages, cocooning himself with his silkworms and what little was left of the extended family.

79

I remember how, meandering through the disarrayed trails of Mount Olympus, the *araba* labored up the unpaved road. I traced it along the foothills where peach orchards webbed out with fruit so large that branches lay about broken from the weight. In the valley below, the fog was hanging like a giant umbrella over the dung-brick farms and Pillars of dung smoke rose from the plateau where flocks of sheep grazed, blissfully oblivious to their imminent destiny.

The *araba* rattled higher up the holy mountain road where bubbling hot springs oozed out of the sulfurous earth near the precinct called Grasshopper. The snowy peaks widened there, thawing into a landscape of silk plantations, where wild lavender and pink hyacinths scented the air, thinner and more damp at this higher altitude, prime for mulberry—and silk, of course. The best of its kind.

Ambling through the avenue of white oleander hedges, the *araba* finally turned into the courtyard, lurched to one side, and came to a jolting stop. Cadri got off, took in the mountain air, and once again observed the complex of pavilions with colossal arches and columns shaded by cedars of Lebanon, surrounded with reflection ponds, small cascades, and fountains.

I could sense the eyes darting behind the lattices. Shuffling of light feet along the corridors. Whispers. The doors opened as if by magic and a bevy of women—wrinkled old ladies with irrepressible babushkas, golden-teethed buxoms with gold bracelets jingling up to their elbows, the matriarchs with elephant legs—wobbled in through the great wooden doors.

Cadri helped a young woman still in city clothes climb down the *araba*, followed by a maid holding the hand of a little girl.

The women took a quick peek at the wife—rumors flying around. And, of course, later ogled the little girl, their latest progeny, passing her from arm to arm and lap to lap, pinching and kissing and squeezing until the child rebelled, burying herself under her mother's armpits. Who could blame her uncertainty?

Camilla would describe Mihriban later as a woman "with dehydrated skin so taut you can stretch a drum." Mihriban's eyes watered, seeing the child. She extended her bejeweled hand and baptized her with a flask of attar of roses.

"The resemblance is uncanny. . . ."

"Enough, enough," the child shrieked as she rubbed her scratchy eyes; burnt with alcohol. But promised sour cherry sherbet made from the mountain snow, oh, she smiled, exposing two missing front teeth—uninhibited by the huge gap, seeing herself through the other's eyes full of inexplicable adoration. She indeed was adorable.

"So, what's new?"

"Oh, the General is just back from Korea. Missing an eye," Mihriban explained.

"Yes, yes, we heard. How awful that is."

"Aida went off with him to visit his mother. They should be back tomorrow for the Feast of Sacrifice."

"And their boy?"

"No good," Mihriban whispered to Cadri. "Like he's swallowed a bad seed or something. Aida can't tame Osman. But maybe now that the general is back, who knows?"

Cadri and Camilla exchanged meaningful glances as if they shared a secret.

Mihriban kept staring at the child. "*Maşallah*. May the evil eye stay away from her angel face. How old are you now, Amber?"

"Six and ten months."

"May the angels protect her, Cadri. Such a smart little girl. Is she doing well in school?"

"*Chok*. Already reads and writes and knows the numbers. Prefers books over dolls. Reads all the time. Likes to draw pictures. She has curiosity for sure."

"*Maşallah*. A thousand blessings on your mother, Cadri. If she could only see us all like this!" Then, more tears and the sound of rolling worry beads.

"I think she can," Amber cut in unexpectedly.

Heads turned around with sudden alarm. The child obviously crossed to the invisibles like the others but she should be made to forget them. She should be distracted. Or else she'll grow pixilated. Like Esma.

A sudden telepathic force swarmed above them, like the kind that begins and ends frogs' songs or a flying goose taking the lead of a flock. Whispers faded into a gradual hush. The old man had entered the room, wearing a full-length bearskin—Iskender's thermostat was reversed—cold in the summer, hot in the snow. Leaning on his walking stick, shifting his weight, pushing off with the silky smooth movements of an eagle gliding. Remote and elegant, he passed his hand around the room with an air of indifference until the little girl kissed it at her turn, touched it to her forehead, and caught his eye as she lifted her head.

"What is your name, child?" His voice cracking slightly, obviously touched by the resemblance.

The girl took his hand and wrote the letters with her index finger inside his palm.

"A-M-B-E-R," he spelled. "Amber. The divine liquid of great purity. It becomes you." Then, he turned to her and smiled a smile worth a thousand smiles.

No one had thought he'd ever smile again. Iskender had not cut a smile for so long. How many years? One forgets. Since Aida's beauty contest maybe. Or before, when he and Esma were estranged. How touching that was.

"You have crooked teeth," the child told the old man and he looked very sad for a moment, then leaning on his cane left the room for another distraction. Or maybe to find some solace in his confused heart.

"You shouldn't have said that! You should never say such things to your elders," Camilla scolded Amber. "You made him leave."

"But he does. It's the truth." Darkness came over the child's face, a deep sadness children are immune to.

"She's tired. She needs a siesta," Camilla apologized. "I'll take her away."

The young family lingered on a verandah the rest of the afternoon, enclosed in steaming glass like orchids. They were meditative and languid, stretched out on the sagging wicker chairs with loose joints, listening to the sounds of the fountain playing through the French doors. Gonca fanned the child while Cadri wrote in his little black diary and Camilla crocheted a bonnet for some relative's baby until she was unable to move her limbs or lips.

Amber tried to ignore the flies, burying herself in a new coloring book, *The Great Women in History*, line drawings, identified as Cleopatra, Queen of Sheba, Florence Nightingale—all glamorous like movie stars. But it was Joan of Arc that she was transfixed on, hands tied, face anguished, peeled by flames—or so it seemed. Amber wondered what it would feel like to burn so much, like a lamb turned on the spit. How it would sizzle and fizzle, the way it did the time she stuck her hand on the brazier and touched the embers breathing with such beauty. An early lesson. When you play with fire, you get scars.

As the setting sun smudged the sky before vanishing behind the mountain, the pounding of the distant kettledrums reverberated through the valley. A hundred times, announcing the end of Ramadan. They immediately broke their fast with a ritual olive, wrinkled and greasy, mumbled blessings, gulped down the rosewater with roasted pinions. So ended the thirty days of fasting, what awaited them now was a great feast.

Aida's son Osman arrived late from quail hunting with the caretaker. He was a slight lad, beginning to get fuzz on his face, and his voice dropped to a pebbly baritone. When he sat down, a heavy silence surrounded the table as if their unity was disturbed, as if they feared to agitate him, as if to avoid his tantrums.

"Tripe again!" he groaned, making a farting sound. "Never anything decent to eat around here. Either tripe or trout."

"What's tripe?" Amber asked.

Osman looked at her with a chilling hunger, as I witnessed the culmination of my fears.

"Where their shit travels before coming out," he carried on, something obscene about his mouth, his lips like the inside of a snail.

"Don't listen to him," Cadri interfered. "He's shameless. Tripe is the stomach, not what he says it is."

"I'm not eating," Amber whined.

Camilla crossed her worry lines together. "A guest must eat what she's offered."

Amber shook her head again. Camilla dove with her spoon into her daughter's soup, stuck it in the girl's mouth. Amber pushed her hand away, splattering the soup on the freshly starched tablecloth. Camilla's hand hit her cheek.

"She doesn't have to eat it," Mihriban told Camilla. "It's all right. Children don't have much taste for tripe anyway. It's all right, you see?"

"But the tablecloth."

"Don't worry. It will come out in the wash."

As the family dispersed after dinner, Osman talked Amber into going with him to the library. Something inside her told her not to but she went anyway. She was testing the boundaries of her fear. He showed her a children's illustrated version of a Koran with pictures of different prophets and saints. Moses, Jesus, and Mohammed.

Osman pointed at a white-bearded man wearing a dress like a burnoose, looking at a sheep hanging down from the sky.

"This is Abraham. God asked him to sacrifice his son, a boy named Ishmael, to prove his devotion. Abraham loved God so much—much better than his sons, better even than his own life—so he agreed. He took the little boy—who was about your age—on top of a mountain just like this Mount Olympus here and was about to cut his throat," he made a slashing gesture.

"But how could he do it to his own son?"

"Parents are evil."

Amber wanted to get away, to disappear but the hallway was long and dark. He would follow her and catch her. He was so much bigger. Then, they heard some footsteps.

"But Allah lowered a sheep from the sky. So, Abraham sacrificed it instead, winning God's love," Mihriban interfered. "That's why we sacrifice sheep every Bayram, to give our thanks for saving the little boy's life. Come with me now, sweet child. Let's go to the *hamam*. We'll do some henna and I'll tell you more stories."

Maybe she also possessed a sixth sense.

کرے

The *hamam* is decorated entirely with tiles—tiles of birds, of flowers, and an enormous tree of life—all fired in Kutahya, the slim Byzantine columns supporting the stained glass dome, remnants of the legendary Theodora's basilica. Underneath, the natural sulfur springs are still bubbling. Around the edges of the pool, a rust color had formed from the persistent steam.

"Smells like rotten eggs," Amber complained when she came in, pinching her nose.

She watched through a curtain of mist, the women wrapped in *peshtemals,* undressing in the tepidarium. Stubby legs, fat hips waddled around sideways. Fat so unkind to flesh in age.

Mihriban pumiced Amber's back. Lots of tension in the little body.

"Did you know Cleopatra and the Queen of Sheba bathed in this pool?"

"They did?"

"Oh, every thermal town in Asia Minor claims the same," Camilla interfered.

"They sure did," Mihriban continued ignoring her. "This water is so precious that once upon a time, long before even Cleopatra and the Queen of Sheba, a vicious dragon with seven heads guarded it, not allowing a soul near its source."

"Every spring the people had to sacrifice a maiden so that the dragon would spare them some water. Without water there's no life. You know that, don't you? Without water everything dies. So, they had no choice but to sacrifice their daughters to the dragon until the women stopped rearing children, terrified of giving birth to girl babies.

"Hearing this tragic and unjust story, a young lad traveled far from another land beyond the Aegean. He arrived at the fountain just at the moment the last maiden was tied to a rock, about to be sacrificed. This daring young man confronted the dragon, unsheathed his sword, and with one strike, slush, slash, he decapitated the monster, rescuing the terrified maiden."

Mihriban had told the story so many times that she had come to believe that it actually had happened.

Amber opened her eyes, "And then?"

A girl was passing around a pot of the greenish mud-like stuff—all except Camilla were dipping their hands and feet in the pots and sliding into mitts. Amber too held out her hands.

"You'll have bright-orange hands like peasant girls," Camilla said.

"I don't care. I want to be hennaed."

"Your friends will make fun of you when we go back."

"I don't care."

"Go ahead then. Have your hands done, see if I care, but not your feet because I don't want you to slip and fall when you get up in the middle of the night to pee. You'll break your neck with those mummy bandages on."

Amber turned to Mihriban again, "And then what happened?"

"Then, the townspeople were so happy that they made the youth their Sultan. He married the young maiden and they lived happily ever after and people never worried about water again. The spring flowed freely, bringing healing to people. So ends the story. Three apples have fallen from a tree—one belongs to you, one to me, and the last to the storyteller."

The hypnotic rhythm of the water, the hollow sounds of wet wooden clogs, the soothing hands gliding over her fine skin lulled Amber into a hypnotic slumber as the stories went once again late into the night, turning into women's gossip.

ꕤ

Amber tossed and turned all night in the bed she was not accustomed to—everything of eiderdown. All night long, the eerie bleating of the sheep wove in and out of silence. The chill of her damp hands, the feculent smell of henna, and outside, the sheep's anticipatory cries wove into peculiar dreams until Gonca shook her out of sleep around sundown so that she could see them "do it."

"Children should be accustomed to things like this. It's all part of becoming a grown-up," her father had told Amber. "It won't hurt so much when you see it again. Pain loses its strength with repetition."

Gonca removed the bandages. The child squealed with delight at her bright-orange hands. Rinsing off the henna.

"But how could he do that to his son?"

"Who?"

"Abraham."

"They believe no love is greater than the love of the Divine."

When Amber and Gonca walked down to the meadow, a group had gathered around a black-and-white sheep with a red ribbon around its horns, already blindfolded, its legs tied to a stump. Osman stood next to a man with octopus eyes and menacing black mustache, who was sharpening his knife against a whetstone as the others stood in silence. Amber caught the man's dark gaze. She looked away.

"That man, I saw him in a dream," she told Gonca.

"Murat? He's just the caretaker."

"He was going around with a scimitar, slashing a field of watermelons, which turned into heads of people, separated from their bodies. Let's go away, Nanny. I don't want to watch."

"Be patient,"

Although some plantation hands held down the beast, tensing with all its might, it began bleating as if sensing this holy menace.

"Can't you see, it's crying for help," Amber told Gonca, squeezing her hand. "Please, do something. Please."

"Hang on, child, it's almost over. We must make ourselves

stay to the end. Your parents wanted you to watch, you know?" She pulled the hair off Amber's eyes so that the child could see better. Amber covered her face with her hands but peeked between her fingers—an irresistible impulse.

In a flash, the knife hit the jugular; an enormous fountain of blood squirted out of the sheep's throat as it convulsed and shook, convulsed and shook. The blindfold slipped; its eyes became fixed on an invisible spot somewhere in the distance, at the last moment opening its mouth to make a sound but squirting a flood of red flourish instead.

No one remembers what happened at that moment but suddenly Amber was kneeling next to the sheep. She put her hand on the animal's throat where a stream of blood was gushing. Although Gonca caught up and steered her away from the dead animal, a bloody imprint of the tiny hand remained on the stump for some time, which they were unable to remove.

Murat had already removed the skin and slashed the belly; the entrails spilled out, delicate membranes of transparent pinkish tubes, vessels, great soft sculptural shapes of kidneys and liver and heart and eyes and sweetbreads and brain. Within minutes, the sheep was chopped into its components, ready to be distributed among the poor who were already gathering outside the gates.

Amber cast a last furtive glance. First time seeing the death of a substantial being. She began throwing up. Gonca rushed her to her room and gave her some chamomile tea. She washed the child, painted her toes with blood-red nail polish, then, dressed her in her new *Bayram* dress with purple pansies, a giant bow in her hair of the same fabric. When Amber saw her image in the mirror, she began to cry.

"I don't know why," Gonca said. "Please, don't cry. I won't tell your parents what happened. And no one, no one else will

know. I promise. Run along now. Kiss everyone's hands and collect your loot. But you're not supposed to count it till you're
alone."

In the *lemonier*, jewelry discreetly chimed, the women were
basking in musky perfumes as they fanned themselves. Amber
went around the room kissing hands and collecting a handkerchief from each containing coins while they fussed about her
new *Bayram* dress. "*Çok güzel, çok yakişmiş. Maşallah.*"

After it was all over, she slipped out onto the verandah
where she could be alone to count her booty. She did not notice
that she wasn't alone.

It was mostly brass coins with a hole in the center. Thirty-
two liras in all. Quite a score! She dreamed of the chocolate
gaufrettes she could get that came with trading cards of movie
stars—Esther, Liz, Marilyn, Gina, Elaine Stewart, Patricia Med-
ina. She dreamed of a Faber watercolor set with forty-eight different colors. And lots of paper to draw houses.

Suddenly, she became aware of the other presence. Iskender
was watching her. "How much have you collected?" he asked.

"About fifty," Amber lied, startled somewhat.

"You could do better. Maybe more hands to kiss?"

Amber took the wrinkled hand with the beautiful blue
veins, touched it to her lips, then her forehead.

Iskender squeezed her nose. "Close your eyes." He slipped
something in her palm. "Now open your eyes. Hold it to light."

A yellow transparent stone, the size of a plum. Inside, a perfectly preserved moth, the facets of its eyes, veins in its wings,
even the combs of its antenna as vivid as life, climbing out of its
cocoon.

"It's beautiful. What is it?"

"Amber. Like your name."

"Where did it come from?"

"No one knows."

He explained to her that amber originally was ambergris but afterward, through some confusion, came to mean this translucent fossil resin that entombs insects. "In French amber *gris* is gray amber; amber *jaune*, yellow amber. The Greeks called it *elektron*—where the word "electricity" comes from—or "substance of the sun."

"When you hold a piece of amber to the sun, it attracts the sunshine to itself and explodes with celestial brilliance. The first people made fire by rubbing two pieces of amber together. *Zip-zap*. Without amber there would be no fire. And without fire, no civilization."

"But where does it really come from?"

"Well, a long, long time ago, there was nothing but trees. Great broadleaf conifers interspersed with hardwoods formed vast forests on the earth. When it rained endlessly, lakes, rivers, oceans formed. These trees felt the fate of the world (by fate he meant kismet, of course) and wept resins. After the ice melted, the entire surface of the earth was covered with amber. Yellow fossil glazed the surface, the rocks, even the tops of old trees. Can you imagine what it must have looked like?"

"Lemon candy?"

"Liquid gold. Anyway, many, many years later, the waves eroded the coastal sediments, revealing amber-rich layers of earth. You see, amber is so light that it floats in saltwater. So, millions of pieces of amber, trapped in seaweed, washed up to the beaches, especially after tumultuous storms—hurricanes, monsoons, tempests, typhoons, siroccos, tsunamis."

Amber peered again in deep fascination at the tiny moth emerging from the fluffy white cocoon, all happening so fast that the moth had not been able to escape before the resin had hardened.

"Is it the silk moth? The Bombyx?"

Iskender slouched forward, leaning on his cane with both hands, and laughed. "How did you know about the Bombyx?"

"Everyone knows."

"No, not exactly. But since you asked, it's an ancestor, I'm sure. Millions of years old. Here, take it. It's yours now but promise not to show it to anyone and not to betray your fate. Promise?"

"Why?"

"Because it has great fields of attraction and ultimately can be taken away from you. Adults don't like children possessing such powerful things."

"Why?"

They heard Camilla calling Amber. She came out to the verandah, seeing the child and patriarch in such intimacy.

"Amber, what are you doing here? Iskender Bey, I hope she's not intruding."

"Not in the least. We're already old friends."

The mother snatched the girl away. As Amber waved goodbye, something in the casual way she dangled her wrist threw Iskender back in time. He saw fragments of his life flash before him. Everything condensed into a second and everything in motion.

Visitors poured in and out all morning, saying little while the İpekçi women scurried around with plates of pistachio marzipan, Turkish delight, and served homemade fruit liquors, which even the children were allowed during the *Bayram*. With each guest Amber toasted a shot of banana liquor, which she savored.

At lunchtime, they served the lamb roast on a bed of mint. Amber felt sick.

It must be all the banana liquor, Camilla thought. Gonca suspected the memory of sacrifice.

"It's not the animal you saw," she told Amber. "People never eat their own sacrifice. This is a gift from another plantation. It's a sacrament to eat it."

The child was noticeably distraught. Maybe she had affinities with animals, animist tendencies like herself. Finally she carried Amber to the room they shared, adjoining Cadri and Camilla's suite, the one called "Solitude," and put her down for a nap.

The walls always remained cool and humid from the stone and stucco. The room was furnished like a monastery, white piquet covers on the simple beds and nothing else except a vase of hyacinths. Out of the window, it overlooked a tranquil view of the mountain. Then, the infinite rows of mulberry trees.

Instantly, Amber was asleep.

　　　　　　　　　　ぞ

She woke up midafternoon, an oppressive humidity filling the room, which even the laboring overhead fan could not subdue. Through the crack between the shutters, she could see the small herd of Angora goats tracking up the mountain, hear the music of their bells. As she lay on the bed observing the moth inside her amber rock, she suddenly sensed her aloneness. Camilla and the other women still had not returned from visiting relatives. Gonca was helping in the kitchen. And Cadri? Time when he would retire to his room to write poetry, a luxury he hadn't had for a long time.

Amber jumped out of bed, ran across the corridor into the *selam*, the men's quarters, shouting, "*Baba, baba,* where are you?"

A strange music drifted out of one of the rooms and the smoke of olibanum rose through the corridor. The door a crack open. She peeked into a jungle of velvet drapes, Buddha heads, carnivorous plants, golden braziers, ancient tombstones, assorted smoking-pipes, maps, musical instruments, peculiar ephemera. An ancient map of Asia Minor was titled "Map of Turquoise." Clumps of brown photographs pinned on the walls. One showed two men dressed in Bedouin clothes smoking *nargilehs* in front of a coffee shop somewhere on the Silk Road, a backgammon board between them. Another showed Iskender on camelback dressed like a sheik.

In a corner of the room, Iskender sat cross-legged on the floor, in awesome concentration, writing on a lacy tobacco leaf with gilded ink. Without lifting his eyes from his work, he told her to come in. Amber walked over to his table, peered at what he was writing.

"What brings you to the men's quarters?" he asked in a sonorous voice.

"When I woke from my nap, no one was around. I came looking for my *baba*."

"Things have a way of disappearing when we sleep, don't they? That's why I stopped sleeping."

"You don't sleep?"

"We sleep only to dream. But if you can learn to dream while awake, sleep becomes unnecessary."

"But how do you learn?"

"Sometimes we might stumble upon a passageway into dreams."

She looked intently at his face. His right eye much brighter than his left. She had not noticed it before. In fact, one eye was blue, the other yellow.

"Just like the Angora cat at my grandparents Taşpinar's house," she told him.

"What is?

"Your eyes."

Iskender smiled. He cranked up, raising himself with grace unusual for a man his age, faced the little girl.

"Your father's gone walking to the silk hatcheries. But I'm here. You have nothing to fear," he reassured, shaking her hand like an equal. Instantly, the difference in age melted between them. "Now, look at my hands," he went on. "What do you see? They're empty. Right?" In the air, he painted strange movements, then flashed a transparent scarf in violet. Indigo and blue followed. Green, yellow, orange, and red. Seven colors of the rainbow, seven veils. "Here, feel them. Just feel them. Touch them against your cheek, feel the warm supple beauty of their fiber. My finest silk spun by worms I've been crossing for decades to produce the most luminescent spit. Feel it, Amber."

Amber stood across rubbing her cheeks against the silk with the tentativeness of stroking a fledgling dropped out of its nest.

"You'll never feel anything finer, Amber," he continued. "Our silk is better than the Chinese, which is the best in the world. Not many get a chance to touch the royal silk, you know, the spin of the queen moth. But a lucky star is following you all your life. Good thing, too, you'll need it to balance your difficult kismet. But you better go now. I have a map to draw, hours to contemplate. Tomorrow I'll show you how silk is made. All right? Go, now. Go, look into your amber stone. Maybe it will help you to learn to dream while you're awake. Tell me later what you discover."

Amber caught a glimpse of Iskender as she labored to close the heavy door. The old man readjusted his body, settled into a recline on a divan. From a small box, he pinched a piece of black paste, rolled it into a pea-sized ball, and stuck it into his strange-looking pipe. Then seared it with a hot poker from the brazier, inhaling the smoke.

"What is it?" Amber asked before shutting the door.

"Oh, the white poppy. Tastes like dung."

"Then, why are you smoking it?"

"I close my eyes and watch images pass like an endless procession of caravans. So many worlds besides this one, Amber. Just a matter of finding your passageway. And some ways are better than others."

Iskender propped himself up against dozens of pillows, keeping his gaze on a fern plant. He seemed transfixed. Looking at it, Amber saw at that moment what he saw. The sense of time had slowed down to such a degree that Iskender could actually see the young leaves uncurl into spiky fans. He could see plants grow like time lapse photography. Through his eyes, she saw the same.

It rained that night as it always did after the sacrifice, washing away the blood of the beasts. The rain concealed the slightest hint of the morning's ritual—even the little handprint that had threatened the caretaker had been washed away by the incessant movement of water.

In the morning, while the women gossiped over breakfast, Amber slipped away, bouncing from pavilion to pavilion, from room to room, in pursuit of secret passageways—an escape hatch, a closet, a mirror. She opened door after door, seeking hidden worlds behind.

She entered a room, a woman's room, atlas blue with painted stars. Garments of silk, colors of the moon. An ornately carved three-leaf vanity, inlaid with gems, reputed to have belonged to Aimée de Rivery, the great French Sultana.

Aida found the child in front of the mirror—smeared with rouge, kohled eyebrows, resembling the rambunctious shadow puppet, *Karagöz*, the Black Eyes. The vanity, the floors, Amber's *Bayram* dress were all covered in pink dust. The blue perfume bottles were tipped open and an overpowering scent of lilac and violet filled the air. Amber was about to pass out from the scent when Aida walked in. Amber recognized her aunt immediately. She'd seen Aida's pictures everywhere. In bathing suits and ball gowns, even one dancing with the great Atatürk. Amber pouted, cast down her eyes, expecting a reprimand. But Aida smiled, sat next to her, their image reflected in the mirror side by side.

This was the first moment Amber recognized her own vanity.

"Your scent, my little passion. You should never give it away. If anyone steals your scent, they can steal your soul, you know?" Aida explained.

She took a bottle, rubbed the little crevice between the child's nose and lips. "Smell this, Amber, she said, you know what makes it so potent? Ambergris. Like your name. You know where it comes from? From the intestines of the sperm whale—a big, clumsy leviathan exuding this sensuous substance. Imagine! They kill big giant mammal-fish just to get this precious substance? What tragedy! But take a whiff. Isn't it to die for?"

Amber still pouted, peeking at her beautiful aunt, filtered under her baby long lashes, noticing Aida's peach skin, the low-cut dress, exposing the half domes of her faintly freckled breasts. The left one had a birthmark, a crescent and a five-pointed star. She touched it unself-consciously and made tiny circles with her fingers.

"How did you get this?"

"A gift, Aida said, from the great genie. Remember, always put the lid on a perfume bottle immediately after using one! You know why? Because genies live in perfume bottles. When you open the bottle, the genie's breath slowly escapes. That's what we smell. Genie's breath. But if you leave it open for too long, he loses his breath and has to escape to find another bottle. Once a genie leaves, he can never come back."

Aida, put her arm around Amber, wiped her cheeks gently with a handkerchief until the harshness of red rouge began to fade. Two faint circles appeared, one on each cheek.

"There," Aida said. "Not too much, nor too little. Beauty should never appear artificial." She spat into her handkerchief, wiped off the kohl smudged all over Amber's forehead, tried again. The blackness finally faded. "See how lovely you look now? My little sultana. And just a little lipstick now. Wouldn't you like that?"

"Yes."

"Of course, you would. But you shouldn't purse your lips like wrinkled figs. Give us a smile now. Smile."

Amber grinned to stretch her lips while Aida filled them with brilliant red, holding the tiny chin, lifting the child's face up to the morning light, straying through the empty spaces of the lace curtain.

When Amber looked at the mirror, she grinned a toothless grin, pleased with herself. Her first vanity lesson. From her aunt, the former beauty queen.

Aida then led Amber to the reflection pond where she told her the story of Narcissus. How sooo beautiful the lad was, how he had fallen in love with his own image reflected in crystal clear water. "But when he wanted to possess this image of himself, he fell into the stream and drowned. You should never allow yourself to peer so deeply into anything that it could drown you, promise me, sugar peach?"

"All right."

The following morning, Amber was initiated into the mysteries of sericulture. Iskender showed her everything—harvesting the cocoons, removing the chrysalis, setting free the moths so they could make more eggs.

"With patience, mulberry leaves become the finest fabric,"

he explained. "Silkworms dislike eating wet leaves; therefore, you should never feed them when the leaves have dew but also be careful not to when the sun begins to warm the earth because they dislike eating hot leaves as well. When the silkworms have just been born you should keep them far from the kitchen, in a place where smells cannot intrude because they dislike having fish or meat nearby. They dislike grains being pounded. They dislike resonant objects like drums being struck. They are not happy when a woman who has recently given birth becomes their keeper; they are jealous of the baby and they can smell the milk in her breasts. They dislike it when a man making wine gives them mulberry leaves to eat; they dislike smoke and the smell of coffee. They dislike the smell of *raki* and of the seven sour herbs. They dislike rancid smells, the smell of musk, the smell of sex. They dislike it when dirty people come into the breeding house. They dislike it when, in the daytime, a window is opened to the wind. They dislike the light of the setting sun. When it is hot, they dislike a violent wind or a sharp cold. When it is cold, they dislike a sudden and excessive heat. They like silence."

As the old man and the girl strolled through the mulberry groves, she asked why there wasn't any fruit on the trees. "The one in our garden makes sweet purple berries," she told him. "When they ripen, we lay sheets underneath, shake the tree, shake it until the berries rain from the branches. I love the taste of mulberries."

He explained that his trees were of a different sort—the white mulberry, *Morus alba*, which bears neither flower nor fruit. Once upon a time it did, but this took so much vitality from making leaves that they had to be sterilized. Now, the essence of the tree is concentrated in its leaves instead. Look how thick and broad the leaves are. Tastes different, too. See? He put the leaf in his mouth, slowly chewed and swallowed it. He gave Amber a leaf as well but she made a face and shook her head. Then, they both burst into giggles.

Iskender told the story of every tree and stone, reinventing everything on the spur of the moment, spinning stories until they became completely ludicrous but still credible. He watched Amber's face, roared with laughter at her gaping wonder.

He told her stories of the Silk Road, of places where people were yellow, where they ate monkeys. Of giant ants guarded by griffins digging up the earth for gold, of pearl divers who found treasures buried beneath the sea in dark and sinister caves, of skinny naked men who sat on beds of nails, of people who lived hundreds of years because they drank out of a special spring, of others who reclined in the shade cast by an enormous foot, of giants and unicorns, lions and tigers, jewels scattered everywhere like dust, the cobras that guarded them, and of perfumes and silk that grew on trees.

He led her to the egghouse. "Too small for you to see but look through this magnifying glass." Clusters of silk eggs, pearly blue and translucent like their moths, resembling bunches of minuscule grapes. "We must keep the seeds—that's what we call the eggs—cool and dormant to prevent hatching too early," he explained. "Otherwise, we lose the silk."

Next door, flatbeds stretched for the eggs getting ready to hatch. Everywhere, small white worms were creeping and crawling under blankets of straw while vigorously chomping the fine leaves with their massive jaws.

"They must eat freshly cut leaves day and night," he explained. "The little buggers must always eat. They eat leaves twenty times their size. You know how many times they molt in their lifetime? Four times, discarding their outside skin but a new one grows underneath, giving them more, allowing new growth. You know how long it takes a caterpillar to make a cocoon? Three whole days! It's a lot of work."

Some of the worms were larger and they were beginning to spin cocoons for themselves, releasing twin gossamer threads out of their mouths. A gummy substance, *sericin*, bound the filaments together as well as forming the walls of the cocoon. By moving their heads from side to side, the silkworms lay the filaments in a series of figure eight, gradually building from wall to wall.

"The *sericin* sets hard and the cocoon develops into a peanut shape with the chrysalis inside. In a couple of weeks the chrysalis will break through the cocoon and emerge as a moth—and this we must avoid."

In the cocooning room, large-breasted women, dressed in colorful cottons soaked from the steam that revealed their voluptuous curves, plunging cocoons into boiling water. Venus of Willendorf's descendants.

"Why are they boiling the cocoons?"

"They have to. To dissolve the *serecin*," he explained.

"What's *serecin?*"

"The stuff that binds the silk thread—of course, this kills the chrysalis inside—so that they're unable to disturb the cocoons in their struggle to hatch."

A woman caught the lead thread, began unwinding it. Then, attached it to something like a pulley. Another pulled out with a tweezers the dead pupas, wingless, eyeless moth embryos. One by one she cast them into a basket so that they'd become fertilizers for the mulberry.

"But I don't like them killing those baby moths," Amber told Iskender.

"They're not born yet," he reassured her while grabbing a basket full of pupa. "They haven't yet captured their spirits. It's the life cycle, unavoidable. Come, let's go feed the peacocks now."

Sitting under a mulberry tree waiting for the peacocks to come out of their roost, Amber asked him about the passageways again. How to enter those other worlds.

He read her a story about a girl named Alice who followed a white rabbit into his hole, finding herself in a strange, mysterious world. About this caterpillar who talked to Alice. Pictures in the book showed deformed creatures. A girl with a very long neck, an ugly man with an enormous top hat, a caterpillar sitting on a mushroom. "In the East, there's a special breed of caterpillars that smoke hookahs."

"Do caterpillars have dreams?" she asked.

"Certainly. The most amazing kind."

"How do you know?"

"You have to be very, very old to understand that. Plants, animals, people, gods—all share the same dream."

~

"What do you do when you go off with Uncle Iskender?" Camilla asked as she braided Amber's hair before tucking her in at night. "Where do you go?"

"Nowhere. We wander around. Seeing things."

"What things?"

"Silk houses. Moths and caterpillars and imago and pupa." (The way she pronounced those words!)

"You should be playing with children your age. Your cousins, for example. Maybe you ought to go with Osman to shoot pheasant tomorrow. He offered to take you."

"He's creepy. And I don't want to see dead birds. All you want me to do here is to see dead animals."

"But you should leave Uncle Iskender alone. If you get too close to old people, you begin to smell like them, your skin shrivels. They feed off you. Besides, the mulberry groves are alive with black, deadly poisonous snakes. I don't like you vanishing all day long. All right?"

Amber continued disappearing and every day after she returned, Camilla probed, "What else do you do? Where else do you go?"

"Sometimes to the hyacinth garden; we smell each and every hyacinth. Sometimes we sit all day long by a brook, watching everything that floats, the leaves, the bugs, the twigs, and things like acorns, like peach seeds, and stuff. I saw a chameleon that changed into the color of purple hyacinths. I even saw a camel being born."

"My God! He made you watch it?"

"The baby camel came out in a milky sort of a cocoon. The mother licked it, immediately it stood up on four wobbly legs. It's really cute, *anne*. Uncle Iskender said I can have it."

"He's lost his marbles," Camilla said exasperated. "Senile old creature. He knows it's ridiculous. He knows camels are not allowed in modern cities!"

"He said he'd keep it here for me. I could play with it when we visit again."

"It's all so weird. And look, your skin is getting parched like leather. You're under too much sun. You'll suffer sunstroke. Look at those dark circles under your eyes. From now on, you're going to take a siesta every afternoon. Every afternoon. And castor oil three times a day. Understand? Tomorrow you'll go off with Osman."

That night, after the grounds settled into a surfaceless silence, except for the occasional hooting of owls and the eerie symphony of singing frogs, Cadri and Camilla sat out in the

East verandah in darkness, smoking an endless chain of cigarettes.

"He took her to see a camel giving birth," Camilla told Cadri in a whisper. "Can you believe it? She shouldn't watch things like that; they will contaminate her mind with disturbing images. She'll never forget such things."

"We made her watch the sacrifice."

"That's different. It's tradition. It has meaning."

"And you want her to go hunt pheasant with Osman?"

"That's a sport."

"He's a bad kid. Troublesome."

"I think he is just neglected. Aida couldn't bear losing her first child. He needs friends. He needs assurance."

Cadri took a long puff of his cigarette. Obviously, he did not want to waste time in contradicting Camilla.

"I'm tired of this strange place. It gives me the creeps to be here with that weird uncle of yours. When are we returning to Izmir?" Camilla asked.

"He wants us to stay till the colors turn."

"We can't stay that long. I can't stand it here. I don't like what's happening to Amber. I want to leave right now, Cadri. Yes. Tell him, I'm ill or something."

Amber spent interminable hours lying in bed, looking at her amber and the moth that had almost succeeded in escaping— but only almost. One-half was still inside the cocoon. She dreamed of the Stone Age shamans on the Black Sea coast, carving small, curious amber figurines with expressionless faces that Iskender had told her about. Or the Amber Room in the palace of *Tsarskoye-Selo* with walls covered entirely in a jigsaw puzzle of a hundred thousand intricately cut, perfectly matched pieces of amber. One day, all the amber had mysteriously disappeared never to be found again.

The next morning, she resisted going hunting with Osman. She resisted as if some instinct was warning her of a sinister and mysterious intrusion. He scared her, poking around with his rifle like a bad soldier, pretending it was a bayonet.

But there she was walking behind him as he slashed the gentle wheat grass, the wild hyacinths. Stamped on them. Shot at songbirds like nightingales and shot rabbits.

Osman was a ruthless soldier. Once they had strayed away from the sight of the buildings, he led Amber into a silo where the extra cocoons were stored. He put the rifle down, his hands pushed her on the ground. She was wearing a yellow eyelet dress.

"Take off your dress." he ordered. "I want to see what you have underneath."

Who knows what kind of an impulse led Iskender to the silo that morning? A fateful twist. He had hurried all the way from his pavilion to the silo with the velocity and vigor of a young lad. He materialized like an old wizard, see all, know all. He was as fierce as the God who had ordered Abraham to sacrifice his son. He took the gun and shooed the boy with his stick—the one in which he had smuggled the silk eggs. And scooped the little girl off the ground, before she had known shame, with the tenderness of an archangel.

"The ice lands of Kars is where the boy belongs. Bad eggs should not be allowed to hatch," he mumbled, fuming. "I'll keep him locked up for forty days and forty nights in the silo."

Amber had aged years in those few moments of terror. She felt gravity compress her body. Iskender was her only ally. She took his hand, together they walked to the reflection pond, her favorite place, watched the way the colors caught in the lacunae of the surface. Liquid hours passed drowning in each other's eyes, each impulse drawing them closer to a world outside of this one, surrounded by an invisible shield that allowed no one else to perceive them. They uttered sounds, danced dances without the limitations of their bodies, sculpting perfect environments to nurture their play.

The others wondered where the old man and the little girl went, why they never saw the two. It pleased them that the patriarch had found happiness once again but the bond between the two became an object of curious jealousy. In fact, Iskender and Amber often walked in everyone's periphery but no one ever noticed. They had drifted into an invisible world of silk.

"Let's go to the house of colors today," he told her gleefully. "It'll cheer you up."

From sky-high rafters hung yards of white like snow, the red like the flames of the setting sun, the blue finer than the feathers of storks, the black like a fluttering raven. The living colors reflected their opposites like *changent* taffeta as the cloth moved, shifting hue with each quiver. Finely woven webs as brilliant as emeralds, silk brocades with flowers in seven colors, atlas blue and turquoise satins, shimmering fabrics woven with carnelian thread, embroideries of turquoise stones set in gold. Colors had awakened, spreading everywhere.

"Many come from fruit rinds and tree insects," Iskender explained, lost in their resonance. "The purple I get from crawfish, the red from sumac. Burgundy from madder. The orange from golden chanterelles. But in each, there's a secret element. A secret only I own."

"Tell me," she said.

"Watch me," he said.

They steeped a sheet of *crepe de chine* in the bubbling pools of color. Amber soaked the raw silk in the yellow liquid. When she pulled it out, the color had turned into a bright canary. Iskender told her to dip it now into the blue pool.

She watched it transform into a green like the tiles of the

Emerald Mausoleum, like the center of a peacock's feather. She submerged another sheet in the red and the blue pools, which made it purple as eggplant; red and yellow together turned orange. She asked him if this would happen every time she mixed colors.

"You have to find out for yourself. Colors have their own secrets, you know?"

That same afternoon, Cadri and Camilla sat by the fountain so that their voices would be muffled by the running water while a houseful of relatives wandered about the gardens.

"Where do they go? What do they do? What does he want from Amber?" Camilla nagged Cadri.

"Calm down, Camilla. He adores her. He's an old man. Obviously, they have an unusual connection. Maybe she reminds him of my mother. Who knows? He never forgave himself for what happened to her."

"What do you mean?"

"My mother had a lover. Uncle Iskender sent him away."

"I can't believe it. Your mother seemed so . . . what happened to the lover?"

"No one really knows. Most likely killed in the Liberation War. He never returned. It destroyed my mother. She had a child by him. She had to give her up, too. Mihriban and the Pasha pretended she was theirs to save face."

"Aida! God almighty. You never told me these things. Why did you never tell me?"

"No one had ever told me either. But some things you just know. Everyone does, no one talks about."

"Things begin to make a little more sense now. Wish I'd known . . ."

Only the water filled the long silence that followed as they inhaled their gold-tipped Sobranies, deep in thought.

"He's a selfish old man," Camilla continued.

"He's my uncle."

"A lecher. Four wives. Selma was sixteen when he took her. Don't forget that."

"That was a long time ago, Camilla, for heaven's sake. People got married early in those days. My mother was fourteen when she married my father. And you know how old he was? Forty!"

"Perverts. Can't you see the fire in his eyes when he looks at Amber. We have to separate them, Cadri. It's unsavory."

"You're misinterpreting the ways of the spirit."

Cadri stood up and went through the trellised garden gate and walked down a tidy path edged with pale hydrangeas, flat and tiny like a paper doll, already pudgy and slouching though he had not yet reached midlife. As always, even when he had been a little boy, he was impeccably dressed in a wrinkled linen suit, two-toned shoes, dark shades, and Panama hat. He paused for a minute to clean his wire-rimmed glasses with his handkerchief. Maybe it was best they left this place soon. Camilla's anxiety was beginning to creep under his skin although it pleased him to no end to see the patriarch and the girl wallowing in such bliss.

Amber was sitting in the "Silence" pavilion, drawing pictures of the buildings. She seemed to have an extraordinary sense of perspective and space, an uncanny ability to transform the ordinary lines into magic. She knew how to draw houses. Now she was putting color on all things.

Cadri called out her name. He had a passion for panoramas, rather what they evoked. Time for the daily catechism before sunset, she knew. She ran down to join him. They walked hand in hand to the edge of the plateau. Cadri pointed at the domes, the minarets of Bursa in the distance, the toy city beyond the dust-covered valley.

"See that green mosque with two minarets?"

"Yes."

"You know what it's called?"

"No."

"The Emerald Mosque. See the green mausoleum next to it?"

"Yes."

"You know what it's called?"

"The Emerald Mouseleum?" *Is that where they keep mice?*

"Excellent. Good sense of deduction. Now, see the green city stretching below us?"

"Yes."

"You know what it's called?"

"The Emerald City?"

"Nice simple logic. Bursa, the verdant city. Once the capital of the Ottoman Dynasty, the most illustrious empire of its time. Once the center of the world. Now, tell me who built the mosque?"

"The Emerald Sultan?"

"Good try. But no such person," he laughed. "It was Sultan Mehmet I. And he was?"

"A Padishah?"

"Good. What number?"

"Number seven" (she guessed).

"He was the fifth padishah of the Ottoman Empire. He is buried right there in the Emerald Mausoleum with eight others— they say one was a mysterious Byzantine sultana. What are you holding in your hand?"

"Nothing."

"Come on, let me see."

"There's nothing."

"Let me see." He pried her hand open and pulled out the amber egg. "Where did you find this?"

Amber shrugged her shoulders. Cadri held it up to the light, then looked at it more carefully under his magnifying glass. He had a disturbed look on his face.

"Do you know what this is?"

"An amber egg with a moth inside but it isn't the Bombyx."

"Who gave it to you?"

"I found it," she lied. "I found it there," she pointed to the orchard.

"Does anyone else know you have it? Have you shown it to anyone?"

She shook her head.

"You mustn't tell anyone," he warned her as he slipped it in his pocket. He seemed serious and contemplative.

"Give it back. It's mine. I found it," Amber fought back. "Give it back to me. I'm not supposed to part with it."

"I'm your father. I'll keep it for you. I can't let you lose it. Besides . . ."

"I found it. I won't lose it. Give it back. Give it back to me, *baba*, give it back."

But when Cadri walked away from her, Amber realized she had lost her precious gift. Iskender had warned her. He had warned that it could be taken away from her. She walked away, crushed under a sense of betrayal she could not name. She bit her lips till she drew blood but did not cry.

ॐ

Cadri walked to the men's quarters to see his uncle. As they took their meal alone, he told Iskender that this was their last supper together. They had to return to Izmir earlier than expected. Camilla was ailing. The mountain air disagreed with her. The altitude lowered her blood pressure, she was prone to fainting spells.

"I can send for a doctor or a witch."

"I'm afraid she won't see anyone but her own doctor. As for a witch, she's repelled by them. Besides, I have a great deal of work to do."

"If you must, then you must. But leave the child here for a while longer. The mountain air agrees with her. She loves the silk. She's happy here, Cadri. Let her and the maid come back to Izmir later."

"I can't. Camilla couldn't consider being separated from Amber. She doesn't even like letting her out of her sight for a few minutes."

"You have a stubborn wife—unnecessarily possessive. This will only chase away the child. Don't forget, dreams of a six-year-old are so vast they could encompass her whole future. They could determine her journey through life. Amber has deep imagination. I read her forehead, which makes me think she's got the *mana* to be a matriarch someday. Once, I'd hoped the same of your mother, then of Aida, but they both disappointed me. I pray Amber will be different."

"It's a great deal to expect from a small child."

"Surely, you too must sense it."

"Yes," Cadri said. "I do."

Amber listened behind the latticed screen to the unfathomable murmurings, trying to make sense. What was *mana?* Something in her that would turn her into a matriarch. Into an old crone like Mihriban, into one of those wrinkled women, dried-up beings resigned from this world who sat on their chairs day and night, watching the doves mate, contemplating the death angel? And did they think she was an old ghost? She was possessed?

Cadri returned to their quarters. Amber left her hiding place and went to Iskender's room.

"My amber egg is gone," she told Iskender. "He took it from me."

"Who did?"

"My father. I want it back."

"He did? Don't worry. You'll get it back. I'll see to it."

After sundown, as she watched the goats wandering up the mountain, Amber noticed Cadri in the shadows talking to a man in rural clothes. The two men made angry gestures at one another, arms thrust violent slashes in the air, spit glistened, lizards poured out of their mouths. She recognized Murat, the caretaker, the one who had cut the sheep's throat, the one who slashed the watermelons in her dream.

Cadri threw his hands up in the air, began walking away but Murat followed him, cut in front. The hands violated the air again. Then Cadri shook his head for the longest time, paused for a moment before reaching inside his pocket. He pulled out something too small to see from such distance. Gave it to Murat. Murat held it in the light. They looked at each other for an excruciating moment without a word. Murat put the object in his pocket and walked toward the men's quarters.

That night Amber lay on her bed, pretending to be asleep until the common breathing of everyone confirmed they were no longer awake. Leaping over snoring Gonca, she slipped quietly out the side door, her knees weak. As she crossed the corridor, it felt as though invisible hands were reaching out of the walls. A black night; nothing in the sky. Though she could not see her way clearly, she kept walking, her heart about to leap out of her fragile chest.

Iskender was waiting at the lemonier. "Don't be afraid," he said. "Here give me your hand. You don't need light to walk in the dark. Hush. Just listen to the night's voice. Extend your arms when you take a step. Make sure you always check the three directions and know what's behind you. Breathe calmly. Imagine in your mind what you want to see and you will."

"Where are we going?" Amber asked.

"It's a surprise. Follow me."

"I'm afraid. I can't see anything. I don't want to step on a giant black snake or anything."

"No snakes here, child. That's why we have so many birds."

"My mother said there were big black snakes."

"She was lying. Not one snake here. Nothing to be afraid of. Here, take this key. As you go, scratch your initials on trees if fear grabs you. Writing your name has the power to protect you."

So she did. ASI. ASI. ASI. Over and over and over.

"You know what your initials mean? They mean a rebel. *Asi*. Are you a rebel, Amber?"

"I don't know."

"I think you are."

The night walk seemed interminable. Despite Iskender's confidence, judging from the way they avoided obstacles, the pounding of Amber's heart was strong enough to agitate the quiet night.

Iskender stopped abruptly. "We're standing at the edge of a cliff and you can now see them down below in the ravine," he told her. "Look."

They began to materialize like stars in the early evening sky. One, at first. Two, five, a dozen, hundreds imperceptibly but unlike stars, they moved against the fatal background, flashing themselves, dancing around, disappearing and reappearing until they surrounded Iskender and Amber as if nibbling their shadows. Her dress was covered with hundreds of twinkling fireflies.

"They're beautiful," Amber gasped. She caught one. "Can I keep it?"

Iskender emptied the powder in his snuffbox and gave it to her. "If you like, but you might be disappointed in the morning."

Amber stuck it in the box.

"But I have something for you that's indestructible," Iskender said. "Close your eyes and open your palm."

She did. But the unexpected happened at that moment. Iskender lost his balance and the object went flying off.

"Oh, no!"

They began searching the ground for the amber egg. They crawled and felt with their hands but the amber egg was nowhere to be found. Amber began to cry.

Iskender conforted her. "Now, now, no tears. Don't worry. Tomorrow when the sun comes out, we will find it. Please don't worry."

He took her hand and they returned long past midnight.

Gonca was at the gate, carrying a flashlight; she grabbed and shook Amber. "Where have you been, Amber?"

The lights were on in Cadri and Camilla's room. Camilla was lying on the bed, pale and limp, while Cadri was making her sniff a lemon. She jerked a couple of times, then opened her eyes, looked at Amber, her eyes swollen from crying. Dropped down again.

Cadri was angry. "Where have you been?" he asked. "And what is it in your hand?"

Amber opened the snuff box. Inside an ugly little bug like a mosquito was crawling, half dead. Twinkle gone. The light expired.

Gonca gave Amber a tincture of valerian. All night, she was delirious. Spirits, jinns, öcüs, dead saints, ghosts danced around her, flashing themselves occasionally like holograms. When horror struck unexpectedly at every turn, she remained calm while Draculas in satin capes, werewolves, and Frankenstein monsters with flowers in their hands raised hell. Good fairies held her hand but the Silk Woman wanted to trap bad children inside enormous cocoons. Giant, monstrous caterpillars with horns spitting fire in the dark, like the vicious dragon in Mihriban's tale that guarded the spring. She heard strange whispers, saw lights moving around in the fields. Shadows of unspeakable things danced behind the curtain that flapped wildly against the taunting wind rising up the mountain in uneven spirals. She saw all the unseen.

The caretaker appeared again in her dream. This time climbing into her room through the window with a ladder. He carried an empty sack. "This is for you," he said. "Climb in." Then his face changed to her cousin Osman in the silo. He threw the amber egg on the marble floor and it shattered into thousands of pieces. A moth came flying out and threw itself into the fire.

She woke up to see Murat actually in the same room. Her parents and Gonca were already up and dressed. It was almost dawn but still dark.

"Come this way," he ordered them. Follow me.

The sound of tiptoeing feet, whispers, things moving around. Camilla was bundling Amber in something warm. Cadri lifted her up and belaboredly carried her downstairs. Camilla and Gonca followed.

"Where are we going?" Amber asked.

"On a secret adventure."

"Where?"

"We're going on a night journey. Do you know what happened to the Prophet when he went on a night journey? Angel Gabriel appeared with Elboraq, a silver mare who was half human, and they rode through the colors of the rainbow to Jerusalem."

"Why are we leaving?" she asked. "I want to stay."

Cadri talked in a restrained voice. "We sometimes have to make sacrifices," he explained. "Like the sheep. This is one of those times. And now, we have to make another sacrifice. We must go home, my dear daughter."

As they went out the door, Amber felt the damp air on her skin. The caretaker led them through the endless pavilions. The iron gate clicked and on the other side, the snorting of a horse. Sound of hooves. The hiss in the air. Then came great silence.

The Spinster's Apartment

❧

(1959–1960)

To those of moist temperament, and especially women, coffee
is highly suited. They should drink a great deal of strong
coffee. Excess of it will do them no harm, as long as they are
not melancholic.

KATIB ÇELEBI, The Balance of Truth (1650)

las, Iskender Bey's fortune melted like a candle.
Too much of an old silkworm to make the adjustments
to a chameleon world that had left him behind in an
oasis of loneliness he, in turn, had abandoned the world that
could not remember its past nor recognize its own reflection in
the mirror.

No one ever mentioned the fire that had killed Iskender Bey
and devastated the plantation. So, I cannot say. Your guess is as
good as mine. But being the oldest male relative, Cadri succeeded Iskender Bey as the patriarch. Familiar with the process
of silk, which had encouraged his lepidopterist impulses as a
child, but unlike his cousins Aida, Sibel, and Papatya, all women
of silk, Cadri lacked the knack for its stuff.

The three sisters trusted Cadri's kindness and his scholarly
gifts, less certain of the patriarchal ones. Nevertheless, they had
little choice. As women, not allowed to participate in business,
despite their husbands' objections, they placed the family's as-

sets in Cadri's hands, nicknaming him the "poetriarch," first as a jest but in no time at all, everyone had almost forgotten his real name.

Oblivious to their sudden changes of fortune, the family members continued their lives in the manner they were accustomed to, with their servants, multiple houses, and flamboyant ceremonies until an April day when Cadri gathered them in a vacant lot in Ankara, a dusty city in the arid Anatolian plains, the ancient Angora. (Better known as the domain of shaggy goats from whose fleece fuzzy sweaters are made, and snow-white long-haired cats with two different color eyes and fearless of water, and that swam in the rapids.) A nomadic inland rumbling with blood memories of human sacrifice for rain, a modern city reborn out of a need to find fulcrum for the revolution, a city of new beginnings that Atatürk had elevated overnight to the status of the new Turkish Republic's capital.

"I tried to conceal it from you as long as possible but the truth is, the family is badly in debt—worse than any of us could have feared," Cadri disclosed to all the İpekçis. Besides the sisters and the families, there were cousins and aunts and uncles who were part of the clan. "So I had no other choice but to liquidate our assets. Almost everything—the summer yali in Moda, the fig orchards along the Aegean, the hunting lodge in the Belgrade forest, the villa in Pamukkale Hot Springs, the vineyards, the weekend house in the Prince Islands, our own respective houses—and even, even the silk plantation—what's left of it after that wretched fire—now belongs to strangers. It broke my heart to pieces to lose those places. But we'll never lose their memories. You must understand, it was the only way to pay our debts."

At first, no one seemed to grasp the gravity of the situation, no one could identify with the finality of Cadri's words.

"Luckily, a handful of remaining *liras*—just a little scrape off the top—will make it possible to build an apartment complex for all of us to share, right here where your feet are touching the ground, to start a new life here in Ankara where opportunities are greater, where better schools exist for children, and better jobs for men. Everything is new and modern in this city. Everything sanitary. Every sign of progress exists. I know, all this may seem tragic at first but believe me, it's best for the family because we have no choice except to pool our resources together. Remember, my loves, disasters bond people."

"How we'll lose face when everybody finds out," Sibel yelped.

"It's up to us to regain it," Cadri replied. "Simply, with our own intentions."

"They will laugh at our misery. They will get pleasure out of our loss. Somebody must have cast us the evil eye. It's not fair."

So it was that I was built, one of several in a grand row, all more or less identical, cement colored, six stories each—mutant progenies of urban functionalism, ghostless and hollow inside. Low ceilings and tiny holes for windows to economize heat. Water hissing out of the radiators. Pragmatic like most of their postwar relatives elsewhere, built to last no more than ten or fifteen years, then self-destruct. Nomads resist the threat of permanence.

Years later, when I was demolished and they excavated the foundation, the workers uncovered terra cotta artifacts—Neolithic pots and pitchers, the remnants of six thousand years ago, way back from the matriarchal cultures that existed even before the Hittites. The law required that antiquities be donated to the Museum of Ethnography but Cadri, convinced that the family would take better care of such things than the government and prevent thieves from smuggling them out of the county, concealed them in a vault in the boiler room chained to the foundation. (Years later when the building was demolished, they could neither remove nor destroy the vault. Of course, its contents had already disappeared.) Little did anyone know that underneath, less than twenty meters, a whole ancient city lay not yet uncovered. So, after all I was an old soul deep down. Despite the mask.

A sunless winter afternoon, Cadri, his wife, and the girl stepped off the Citroen at the corner of Atatürk Boulevard, climbed up the Yüksel incline to Meşrutiyet (Constitution) Avenue, a cul-de-sac closed to traffic. They hurried up the narrow steps out of breath and arrived at the entrance just as a painter was finishing up the plaque above the entrance that read "Spinsters Apt," aptly named, although obviously the family had buried their spinning impulses with the former patriarch.

To distinguish us buildings from one another, people gave them names. The frilly one next door, for example, was called Boğa, or bull, which defined the business of the family who owned it. The tall one across the street was "Safran" (belonged to the family in the saffron trade). Or named after the people's ancestral place during the Empire like Vardar, Özbek, Milas, Damascus, Caucuses, and Cyprus, etc. They were like palaces, in a way, of big nomadic tribes—Tartars, Mongolians, the Huns, the Semites, the Seljuks, names flaunting their own prestige.

"We'll plant some acacias and plum trees and put up some swings for the children," Cadri reassured Amber who seemed distressed with the bleakness. "Meanwhile, you'll have to make do with playing on the street, my sweet, or play at home. You'll have lots of children to play with now. You're no longer an only child."

Just then, a window opened on each story, faces filled its

frame—faces of aunts, uncles, cousins, the matriarchs, the maids, singing, "Welcome, you sweet loves. Welcome to our midst. We'll share with you our bread and hope you'll do the same."

Through the stark courtyard leading up to the concrete stairway, wafted the scent of roasted eggplant and of lamb stew. Evil-eye charms adorned the hallway and the stairwell. In front of every doorway lay castaway carpets and kilims of extraordinary value, smelling of mold from having been exposed to the elements, that eventually ended up serving as bedding for vagabonds, beggars, and gypsies. The family had come to the conclusion that they had no use for them anymore. America had introduced wall-to-wall carpeting to the developing economy; synthetic pile of "Harvest Gold" and "Autumn Whisper" displaced the precious Shiraz and Isphahan, Hereke, and Isparta.

Everyone settled in their respective units while America insinuated itself further into their lives, seducing the women with Frigidaire and Hoover. Also brought along the virus of Time and virus of time, the imaginary. The first item on time: a Miele washing machine for Camilla, with a pot belly and a revolving wringer to feed through.

The day it arrived, the children eagerly returned early from school, just to see it delivered to the fourth story through the narrow stairway. After that, all the women spent months neglecting other tasks to use Camilla's Miele, mesmerized by its rhapsodic churning, exhilarated by the joys of automatism. Then, the toilet paper arrived in rolls of mud color or dirty pink replacing the pieces of newspaper that had formerly served the same function (the old ladies still used their hands, of course, but they knew how), and Kleenex nose tissue followed, enticing them to give up their beautifully embroidered handkerchiefs of the softest, finest linen and silk in lieu of coarse paper crepe.

Civilization also gifted every household with a modern bathroom of lavender, turquoise, or flamingo faience, chrome fixtures, *à la Franca* toilet, bidet (used for washing dirty socks and underwear since nobody ever quite figured out what it was for). Linoleum tiles. No tulips. No tree of life. No more communal bathing, the respiratory bliss.

Camilla told Amber she was old enough now to learn to wash herself as she handed her a scouring mitten and a bar of pink Puro soap, shut the door, and left her alone to fend for herself. Amber felt insignificant, dwarfed, sitting inside the enormous coffin-shaped tub, sliding around its sleek, slippery base. Afraid of drowning. Afraid of the door getting stuck and not being able to get out. Afraid of getting sucked down into the drain. Missing the hands that preened and scrubbed and washed her. Missing the primate creature warmth. A moment in which bathing suddenly became the emblem of loneliness and desertion.

Cousins, above and below, just a year or two apart. Real children to deal with after life with invisible playmates, apparitions, and animal spirits. Certainly an undesirable intrusion. She buried herself in drawings instead, but unlike the other little girls who drew princesses in pretty dresses, Amber drew houses, enchanted places with doors and windows and gables leading to other dimensions hidden behind ivy and vine, towers and cupolas and secret gardens. She drew every single room in the building, establishing her own fictional universe peopled with imaginary beings, imaginary dwellings, except for the paper dolls.

She moved from room to room following the impulse of her hands as they searched for colors and brushes and empty surfaces, filling them with images as though a voice inside had freed her from the limitations of being a child. She mixed yellows with reds, and blues with reds, and blues with yellows, spinning the color wheel that Iskender Bey had made for her like a roulette. She discovered that opposites mixed nicely into oranges, greens, and purples. The complementaries created colors of inexplicable darkness—red with green, yellow with purple, blue and orange, all such murkiness.

On Mondays, when all the women pilgrimaged to the great farmer's market, she stayed home. Watercolors spilled everywhere, the carpet tinted with the dust of the pastels, charcoal smeared on the yellow walls, and the drapes in the salon dripped with turpentine, the kitchen slicked with linseed oil, even drippings of oil stained the runner in the anteroom.

When Camilla returned into the chaos strewn with Amber's creations, she began to yell at her and threatened to take away her paints if it ever, ever happened again.

Cadri continued his peregrinations to the obscure silk provinces in Anatolia, being now simply an employee of the national silkworks. On these journeys, he visited factories and searched for solutions to ever-growing problems between labor and management. He returned debilitated and distraught, having been trapped in a life that did not seem to be of his own choosing. But he had convinced himself that family was inseparable, invulnerable, and permanent since nothing else seemed to be. Yet he could not account for the absence of his own brother Aladdin, who had been intended as the other pillar.

"A fluke, an error of kismet," he justified.

"What if we all had kismets like that?" Camilla asked. "What if kismets traveled in clusters?"

"Not very likely," Cadri argued.

But in retrospect, they were sitting in its shadow.

Once, when Cadri was away, noticing the door to the *pensatorio* a crack open, Amber walked in on Camilla, struggling with a screwdriver, picking the lock of Cadri's cabinet where he kept his private icons and harmless male secrets. Startled, Camilla stuck out her tongue like a lizard, snapped at her daughter.

"Always knock on the door before you enter someone else's room," she scolded.

"But this is not your room, mama," Amber responded.

"Don't talk back to your mother. I'm not doing anything to either shame me or harm anyone else. If you want to see the movie stars, just shut up. Will you?"

So Amber followed her mother into the sewing room and plopped herself next to Camilla on a divan. They cuddled together and leafed through the pages filled with stars fashioning Nazi haircuts, shoulderless dresses, slink and brilliantine in an atmosphere of ocean liners, tennis courts, and rooftop apartments overlooking illegible neon signs at Times Square or the Paramount Studios lot.

Amber seemed fascinated by the pictures of a woman who had an uncanny resemblance to Camilla.

"Oh yes, that's Dolores Del Rio, your father's favorite."

"She looks just like you."

"That's probably why your father married me."

"Really? So, who is your favorite?" asked Amber, turning the pages full of men and women in various forms of posed embrace and silent posturing, trying to make sense of the mystery called attraction.

As she flipped through the pages to the picture of a shirtless man, muscular but with hairless skin—unlike the Turkish men Amber had seen on the beach, who had tufts sprouting off their chests, arms, and even their backs—Camilla's face beamed. He was wearing a scarf and an earring like the gypsy men she'd seen around the Ankara citadel who pounded copper. In his hand flashed a sword freshly removed from its sheath, so shiny that a star twinkled out of its tip.

"Cornell Wilde," Camilla cooed. "He was *my* idol. Look at him. Look at his chiseled features, sensuous lips, look at his gorgeous mustache!" Another picture of Cornell hovering over Linda Darnell with moist lips, oozing with melancholic lust. "You know, I named you "Amber" because of the book *Forever Amber.* It was made into a wonderful movie with Cornell. What a man! (Ironically many years later, this virile idol of her mother's youthful dreams would become Amber's friend in real life, by then a sad, mummified old man, on the verge of leaving this world.) I've seen it ten times at least, sneaking out of the house while your grandmother Esma took her siesta— she didn't like me going out by myself. Mothers-in-law like controlling their sons' wives. I hope you never get one like that. So I'd sneak out while she snored—God bless her soul—meet up with my girlfriends to catch the matinee at the Alhambra Theater in Izmir."

Something about the image of Cornell had touched a yearning in Camilla's heart, that place of desire despite its evident impossibility. She was not the only one—Papatya, Aida, even the sourpuss Sibel seemed under the spell of this matinee idol's charisma, having harbored fantasies of Latin lovers in movies, whose songs came through His Master's Voice.

Like all collective dreamers, one of them would inevitably trespass the dream. But it was not Camilla.

❧

How Rodrigo entered the lives of the İpekçi family and became intricately entangled in their kismet seems almost scripted, a cliché. Even who he was, the way he dressed, how he had the fortuitous resemblance to the women's idol. Perilous from the start to have someone so erotically inclined entering the inner sanctum. No question about it. But they say if you avoid peril, peril sneaks into your bed. And peril did.

It all started at Sibel's boys' circumcision. For weeks, there was a great fuss of food mania, a retinue of porters carrying enormous baskets on their backs delivered the cornucopia, day in and day out for months. The older women wrapped their fat legs around low round tables, rolling enormous circles of dough, so thin that one could see through it. Trays and trays of boereks and baklavas and yogurt cakes were carried off to clay furnaces and greasy pilafs with roasted pinions and currants stuffed into every imaginable vegetable, shellfish, and fowl—eggplant dolmas, sweet pepper dolmas, tomato dolmas, green squash dolmas, grape leaf dolmas, artichoke dolmas. Quail dolmas. Mussel dolmas. You-name-it dolmas.

The General's *gedikli*, the errand boy Memed, brought a small flock of baby lambs from his village, which they kept in the backyard. The children took turns feeding the animals until the time for slaughtering. Gonca and her sisters cleaned and scrubbed their trendy linoleum floors, washed by hand all the embroidered linen from the women's worm-eaten hope chests, kept in mothballs and used only for special ceremonies, refusing to conform to the capricious ways of the newly acquired hand-crank Mieles that by now every household possessed.

The men negotiated with puppet masters, magicians, and phaeton drivers, for entertainment. The boys were washed and scrubbed, their heads shaved—all the children deloused—the nails trimmed, the bodies rubbed with aromatic oils, and kept home from school. The girls, however, were suddenly ignored by everyone, which made them needy and envious, especially when they witnessed the arrival of the mountains of presents for the twerps that collected at the foot of the circumcision bed.

What they did not know was what exactly happened during circumcision, except some nastiness to their "itsy-bitsy faucets."

They had watched other boys wearing white satin embroidered dresses like girls and, afterward wobbling around with bowed legs, forbidden to play soccer for months. But all this seemed like a small price for the attention lavished, all the worldly compensations.

"Can I be circumcised too, please?" Amber begged Camilla, disturbed by this profound sense of injustice.

"Of course not. Girls don't get circumcised in our country."

"Why not?"

"Because they don't need to be. They don't have the, you know, 'organs.' "

"What organs?"

"They don't have a *bibish*."

Amber contemplated this response briefly, then asked her what exactly was done to the boys' *bibish*.

"They remove the skin."

"But why?"

"Because it gets dirty underneath and shelters germs."

Imagining her poor cousins and the other boys at school, their teeny weenies skinned like the eels at the fish market, or the necks of chickens, the weenies that they had so proudly exposed during communal peeing behind the coal storage stalls, was enough for Amber to change her mind. She felt content to keep her lower lips.

The prepubescent boys lay side by side on a brass bed under a purple satin quilt. White caps embroidered with silver *Maşallah* charms concealed their sheared heads, lumpy and blotchy as if afflicted with a fungus from the stray cats. An evil-eye charm— a blue glass bead with a yellow iris set in a gold cameo—pinned on each shoulder.

Alternating silence and sighs inflated the room as if it were breathing. The boys lay impatient, surrounded by their audience, presents piled everywhere—bicycles, soccer balls, flash-lights, compass sets, and every gadget obtainable on the black market.

Sibel's husband Dursun Bey shook hands with the Circumciser. The Circumciser lifted the lovely quilt, fluffed profession-ally, exposing the frail bodies of the boys, tunics reaching below their knees; hairless, spindly legs, their feet still soiled from the permanent red clay of Ankara. The younger one looked as if he were about to cry. The older one giggled. Others in the room giggled along. Someone whispered to hush. The Circumciser took something out of his bag, a metal contraption resembling a potato peeler. A sunbeam caught the surface, sending prisms of color all around the room.

It was a hot day. The ceiling fan turned sluggishly as if its motor were running out. The boys lay soaked in perspiration. This time of the year, the family would be in Moda where it was cool, where they had a sailboat, a private beach. But now they had to accept the change in fortune that had confined them to humid Ankara in midsummer while the nouveau riche fami-lies replaced them on the lovely beaches.

The contraption slid in between the covers like silverfish. Something stirred in the void. The room reached a silent pitch. The boy clenched his teeth, but not a moan escaped his lips. Steel silence, gasps, and the dangling skin. The Circumciser squeezed the boy's cheek, everyone applauded.

"Little hero," someone yelled. "Bravo."

Although the boy seemed determined not to cry, a fleeting agony escaped from his carefully controlled face. Betrayal, need-ing retribution. Revenge, a matter of honor here.

Aida was standing next to Amber, one hand digging into the girl's shoulder, the other stuffing a handkerchief in her mouth as if the boys' pain were transferred to her own body. She must have been thinking of her two sons. The one lost to her forever and the troublesome Osman in a corrective institution. She recalled his circumcision. Maybe she thought, "If they'd only cut off his penis then."

The Circumciser wiped his knife with methylate. Down it went under the covers again and out came a cry of such hurt that Aida buried her head on Amber's shoulder as if she were watching a scary movie she could no longer endure.

"Mama! My mother!" the boy cried.

"Shush. Shame on you. Be a hero like your brother. You're a man now."

The crying stopped as the Circumciser's hand displayed another piece of bloody skin in the air. People applauded again. The show was over.

Dursun kissed the older boy on both cheeks. Mihriban cuddled the younger one so that the others would not see him sobbing but no attention lavished upon him could diminish the betrayal. His eyes died that afternoon, like the other men of this land. The price of manhood.

Cool sherbets seasoned with roasted pinions were passed around as the boys fondled their presents while watching the screen of thin transparent cloth, illuminated but motionless. It was adorned with a filigreed palace garden, tottering and fit to collapse at the first sigh of its odalisques, or burst of rage from its eunuchs. The screen vanished to the accompaniment of a weird cacophony; Karagöz and Hajivad, the infamous shadow puppet characters, jumped out of their garish paper skin, insulting each other right and left, and came alive.

In the bleak backyard, now decorated with streamers and flags, the men gathered, turning headless lamb carcasses on spits that looked like crucifixes. In this setting, Rodrigo arrived, dressed in a black satin shirt and black trousers, carrying a gui-

tar. The men ignored him, which was an insult. The younger
women watched him discreetly. The children thought he resembled Zorro.

He tuned his guitar and "La Paloma" escaped out of his
lips like a real dove. The tremor of its wings caressed the sleeveless arms of the women. He sang a couple other songs and then
disappeared. No one knew who he was or where he had come
from. But they shared a strange intuition that they would see
him again.

The smell of horseshit mingled with roasted lamb as the
children were packed into the phaetons. A little girl sat on
Amber's lap. Horses decked with red and green tassels, embroidered vests, good-luck talismans trotted clickety clack on the
cobbles, the jingling of their bells accompanied by large kettledrums and high-pitched flutes. They watched a dancing bear
with a guard around its snout. The gypsy owner held on to it
with a rope as he beat his tambourine. *Yallah, Sülüman, Yallah, Yallah. Hele bak, bak, bak. Yallah, Sülüman.* Poor Sülüman, the bear, pitifully flea-infested and fatigued, appeared disinterested in the
world around him but when the whip hit the ground he stood
up on his hind legs, began to sway from side to side, and played
his tambourine.

Yallah, Sülüman, yallah, yallah!

Sülüman tried coming down. The children screamed. The
whip hit the ground again, he growled as he stood up and
passed the hat.

The braver of the circumcised boys, disinterested in the
bear, clutched a transistor, Elvis singing "It's now or never," and
flaunted his new Donald Duck watch.

It was late afternoon by then. The young bucks and pretty
girls accompanied by their families, promenading down Atatürk
Boulevard, dressed in wild colors of courtship—bright florals,

ribbons, and gauze. The phaeton trotted down a badly paved street of this unexceptional city of terra-cotta roofs, the red arid dust. In the distance, stood the sparse silhouette of the enormous scaffolding that would eventually become *Anit Kabir,* Atatürk's mausoleum.

Later that evening when Gonca came to tuck Amber in, she pulled a piece of paper out of her bra.

"Amber, can you keep a secret?"

"You know I can."

"Promise me over your dead mother and father and all your other relations that you won't ever, ever tell anyone what I'm about to show you."

"I promise over my dead mother and father and all my other relations that I will never ever tell anyone what you are about to show me."

Gonca then handed Amber the piece of paper.

"Read to me what it says."

Amber looked at the printed letters on powder-blue vellum perfumed with a pressed violet.

"Lovely Gonca,

How are you? I'm fine except I can't sleep at nights thinking of you, your cherry lips, your apple cheeks, your almond eyes . . .

Amber began to giggle. Gonca slapped her hand gently and said, read on. So she did. The letter was unsigned but the child's intuition guessed it was from the General's *gedikli,* Memed, the shy, rosy-cheeked lad (who helped her mother since Ayşe's disappearance with a ragseller soon after their arrival). The one who had brought the flock from his village for the circumcision. That night and many nights to come, Amber lent Gonca her child's handwriting, her crooked capitals, misspellings, became

Gonca's voice and her secret love, Amber's own secret. That's how she learned to write love letters.

But no secret lasts forever. Memed's military service was coming to an end and he would have to return to his village in Çemişkezek with a wife from the big city. The family gave them a wedding at the Army Club, after which the young couple moved down to the tiny studio in the basement and Memed was promoted to the status of my guardian and persuaded to stay. Thus Gonca remained attached to the family till the very end, until the lizard fell into her glass.

﷼

After it was all over, Cadri would say that Rodrigo was no more than a rascal, a crafty con artist, one who became so good at it that his act ceased being a con and turned into his destiny. But the image of himself as an impostor was so deeply imprinted in Rodrigo's heart that it would never occur to him he had an option—even when he fell in love. An illusionist who, when his illusions became real, could not tell the difference. A dreamer who'd stop at nothing. A rogue who would not hesitate to take a shortcut through a cemetery at night to get where he wanted to go, but always carrying a rose, just in case.

During the languorous siesta hours, the younger women often escaped to the Blue Angel pastry shop across the street. Underneath the shade of green-and-white-striped awning, they licked profiteroles while exchanging gossip like a cat's cradle. Uncluttered now by the dark-scarved matriarchs who presided on their bridal thrones at family gatherings, they sipped café glacée, served with silver straws, dunking their petit beurres and bitter-almond cookies while whispering secrets to each other with bubbling enthusiasm.

While they swore faithfulness to their husbands, their libidos were titillated with the images of their matinee idols, as well as their look-alikes who seemed to materialize in the most unexpected places. Sometimes they took the girl children along, not bothering to censor verbal confidences since children were assumed to be deaf to things they were not supposed to hear. The children themselves, accomplices in this, feigned invisibility, the best way to discover mysteries they did not quite grasp.

The women chattered about the Robert Taylors they knew, the Clark Gables, and Tyrone Powers. They giggled, pointing at the third floor of the apartment building across where a Ray Milland lived. But none of them had much respect for this Ray Milland, who never seemed to work but instead sat all day long on his balcony in his striped pajamas, reading *Ulus* (*The Nation*) and chain-smoking government subsidized Yenice cigarettes while his two pretty sisters departed early in the morning and returned at dusk, their skins paled from a day's work under fluorescent lights. This Ray Milland they called "the lazy man." Handsome but lazy. What a horrid waste!

That afternoon at the Blue Angel, Papatya, often silent and inexpressive, chirped with wicked enthusiasm.

"I saw him again," she told the others. "I saw him."

"Who?"

"That mysterious man who came to sing "La Paloma" at the boys' circumcision. I saw him at the music store buying paper and we talked."

"No joke!"

"What can I say? He's divine. Looks like Cornell Wilde, dances like Carlos Gardel, and sings like Mario Lanza."

"But who is he really?" asked Aida.

"No one knows for sure. Some say, the son of the Bolivian

consul who left home one day, no one knew why, taking with him only his guitar. They say he slept in alleys and stood at street corners passing the hat, playing his music. A true artist. Not the ordinary vaudeville kind, you know. Nor gypsy. So elegant and exotic in that gaucho outfit, singing songs in a language of passion like some performer out of *Flying Down to Rio*.

"So, he's a street musician?" Sibel stirred, raising her eyebrows.

"Not any more. Çhardaş, the Hungarian club owner discovered and hired him to sing and dance the samba and mambo and carioca at the Circle d'Orient."

"But won't he need a partner?"

"Like Fred and Ginger."

"They are looking for one."

"Too bad you had to stop dancing, Papatya, you'd be perfect," Sibel addressed her sister, condescending.

"What's his name?" interrupted Aida.

"Rodrigo. Rodrigo Cavallero."

They all ululated. "Rodrigo Cavallero. *Vallah! Vallah!* Cavallero! Ah!"

"Cavallero," said Sibel, "means horse in Spanish."

"A horse rider," said Camilla.

"He has many other names, all so very long. Çhardaş thinks he's really a prince from Bolivia. No, Argentina. No, no, Chile. Oh, I don't know, maybe it's Brazil. Anyway, one of those Latin places down there where they have winter when we have summer." She rolled her eyes. "Makes them warm blooded, you know? Most likely he sleeps all day long and up all night." She mimicked the Andrews Sisters singing "The South American Way."

They all giggled, their eyes alive.

"Is there a Madame Cavallero?"

"I don't think so."

"Maybe we can talk Cadri into taking us to the Circle d'Orient tonight so we can see him sing and dance."

All clapped. Except Sibel, of course. The sourpuss. Every family has to have one of those to tip the scale. Yet they are always so predictable.

Amber licked her chocolate-covered fingers from the profiteroles as she observed the women's feet under the table. All had new two-toned summer shoes on, all with perforations and holes—navy and white, brown and white, black and white, or red and white. Sibel's legs were already thick and straight like tree stumps, dark prickly hairs sprouted out of her skin. Aida was the only one with real ankles, the kind that tapered gracefully. Camilla had the tiniest of feet like those Chinese women, her peep-toed shoes revealing toenails painted iridescent purple. Papatya's hyperextended arches smoothly blended into her legs, her toes curved the way of a ballerina.

"She showed so much promise," Aida told Camilla later, as they walked back arm in arm. She and her sisters derived great pleasure taking turns telling stories of their lives before Camilla's arrival into the family, embellishing every nuance, and Camilla listened intently, her heart pounding, absorbing what she could concerning Cadri's past.

"Her body was so transparent," Aida continued. "She really had a dancer's heart. They sent her to dancing lessons with a White Russian woman, Madame Ouspenskaya—her husband was a mystic of some sort, Ouspenski. She danced with all of herself, defying gravity until the most unfortunate curse of puberty brought on the changes in her body. When father saw her in her tutu, her tiny tits perked up from rubbing against the silk camisole, he figured it was time to bring this deal to an end before they grew big enough to dangle like watermelons.

"So, one day, after rehearsal, my parents picked Papatya up at the dance studio and took her to a photographer who tortured the poor thing into interminable pliés and relevés—the ones in Cadri's picture book, you remember? When they came home, they ceremoniously burned her tutus and toe-shoes in the brazier. The whole house stunk. 'Passions are in need of pruning, not cultivating,' father told us all. No more dancing for Papatya after that. No way he would have allowed me to join the beauty contest if he were alive then.

"Anyway, after that, Papatya began to get plump, dragged her fanny around the house. She took up singing instead, because she could sing in her room and they would have to cut out her tongue to stop her. As long as her voice did not drift out to the street and arouse the pedestrians, the family tolerated her chirps. But, no matter what you do, you can't change one's fate.

"One day, a young olive-oil broker named Tarik, small-boned and pin-mustached, was walking down the street when he heard a voice as sweet as halvah, wafting through the cracks of the closed lattices, a voice that sounded like a prepubescent boy's just before it dropped. You know, that sweet castrati voice, the child soprano. He stopped to listen and, enraptured, returned every day for more. He never saw her face but the voice had conquered his heart, convincing him that he would have her as his sweet wife.

"Once again, görücü appeared at our threshold. Sibel, Papatya, and I came out to serve them the obligatory Turkish coffee, sherbets and all. The görücü's eye locked on me and she oozed with satisfaction, assuming I was the bride-to-be. As it slowly dawned on them that Papatya was the one, the one with the chubby cheeks, mouse eyes, and muscular dancer's legs—you know I love my sister but I'm not going to pretend she's much to look at—their enthusiasm withered rapidly. But a promise was a promise and Papatya was soon betrothed to Tarik Bey. Of course, they'd never met before.

"At last, Tarik saw the shutters open and his nightingale appear at her balcony; he was so disappointed that he turned away instantly and disappeared without even glancing back. Imagine, their first encounter. Imagine! Poor Papatya, she thought he'd never return, which probably would have been a blessing, but Tarik was an honorable man in his own way and he did return and married her.

"Papatya and Tarik spent their lives under the same roof but in separate rooms, avoiding each other's bodies, connecting only through songs she sang unseen. She made love to him through her voice but she herself was unfulfilled. They had no children. Some say Papatya was still a virgin after fifteen years of conjugal bliss. I prefer not to discuss it except to say she's not the sort who'd complain."

Everything about Tarik was oily, his skin, his hair, even the texture of his clothes. His eyes were damp and slippery with a filmy surface. He even smelled like Marmara olives. He often traveled on business, selling olive oil to the provinces, and on the rare occasions he was home, impeccably dressed young men, in tight-fitting powder-blue and pink suits, Panama hats, pin mustaches, neat coifs bleached with peroxide and embalmed in Brilliantine lurked around the Blue Angel all hours of the day.

"My mother says they're sick men," her cousin Maya told Amber. "They are perverts."

"But they always smile," Amber said. "You can look into their eyes. They are soft. They return your gaze."

She did not tell Maya of the time she saw Tarik kissing one of his dandelion friends under the street lamp when she had sneaked out to the balcony after everyone had gone to sleep. They kissed just like in the movies; they sucked each other's lips and put their hands in each other's pockets. She had never seen anyone kiss like that before in real life.

"Do people kiss on the lips in real life?" she asked Camilla.

"Just the Americans. And only in the movies," Camilla told her.

Papatya's face was a sulking wilderness when Tarik returned from his oil-selling trips but when he was away, she was sunny as a daisy, her namesake. (Papatya means Daisy.) Opening all the windows and all the doors, she chirped tremulous love songs with her dramatic soprano voice, which concealed the brittle heart. Sometimes she held recitals, inviting the most renowned musicians of the city, who spilled out during balmy summer evenings from her living room out to the balcony where she had pillows thrown around, and torches lit, chorusing in nostalgic melancholy. At those times, the whole street vibrated with energy.

༃

Unable to restrain her impulse any longer, Papatya wrote a note to Rodrigo, inviting him to sing at one of her recitals. He replied positively.

That day is still vivid in everyone's mind. The Blue Angel delivered confections and desserts with erotic and voluptuous names like Lady's Thighs, Beauty's Lips, Hanum's Fingers, and Woman's Navel. They brought sour-cherry and melon sherbets. Mont Blancs and Pyramids.

In the afternoon, they dashed to Necati's beauty parlor around the corner. Necati pranced around like a swashbuckler, playing their heads like the keys of a xylophone, bouncing from one woman to another, never for a moment neglecting or favoring any one above the others. He said he had brought back a new "do" from Paris, asymmetrical, one side clipped like a short bob, the other shoulder length and curled up like a caravel. Scissors flew in the air snipping wisps of hair; the stink of permanent chemicals blended with cigarettes and Turkish coffee.

They came out several hours later, resembling a singing group in their identical "do's" with a gold streak right in the center, frosted eyelashes, and false fingernails painted shocking pink—that season's favorite color.

He arrived exactly at seven, just after the sun had set but before it became dark altogether. A snug sharkskin suit in algae green with a shocking-pink carnation on his lapel. All the doors opened and the women with identical hair and inflated petticoats rushed out to meet him as though they were his backup girls.

That night he sang like a bird in rapture. His smooth, sonorous voice and vast repertory of Latin songs—"Luna Rosa," "Vaya con Dios"—dissolved into new arrangements. The acoustics were less than favorable, and the street noise interfered with the purity of his timber, still Rodrigo knew how to labialize with his voice and watch the women swoon.

Papatya was at her best. She dimmed the lights, stood under the streetlamp, wearing a trenchcoat, opened her moist lips, and with deep melancholy sang "Lili Marlene." At the end of each stanza the group repeated in unison, "Die eins Lili Marlene."

I don't know what had happened to the husbands that night but they were elsewhere, repelled by the feminine quality of Papatya's recitals. So Rodrigo had the women to himself. He wrenched his heart, he sang for them, and, at the end, invited Papatya for a duet. She resisted first; she played it coy but at the insistence of the guests, melted like butter from a cow.

Their duet metamorphosed into Jeanette MacDonald—Nelson Eddy, singing from *Rosemarie*, as they dashed off arpeggios like confetti.

"When I'm calling you-ooo-ooo-ooo-ooo-ooo-ooo . . ."

After that night, Rodrigo became family, popping up at all hours of the day—most opportunely around mealtimes. You'd find him in the kitchen making a strange concoction of a soup with octopus tentacles and mysterious entrails, flirting with Gonca's sisters, who watched him in fascination, or across the street at the Blue Angel, sipping tea with the women, telling them of all the exotic places he had traveled to—Rio de Janeiro, Maracaibo, Casablanca, Vera Cruz, Shanghai, all of which sounded like the names of movies they had seen. No birthdays, circumcisions, and weddings occurred without the blessing of Rodrigo's sweet voice. Even the New Year's Eve saw him sliding through the chimney into Mihriban's fireplace dressed as Noel Baba, singing "Jingle Bells," crashing and breaking his neck, after which he had to wear one of those special collars, which, instead of making him look ludicrous, gave him even more of a regal demeanor and held his head in place while he sang, "When I fall in love-ooo-ooo-ooo-ooo-ooo-ooo . . ."

He won the women's hearts first, moving all the way up the ladder, from the young ones to the matriarchs, the aging aunts, even the female servants he stopped in the dark during his nocturnal escapades for a purloined kiss.

Gonca's sister Gül told Camilla she didn't really mind. "He knows how; doesn't spit in your mouth like the others nor stick his tongue into your throat like a washrag—does not feel you up in your place of shame (that's what they called a woman's sex organ), like the other gentlemen in the family."

"What other gentlemen?"

"All of them," Gül answered. "Except Cadri Bey, of course." They were not aware that Amber, lying awake in bed could still hear them, trying to deduce what feeling up meant. Up where? Not knowing yet those dark sensations but imagining.

But despite his opportunistic flamboyance, Rodrigo had another kind of a heart for Papatya. Tender and clownish. In Tarik's absence, he visited her often, skipping the steps as he ran up, carrying a bouquet of daisies, since Papatya meant daisy, and whistling. "Figaro. Figaro. Figaro."

Papatya welcomed him dressed in diaphanous caftans and Brunhilde wigs, painted and bejeweled like Turandot or Carmen. They would glide across the freshly installed linoleum singing a mad duet that crescendoed into a striptease with exotic pieces of clothing strewn in every room and ended up in her state-of-the-art, turquoise-tiled shower, reaching the catharsis of their duet, aided by the spray of water.

The tremulous songs rising out of Papatya's flat mesmerized them all so much that the family ignored their ominous impropriety. Everyone knew. Yet everyone kept silent because their hearts were glad that Papatya had at last found something that gave her pleasure. They themselves were envious of the kind of love Rodrigo offered Papatya, courtship and play, not having known it with their husbands, but also not without disquiet.

Once again buried in his paper empire, the poetriarch was lamenting the dwindling fortunes of the İpekçi family—especially since he possessed little talent for such management. He seemed more hunched, rapidly balding, dragging his nose around like a snout. The corners of his mouth turned down like the mask of Tragedy. Everytime he returned, the women immediately descended upon him with slippers, cool drinks, and eager ears. Camilla undressed him and drew him a bath. They stayed in the bathroom together for long hours, as she slowly washed him. Then, in their bedroom, all night long talking in muffled tones that sounded as though they were rolling hard candy in their mouths as they plotted a conspiracy.

Since Esma's death, Camilla had claimed her territory and

guarded it with vengeance but this created a subservience of another sort, one that required constant maintenance. The women existed to serve their men since it was their only chance of acquiring a soul. They were not born with souls but by attaching themselves to a man, they could share theirs thus gaining an entry into the *cennet,* or paradise. But even in *cennet,* the celestial *houris* served the men. No other paradise existed for women.

Rodrigo and Cadri began playing *bezique,* each having been initiated as a child into this ancient court game exclusive to the male sex. Something that Cadri and Rodrigo discovered they had in common though oceans apart. They played so intensely that they resembled the subjects of a Caillebotte painting.

Cadri shuffled a heavy deck made up of four decks of only the higher arcana. Each picked a card. Rodrigo a queen, Cadri, an ace. Rodrigo cut and Cadri dealt nine cards, three sets of three. They arranged their fans with self-important intensity and Rodrigo led. He discarded a nine of clubs, Cadri gave him a nine of diamonds. Rodrigo took the trick. They picked cards from the deck. Rodrigo played a nine of hearts, Cadri took it with a ten of the same suit, and the wooden *marqueuse* clicked castanets. He marked fifty points, for pairing a queen of spades with a jack of diamonds. Two of each would make five hundred, three of each fifteen, and four of each three thousand, or *bezique.*

Amber watched the game, idling from one to the other, scoring her father's points on the *marqueuse,* peeking at both hands; they allowed her, not suspecting that she was calculating the rules, comprehending the moves until she started inside trading in her father's favor.

Rodrigo was annoyed. For a moment he forgot she was only a child, then became one himself. "You're cheating," he scolded her. "Besides, this is not for girls. Why don't you play your own games? Go play with your paper dolls."

So, she did. The most satisfying of games. Out of card-board, she had constructed charming little palaces like the ones in the puppet shows, with filigree and arabesque where she planned lavish parties for her paper dolls that her American aunt Sophie, her uncle Aladdin's Irish-American wife, had sent her. A cast of thousands: Some of them were of real people like Lucy and Desi, Debbie and Eddie, Fred and Ginger, Esther Williams, and Marilyn Monroe. Then, there were the imaginary ones like Betty Boop and Howdy Doody. But in the paper doll universe, they all mingled. Amber dressed them all up in their best evening clothes for a grand ball she gave as in American movies depicting the South—*Jezebel, The Little Foxes, Gone With the Wind*—while talking her stories quietly to herself.

Cadri seemed to be losing. He asked Camilla to make some more coffee. Camilla obligingly closed her *Marie Claire* magazine and unfolded her legs. Rodrigo said he wasn't interested in any.

"Come on, comrade. You'll need coffee to stay awake so I can skunk you," Cadri chuckled. "It's choice coffee. I brought it myself from Antioch. Ethiopian. Not the stuff mixed with dried chickpeas they sell around here."

"Seriously, Cadri, I'm not drinking. Coffee is poison. You're committing suicide consuming such copious amounts."

"Come on, Rodrigo," Cadri exclaimed. "I've been drinking coffee since I was an infant. My mother always said I had a moist temperament, so she filled my baby bottle with coffee. She always said, excessive coffee will do no harm as long as a person is not a melancholic."

"What did they know about health in those days? Coffee ruins the liver, raises the blood pressure, and causes nervousness and hysteria. Even makes a man impotent and turns girls into nymphomaniacs. It's not really the coffee itself but the poison in it called caffeine, $C_8H_{10}N_4O_2$. More than ninety percent of the population is addicted to caffeine, which slowly destroys what is inside you, like a rat slowly nibbling cheese, and then, one day, boom, you're gone. (He feigned collapsing.) Governments know about this but nobody, nobody's doing anything because too much profit is staked in coffee. Too much crime involved. But soon it's all going to collapse because people who know the truth will speak up and nobody will ever drink coffee again because the evils of caffeine will be revealed to the entire world."

"I didn't expect such an evangelical outburst," Cadri laughed, meanwhile concentrating on his tricks as he put a king of spades next to the queen and gave himself another forty points. *Click, click.* Now it was a matter of completing the trump suit before the high points started rolling in.

"I'm not going to beat around the bush," Rodrigo said. "I have a proposition to make. Now, listen to this, Cadri. Carefully. Do you know what is in a coffee bean?" He cited the chemicals ending with the C word—caffeine. "There's a way to get rid of caffeine but still maintain the fine taste of coffee."

"Yes, I read about it somewhere," Cadri said. "They remove it out of the coffee with some chemicals."

"That's not what I'm talking about," Rodrigo said. He put his cards face down and his hands dove into his pocket. He pulled out a small leather sack and slammed it on the table.

Amber stopped playing with her paper dolls and ran up to see. Coffee beans, paler than the usual ones, almost a greenish white. Cadri was obviously waiting for the punch line.

"It's the beans," Rodrigo continued. "Look, each one a golden nugget. See these? My family has been experimenting with them for decades, hybridizing, grafting, splicing, regenerating, and you know what the result of years and years of this labor has produced?"

"What?"

"Minimized the amount of caffeine until we produced this strain without any whatsoever. A mutant."

"Very interesting," Cadri agreed, "but how do we know they are different?" He put down the jack, ten, and ace of spades and gave himself two hundred and fifty points. He was rolling while Rodrigo automatically played his hand, his avarice stranded elsewhere.

Rodrigo asked Camilla if she would dump the coffee she was making and make another instead from his pale beans. Camilla did not like being ordered around. But it was her job.

Cadri skeptically took a sip of Rodrigo's coffee; then Camilla took a sip herself.

"I don't taste anything different," she said. "Honestly. It tastes all the same to me." Cadri shook his head in agreement.

"Ahh," Rodrigo growled, "it is because you both are addicted. Your sensitivity is blunted and you can't even taste the difference, but for someone who is not an addict it's simply a miracle. Besides it's more the effect than the taste. Here, Amber, you try this coffee."

"I don't like coffee."

"We need a virgin for the sacrifice," Rodrigo said and laughed wickedly. "It's just an experiment. Our life depends on your judgment, Amber sweetheart. We're in your hands."

"What am I supposed to do?" she sulked.

"Taste the coffee and tell us if you feel something buzzing, like a bee trapped inside your head or your heart beats faster."

Amber took a reluctant sip, made a face, and said she felt no buzz and it tasted disgusting. Like sewer water.

"You ever tasted sewer water? Give it a chance," Rodrigo told her, "it takes a while, y'know? Go ahead, take another sip."

"But I hate it. I told you so."

"Come on, *tonton* (an affectionate phrase meaning my sweet, chubby one), just one more sip. I'll give you a picture of Esther Williams in *Million Dollar Mermaid*."

"I want some sugar in it, then," Amber negotiated.

He put in a cube.

"Four more," Amber insisted.

Rodrigo, who by now looked as though he were getting ready to twist the child's neck, filled the cup with five cubes of sugar, stirred it. "Try this."

Amber took a sip and just as quickly told him she did not feel any different and went into the living room where Camilla was now tracing a pattern from *Burda* for matching sundresses for the two of them to wear for the Children's Day parade. She liked dressing them the same. Amber dove back into her paper palaces with paper people.

"See, she felt nothing. If there was caffeine in the beans, she'd be buzzing around now. Hyperactive. Look, what I am trying to tell you, Cadri, is that you could grow these beans here and manipulate the world market," Rodrigo pursued. He fondled his coffee beans. "Nothing like this anywhere else. Do you realize that? Nowhere. Do you know what that means?"

Cadri shook his head. "Oh no, Rodrigo," he said. "Many have tried cultivating coffee since it was brought here from Yemen several hundred years ago but no one has succeeded. Coffee grows in hot arid climates and mountains that are cool between the Tropic of Cancer and the Tropic of Capricorn. It wouldn't stand a chance of survival here. The altitude is not high enough nor hot enough. No, sir."

"That's where you're wrong," Rodrigo told him. "You're confusing them with regular beans. We are talking something a great deal more special and capricious. Decaffeinated beans! They need different weather, soil, altitude, humidity. My family tried growing them in Campo Santo but no avail. The poor

plants turned anemic, got scorched, and went hungry. These
beans need much water. Much. They don't like predictable climates; they get lazy. What they need is a subtropical climate,
capricious like on your Mediterranean coast. That's why I'm
here. Don't you think that I wouldn't have tried it in my own
country, with my own people, where I know how to get capital,
with workers whose stomach I know, whose language I speak?"

"Why are you telling me all this?"

"Ahh, my friend, because we are facing similar junctures in
our lives and I know as surely as I know my own name, we are
fated to combine our resources and create a major miracle.
Don't ask why. I just know. You don't think I'm going to make
my living as a canary for the rest of my life, do you? I am also
aware your uncle died not that long ago and now, being the patriarch, you have the enormous responsibility of figuring out
ways to take care of your family. It's all on your shoulders. They
are all looking up to you to regain their respect and fortune."

"If you know all that, you might also know that my uncle's
fortune melted like a candle," Cadri told him wryly.

"I know, I know, but you must have enough assets to plant a
few seeds. You understand? Especially, if you can convince your
women."

Rodrigo and Cadri stayed up late that night storming their
brains about caffeinated and decaffeinated beans and mathe-
matical abstractions as the room got hotter and more dense with
smoke. Amber was all jazzed up from the coffee and cut out
more and more paper palaces and filled them with more paper
dolls until Camilla, no longer able to keep her eyes open, carried
her off to bed and tucked her in.

I'm not sure which came first after that, the thing with Papatya, or the betrayal. Most likely, everything happened at the same time. After all, how could the whole family trust a shadowy Latin singer with a dubious past? But they did. The human need to trust is invincible. Yet stranger things happen in life.

So that night Rodrigo coaxed Cadri, and he in turn the whole family, into mortgaging me and buying some sort of a citrus plantation on the Mediterranean along the Taurus mountains (between Antalya and Alanya) to grow decaf coffee. The entire family agreed willingly, in fact dreamily—except for Tarik, who said that he'd rather put his cash in olive oil any day than bogus coffee beans.

The whole coffee operation had to remain hush-hush outside the clan. They had known such secrecy in the silk trade.

"It should be top secret to prevent anyone spying and stealing the decaf beans and creating competition," Rodrigo emphasized. "Imperative to pretend it is an ordinary fruit operation. We'll camouflage it carefully with banana and citrus trees."

Although the word seeped out and friends warned Cadri against the madness of growing coffee on the Mediterranean coast, he would not listen. Equally obsessed in the dream now as Rodrigo, his already fickle senses could not surrender. The two men went down to the Mediterranean coast frequently and brought pictures of themselves among groves of banana trees in the foothills of the Taurus Mountains. Rodrigo remained in charge of the operation while Cadri returned to Ankara with optimistic reports. The plants were growing well and a fine crop was expected. As soon as it was harvested, they'd flood the market. Of course, Cadri had no notice of how long it took for the coffee to mature.

A sense of spaciousness filled the family members, adult or child, a glimmer that they could retrieve their past glory until that fated evening when Tarik returned unexpectedly from a business trip.

Papatya was not home. Tarik went from door to door, asking for her but no one admitted to knowing Papatya's whereabouts.

"You know Papatya," Camilla tried calming him. "Sometimes she goes to sing with her friends. They get carried away, they don't know how time passes. No harm in it, is there?"

"It's past midnight," Tarik objected. "What kind of friends are these anyway, singers, dancers, low-class scum?"

Camilla and Cadri shook their heads and restrained the panic expected during such occasions.

"I'll go to the police," Tarik told them.

"I'll find her," Cadri interfered. "Don't worry, I'll find your wife. The family name should never be smeared on police records. What goes on behind our walls is no one else's business. We must always stick together with our own. I'll go find her myself."

He immediately departed on the night train.

"It takes only one weed to smother a garden. It was his idea to bring the bastard into the family," Sibel grumbled the following afternoon, as the women stirred their tea at the Blue Angel. "Cadri sweet-talked us into selling everything and buying the stupid decaf plantation. And look, just look what happened!"

"*Yok, yok.* Get your perspective. Rodrigo was wagging his tail at everyone in the family, everyone, long before licking Cadri's you know what," Camilla defended him. "How can you deny your own enchantment with Rodrigo? You all fell for him from the beginning. Don't turn Cadri into a scapegoat now, for God's sake."

"She is right. Rodrigo had irresistible charm," Aida swooned. "Let's face it, I mean, he looked like Cornell. He knew how to treat ladies. He was charming. Talented. He danced beautifully. Sang beautifully. Can't you just hear them singing together? When I'm calling you, ooo-ooo-ooo-ooo-ooo-ooo."

"The neighbor's chicken always looks like a goose," Camilla shrugged. "Admit it."

"Why, of all people, he had to pick Papatya I can't understand," Sibel bitched again, raising her big dark eyes like overboiled chestnuts. "May his shadow never rest. Crow, crow said gawk, gawk. / Climb this branch and look around. / I climbed the branch and looked around. / This crow's just foolin' 'round."

They were all dangling from the balconies, smoking cigarettes, when Cadri returned the next evening. He escorted Papatya out of the Citroën to her flat as if leading her to the inquisition and left her there.

"What did Rodrigo have to say?" Camilla asked when they were alone.

"He said he didn't exactly invite her. Papatya is a big girl. She can think for herself. She came of her own choice."

"And why not?" said Camilla. "With a husband who disappears for several months at a time and chases after other kinds of 'daisies' . . ."

Downstairs, murderous voices rose out of Papatya and Tarik. Sounds of things smashing. More things. A scene from *Othello* when he suspects Desdemona. Her shrieking pain went right through every heart in the building. Then, everything fell silent.

"He's beating her," Camilla wept. "Cadri, you should go see. Oh, my God!"

"Don't get hysterical. One should not interfere with what goes on between a husband and a wife."

"How can you stand it. He's going to kill her!"

A few moments later, Papatya dragged herself out of her flat and limped across the hall, her face black and blue, blood trickling down her forehead, her dress tattered. She banged on Cadri and Camilla's door.

"He threw me out," she told Camilla. "Please, let me sleep at your house tonight?"

Cadri paced in the hallway. "I can't even if I want to. It wouldn't be right, Papatya," he told her. "You should go back to your husband, beg his forgiveness. Things will return to normal in time."

"How can I? I can't. Look at me. I have no place in his house."

"That's your problem."

"But *you* are my family!"

"It's not right to come between a husband and a wife."

Papatya went from door to door begging her family to let her in. They hid behind their doors listening but no one opened a door except for Aida, who came out and embraced her sister before being pulled inside by the General. "Only God has the right to interfere with a husband and a wife."

Papatya ran up and down the floors banging at the doors, crying her heart out. On the other side, her sisters wiped their tears with Kleenex but no one dared step out. They shuddered somewhere between life and nightmare until dawn when they heard her voice.

She sang. She stood in the courtyard and sang the dying song of Madama Butterfly and she hit a higher pitch than ever before, which would have put her among the immortals but instead she ran out the door and disappeared like a will-o'-the-wisp in her tattered white organdy gown with black polka dots. The wind quickly blew her out of sight.

꒰

The days that followed are a blurred confusion since none of the İpekçis wanted to think about or remember what had happened, until the night the telegram arrived. They were all asleep and Camilla was the first to wake up at a persistent knock on the door. Soon, everyone hovered over her shoulder to read the telegram.

"RODRIGO. stop. ABANDON PLANTATION. stop. MONEY DISAPPEAR FROM ACCOUNT. stop. The Manager."

Cadri immediately dressed and left again for the plantation.

"No doubt, Papatya returned to Rodrigo and together they've run off with the money to some exotic tropical place like Havana or Beirut," Sibel projected. "Where else could she go?"

Others were silent.

"The General has good connections in the police department," Aida reminded them. "We could . . . You know?"

But to set the authorities after the lovers would be too mean and scandalous. "Cadri would never allow that," Camilla confirmed. "The most important thing is not to lose any more face than we already have."

So, once again, grinding their teeth and restraining their feelings, the İpekçis stuck together in distress. But this one was to be their last before everything fell apart.

When an expert from the Department of Agriculture was brought to the plantation to analyze the crops, he informed Cadri that nothing was special about the coffee beans. Just ordinary Yemen. As for the crops, no chance of surviving the winter. Even if they did, it would take at least five years for them to yield any coffee cherries. The best thing to do would be to recultivate the soil, and plant more bananas and citrus instead.

The General's connection in the Security Department revealed that Rodrigo was not really a Latin lover but an Egyptian crook named Rashid. He had left a few days earlier on a freighter to Cyprus. And he was traveling alone.

So where had Papatya gone? Silence hovered over every part of the household for days and days. The first Friday of the month, the women gathered in the courtyard, made a circle, and began ululating. They stuck out their tongues long like snakes and trilled. They stopped being women and became sirens, birdlike creatures flapping their wings, desperately wailing. The men were away, of course. They always seemed to be away at such times of women's wildness. The older women sat in their velvet chairs, counting worry beads, whispering the usual incantations while the children leaned against parapets, watching unseen.

That evening while the little ones were shipped off to stay at Mihriban's, the adults confined themselves to Cadri and Camilla's flat and yelled at each other for hours. They pointed fingers that seemed to elongate with each accusation. They even spit on each other, their saliva turning into venom. Children and servants put their ears to the floor, hoping to hear something, but all had turned into a poisoned alphabet soup.

They stayed there for interminable hours, retreating at last into their private quarters only to shut out the rest. After that, they coexisted with the impersonality of neighbors as in any city. The ones who occupied the upper floors deliberately walked heavily, tapped, and rolled things around to irritate the ones below. They vacuumed their floors in the middle of the night. Their kids were allowed to play loud music and even to roller-skate.

No one mentioned Papatya or Rodrigo's name. No more family gatherings, circumcision, or birthday parties. No more *Bayram* feasts. They had even stopped greeting each other except when their paths accidentally crossed in the hallways.

The children took to the street from dawn till dusk to escape the static of mistrust and lose themselves instead in the distraction of play. They played ferociously, trying to pretend ignorance but already brainwashed by respective parents, their opinions stretching farther than words could travel.

On the surface, their world seemed deceptively normal. The girls played "beauty and ugliness" or hopscotch, drawing continuous squares with colored chalk on the cracking concrete sidewalk winding around uneven city blocks, then skipping and sliding slippery stones through the squares, smooth as ice. They argued about where to draw the squares and whether the stones landed on the lines.

The boys played war, pointing their pretend finger-guns at each other, making mechanical groans, incomprehensible to the girls, while slithering and squirming in the dust or the mud on their bellies. The older ones kicked the soccer ball around, their voices in awkward metamorphosis, their legs radically bowed from early hardening. Occasionally, the girls challenged them to a race around the block, all the way to the Officer's Club, bargaining for goufrettes with the movie star cards, always winning since their feminine gravity had not yet arrived, their coltish legs infinitely faster and more agile in their prehormonal confusion.

One day, one of the boys said he wasn't playing any more. He had no money left for goufrettes or marbles. They were all poor now.

"All your father's fault," Maya snapped at her cousin Amber in a tone that sounded as though she was inciting the rest for mutiny.

"No, it's not. He didn't know they were fake. He didn't."

"It was Uncle Poetriarch who talked everyone into a mad adventure," Maya insisted—words that belonged to a grown-up mouth. The attitude as well.

"Not his fault Papatya ran off with Rodrigo or he with our money."

"Shush. We're not supposed to say their names. Uncle Poetriarch brought the family to ruin because he himself had a basic character flaw."

Amber ran upstairs; she could hear Cadri and Camilla, speaking at an argumentative pitch. "You must tell her," Camilla begged, unaware of Amber's presence. "The longer we wait, the worse it will become."

"What if she asks why we're leaving her behind?"

"Then, make up something. She can't yet understand the complexity of things anyway."

Amber sensed that the "she" they were referring to was herself. She felt something horrible was about to happen. They were going to abandon her.

She went into her room, took out all her paper dolls and lay them out for a big party. What were her parents talking about? What could she not understand? Were they really planning to abandon her?

At dinner, as she served mutton chops with thyme and braised leeks, Camilla exchanged funereal glances with Cadri but neither uttered a word. Amber had witnessed this scene before, like every time her parents negotiated with each other which one of them would be the one to punish her. In between enormous bites, chewed and chomped loudly, Cadri cast furtive looks at his daughter as if he was about to say a word but belched instead. Then he began chewing toothpicks. Camilla left the room to get something from the kitchen. Finally, the air formed itself into words and released Cadri's mouth.

"We're moving away," he said.

"Again?"

"We have to sell the Spinster's Apartment to pay our debts."

"Where?" Amber asked him. "Back to the house in Izmir?"

Cadri explained then that he was going to America for a year, to a place called Ann Arbor—which sounded like a movie star's name—to study labor relations, which sounded like something to do with making babies. (Did her father have a mistress? Named Ann Arbor?)

"But why?" she asked him; this distant pursuit mystified her.

"When I traveled from factory to factory, I saw terrible things. The workers live subhuman lives. They need protection of their rights. I'm going to learn ways to do that. Your mother will join me in a couple of weeks."

"What about me?" Amber asked, picturing herself a waifish orphan, missing teeth, dressed in rags like those abandoned kids in *David Copperfield* (or was it *Oliver Twist*?) "You are not taking me with you?"

"No. You'll go to stay in Karshiyaka with your mother's parents for a little while."

"But I want to come with you and my mother."

"America is not a good place to travel with children. Your mother and I'll be busy all day long, working very hard. We have no one to leave you with. You don't know their language. You couldn't attend school. You'd be miserable."

"I want to go with you anyway," she whimpered.

"I told you, Amber, it's out of the question. Besides you'd detest what they eat, what they drink. You hate milk. You don't like carrots. Why, you don't even eat onions; they make you sick. Did you know that all the children in America are required to consume kilos of onions everyday?"

"I'll force myself, then. I don't care if they make me sick. I'll eat onions, if I have to. I'll get used to it," she begged him. "I'll promise anything."

He shook his head. "No Amber, no go. Stop begging. Stop being a pest."

"You don't love me. You don't love me."

"I've had enough."

"You don't love me, besides it's all your fault that Aunt Papatya ran away and our family is broken and poor now. All your fault!"

Steel tears spilled out of his eyes. His bald pate turned crimson, his tongue freakish blue. His hand reached for his coffee cup; he lifted it and hurled it in Amber's direction like a hand grenade.

First, the thick paste of coffee grains dripped all over his nicely starched white shirt, making him lose his composure. Then, the cup flew right below Amber's left eye, burning her cheek like a bee sting. Blood oozed out of her skin as the cup continued flying, flew right out the window, down the street, hitting a beggar over the head who just happened to be passing by, and exploded into thousands of pieces. From the impact, it became imbedded on the sidewalk and formed a mosaic in the shape of a moth.

Even though the İpekçi family scattered all over the world to unrelated destinies by the end of spring and abandoned me and Ankara, there is still a city underneath this site waiting to be excavated. The imprint of the moth still remains on the sidewalk, a great curiosity for tourists who claim it's the silk moth, Bombyx mori. Passersby make up stories about a family of spinsters who once lived here, except they imagine a different sort of spinsters, the kind who spin stories.

The Turquoise House on
Seven Whiskers Street

꒱

(1961–1962)

People separate for a reason. They tell you their reason. They give you a chance to reply. They do not run away like that. No, it is perfectly childish.

Marcel Proust

Y*ou entered me through* an enormous carved door, so warped that to align the sides and close it was impossible. No one ever thought of locking it anyway; the upper shutters perpetually remained open inviting all sorts of flying things but mainly a pair of swallows that built a nest above the brass chandelier.

They laid eggs, the swallows. Once Amber found a shelless one, a translucent membrane with a jelly-bean-like baby bird embryo ferned up inside. Eyeless things. When the eggs chirped, she stacked boxes on top of each other and climbed to peek at the baby birds—ugly beings they were with blind glares and needy beaks. A couple of them fell off the nest. Instantly one of the dozens of cats that trespassed devoured them like hors d'oeuvres. The rest of the chicks gobbled up the earthworms, spiders, and other creepy-crawlers that the frantic parent birds, darting in and out all day long, dropped into the begging beaks. Soon, they learned to fly from room to room, driving the cats to the precipice of madness while inspiring hilarious acrobatics. Then, one day, awkwardly plumed now like spiked-haired teenagers, they followed their parents out the window, instantly disappearing into the vast blueness of the sky, and were gone.

The nest, now a permanent part of the ceiling ornamentation, remained empty until the lilacs bloomed, when the pair returned from their prolonged peregrination and resettled on the chandelier—at least everyone assumed they were the same couple. They repeated this cycle year after year but the summer Cadri and Camilla went to America, the nest remained empty even past the lilac time. The Taşpinars waited and waited in vain but the good-luck swallows had vanished into the realm of forgetfulness.

But other creatures found their way into this household, sensing the open-hearted welcome, and became part of the family during their brief lives. Especially cats. Cats soaking in the fountain—tabby cats from the city of Van that loved to swim and paddled in the trough, out of which Dudu, the ornery goat, drank water. Angoras, conveying dual messages with their mysterious eyes, slyly slithered in the dark, leaving in the air a trace of unease. And grinning Cheshire cats sprawled out on tree branches, flashing their teeth. Cats stalked nightingales among the poppy fields. Hairless cats nervously scurried around, looking for a sunny patch to lick their pink-and-gray sunburned skin. Sometimes Amber rubbed snake oil on their poor flesh to ease the pain. Pretending they were her babies, she clothed them in doll's clothes, little dresses and hats. She rocked them on the hammock, singing lullabies she remembered from the house in Smyrna across the bay, the house where she was born. *Dandini, dandini, danali bebek. Elleri kollari, kinali bebek.*

Then there was the fox. Hamid Bey had trapped the fox one night when she had descended from Tantalus mountains to eat their chickens. Instead of killing her, Hamid Bey kept the fox captive, naming her Scheherazade and teasing her into domestic laws. Although not exactly fond of each other, the goat and the fox shared the chicken coop (which much later in life would become Malika's nest). The chickens, though, kept out of sight because they did not trust the smell the fox exuded when she got excited even though they should have figured out by now that Scheherazade was never allowed to venture out by herself. Chickens are instinctively dumb, anyway.

I am the home of Camilla's parents, the Taşpinars, the fountainheads, Hamid Bey and Malika, or Maria, as she had been known a long time ago, long before the Great War.

Like most backwater families of Cordelio, the Taşpinars spent most of their days outdoors in the garden under the shade of three prolific fig trees, a red, a green, and a yellow one. On the opposite side of the wall, a small alley of Kalamata olives lined up. The night-blooming jasmine entangled with pomegranate vines creeping up the stone wall all the way up the roof terrace populated with potted succulents, cascading into the garden like beaded curtains.

When Camilla brought Amber to stay here, just before her departure to America to join Cadri, she warned her not to go near the stone well from where the water supply came. "Cats have fallen in. Snakes squirm at the bottom. *Odjus* live inside and when they see children staring at them, they open their mouths real wide and suck them in like marrow," she told her, making a sucking and slurping sound.

"I don't believe in *odjus* anymore," Amber responded but still Camilla's warning endistanced her from the lichen-covered well with stones of chevron patterns, until the afternoon she witnessed a private moment of her grandmother.

Malika was drawing water from the well. She stopped suddenly, looked around to make certain no one was watching her. She took something out of her pocket and threw it into the well. She listened to the splash as it hit the water, then closed her eyes; her lips moved as if she was in a trance, talking to someone, like a person in prayer. This, Amber discovered, was Malika's daily ritual. And when she found herself alone by the well one day, she did the same.

Malika was a sinuous woman of silence with flowing streams of white hair concealed in a bun. Never still, her tawny long arms always stirring, sweeping, washing, twisting. Sometimes, rising like a somnambulist in the middle of the night, Malika would descend down to the basement where earlier Hamid Bey and his Sufi friends had gathered to sing and dance until their feet left the ground and they floated like angels in their long white flowing robes and conical hats. Malika sat in candlelight communing with the unseen that the men had agitated, watching otherwise invisible visions from her forgotten past. Sometimes she recited things aloud or hummed in Italian or Greek. She needed the comfort of holy voices to ease out her ever-consuming grief.

How do I know all these things? Because I too never slept. The silence of the night has no wings.

A picture of Hamid Bey as a young man, dressed in a lavishly decorated uniform, hung on the wall across from the swallow's nest. Regal, fierce, untouchable, he'd once been the mayor of Cordelio. Now a neglected notary public and a part-time watch repairer, he occupied a modest storefront in an arcade near the Cordelio boat landing. But when he walked down the street, old men still took off their hats and saluted him and old ladies still coyly giggled, remembering his yellow mustache—"baby chicken yellow" as Maria would say—his Young Turk fez. How handsome he was! And how stubborn.

"Good day, Mr. Mayor. How are you today?" the locals saluted him.

Hamid Bey straightened his gait, closed his eyes, bowed, and took his hat off with old-fashioned dignity as if he were still the mayor. But his chest sank when he remembered how he had lost it all.

༂

Before leaving for America, Camilla consoled Amber with new shoes, and dresses, mother-daughter fashions, matching polka dots, matching stripes, matching eyelet, silk, organdy. She styled their hair the same way, blazing a curling iron on the embers of Malika's coal stove. She sizzled her own abundant curls, then Amber's, Shirley Temple style. In fact, she fashioned her daughter after Shirley, the magical child star.

Amber had already discovered vanity, wished to be beautiful like her mother or her aunt Aida, and she'd blossom when Cadri took their pictures with his newly acquired Kodak Brownie, a gift from his brother, Aladdin. But something changed that summer, just before America. The inextricable cord that bonded the child to the parents irrevocably snapped. In anticipation of the impending separation, Amber drifted into an inexplicable aloofness.

It was the day they had won the Puro soap competition at the International Fair held at the Culture Park in Izmir as the best-dressed mother and daughter and were photographed with the *pehlivans,* the champions of the Turkish wrestling team, Amber sandwiched between Celal Atik and Mersinli Ahmet holding on to their hands and Camilla smiling in the background. Afterward, they took the ferry across to Cordelio and strolled along the serpentine promenade, following the thin blue wafer of the bay, dragging bags full of pink Puro soap, their trophy.

Camilla was beaming as they headed down Seven Whiskers Street through a row of brightly painted houses, eating licorice, holding hands with Amber. Mimosa burst like miniature firecrackers with yellow pollen carpeting the ground and powdering their hair as the tiny puffballs occasionally caught the wind, swirling in spirals. Amber sneezed uncontrollably because the pollen tickled her nose.

"Bless you."

Just then, she noticed on the opposite side of the street a chocolate-colored girl with unusually pale pink lips, identical to Amber except for the color of eyes and skin. The girl was barefoot and had long frizzy braids that jetted out like barbed wire. The two girls' eyes caught each other for a moment and wanted to explore but Camilla squeezed Amber's hand and led her away.

"Who's that girl?" Amber asked.

"She lives in that tin shanty behind my parents' house. You know the enormous dark woman—steals copperware to support her children—her name is Sultan.

"Is she a thief?"

"No, silly. Stealing copperware means glazing it with silver, you know, to give it the reddish patina you see. An absurd name for a woman like that. Well, that little girl is Sultan's daughter. I think they call her Nuria. Those poor kids, always going around shoeless, in rags, snot stretching down their noses to their waists. Gypsies. You know the kid who beats on copper pans every afternoon at five?"

"The one who walks all over town peeping in windows, asking ladies for Nivea cream jars?"

"Yes, that's her older brother."

"What's the matter with him?"

"Terrible story. When he was little some bad kids lured him to the house up on the hill."

"The haunted one?"

"That's the one. It was May, the night of *Hidrellez* festival when strange whispers filled the air, and the light separated from the dark. Well, the bad boys locked the door and abandoned him in the vacant house. Poor kid, he kept banging and screaming for them to come back but instead, from the stairway, descended ugly ghosts, apparitions, phantasms. He was so terrified he swallowed his tongue. Since then, the poor soul only makes sounds, no words."

"Were they real?" Amber asked. "Those things?"

"No, silly. There are no real ghosts and things like that. Just bad boys with sheets over their heads."

When they returned, Camilla asked Amber to stand up on the dining table with her hands sticking out like pokers on each side and began pinning the new yellow eyelet dress for the approaching *Bayram*. Amber fussed. Flies everywhere. The heat.

"Stand still," Camilla ordered, her mouth full of pins. "I don't want to prick you and draw blood. Stand still. Don't fuss, will you?"

"I don't want to," Amber told her.

"It's almost over."

"I don't want to," she repeated. "*Anne*, I don't want to wear this dress."

"What's come over you? It's *çok güzel*, very cute—you said so yourself. Just like the one I have."

"I don't want to look like you, *Anne*. I want to look like myself." Large tears splashed out of Amber's eyes; she was splitting at the seams realizing the separation. "I don't want to," she repeated.

Instead of taking her daughter into her arms, Camilla slowly rolled the fabric into a neat bundle, collected the pins scattered all over the floor, and left the room. She threw herself on her bed and wept. Her daughter had left her.

The next morning, when Amber opened her steamer trunk, she found it empty. All her dresses, sweaters, even the shoes, gone.

"What did you do with my clothes?"

Camilla was packing. She ignored Amber.

"Where are my clothes, *Anne?*"

"You said you didn't want to look like me."

". . . but I liked my dresses."

"Well, they were just like mine and since you told me you didn't want to look like me, I gave them away to the poor who have no cause to complain."

On this note, Camilla left for America on SS *Independence.* Amber and her grandparents stood on the quay waving at the ocean liner as it glided out of Izmir harbor all lit up. The child saw her future at that moment. Someday, she too would leave.

⌇

It would be several days before Malika noticed that Amber never changed her clothes, even when she slept. She had been observing her grandaughter's habits before imposing her own.

"Why are you always wearing the same dress, Amber?" she finally asked one day.

"It's my favorite."

Another night she saw Amber washing the dress and hanging it up to dry. Malika left her alone, obviously the child's security rag. She must be missing her parents. But the children in the neighborhood came around street corners in packs and pinched their noses at Amber and uttered a long *pee-you*. Then ran off in the opposite direction, giggling and chanting, "Stinky Amber fe-ell. Stinky Amber fe-ell. She fell into the cesspool."

Still, Amber was the privileged city girl in their midst, the only one without hennaed hands and pierced ears, without bare feet. The one who'd always worn a meticulously tied butterfly bow on top of her head. The one who read books and *fumetti* during her siesta and drew strange pictures of houses while the rest roasted pinion and scratched olives to help out with the family income.

"Amber, you must tell me, what happened to the rest of your clothes?" Malika asked again days later, staring at the empty trunk. "I just don't understand."

Amber shrugged her shoulders.

"What did you do with them, child? Where did you hide them?"

"I hid them nowhere."

"Then, where are they? Did you give them to someone else?"

"No I didn't. I didn't." She fell apart, on the verge of big tears. "My mummy did."

Malika uttered some incomprehensibles in Greek. "But why? What made her do such a thing?"

"I don't know."

"Your mother has always been a stubborn girl but this is going too far, my little Amber," Malika whispered in her lispy accent. "I just wish I could make you a new dress but I can't afford to buy cloth. Your grandfather doesn't give me any money, you see. And I have none of my own left. But maybe I can take apart one of my old dresses and remake it for you.

It was midsummer by then. Tamarisk trees danced, caught in the sea breeze. Pale asphodels waved like apparitions of flowers and anemones in superbright colors sprung along the cliffs. As

Amber climbed up the rocks, she saw the same chocolate-colored girl she and Camilla had encountered the day of the contest. The girl was skipping stones, her rebellious hair sticking out every which way. But her face was as clean as if a milk cow had just licked it. She was wearing nice shoes and socks, also the yellow eyelet dress matching Camilla's.

Amber looked away, chewing her gum mastic and pretending not to see the girl but there was such little distance between them along the path that it was impossible to avoid her. Nuria turned around and began walking next to Amber, just an air space between them. They walked like this for a long time in competitive silence. When Amber quickened her steps, Nuria speeded hers as well and when she slowed down, so did Nuria.

Finally, Amber stopped, gave her a nasty look, "What do you want?"

"What's your name?"

"Amber."

"Mine is Nuria."

"I know."

"Can I have some of your gum?"

"No."

Nuria shrugged as if she was untouched. "Then, do you want to come and roast pinions?"

Nuria led Amber toward the Promenade to case out the scrubby, gnarled trees, their short, stiff needles oozing with sap. Small nuggets the size of coffee beans burst out of their cones from the heat, yielding hard-shelled nuts that matured and reached full size in August. Most of them had already detached from the tree and fallen to the ground. The girls gathered the nuts scattered among the needles and dirt, competing with each other.

Around sunset, Nuria took Amber to her *gecekondu*, "the

birds that roost in the night," one of those squatters' shacks erected overnight. Three barnacle-like rooms were patched together with driftwood, panels of tin from old olive oil cans, and tarpaper, the windows of oilcloth. Amber was fascinated with this poverty.

Sultan sat on a fig crate outside, surrounded by children, chickens, and laundry hanging to dry. Her pendulous breasts like water-filled balloons, each slung on the opposite shoulder like some sort of an exotic halter top.

"You can't make a purse out of a sow's ear no matter how hard you try," she scolded Nuria pointing at her dress, sticky and tarred now from the pinion dust. "Here take this mutton grease to clean the sap from your hands."

An enormous woman of gypsy descent, Sultan had four children. Yet all that remained from her husband was a skinny gold bracelet made from his teeth, which she protected valiantly. She sat under a grass pergola, spreading a small amount of nuts on a flat surface, then used a flat stone, breaking the hard shells with a gentle rubbing motion. The girls imitated while she boiled the nuts and mashed them into a paste that they spread on day-old bread that the baker had given them.

In the evening, they tossed the cones into the bonfire and swiftly scooped them out with wire because roasting the nuts in their own shells enhances their rich flavor. The aroma strayed like a light feather and reached here.

After that day, Amber and Nuria became glued to each other from the time they woke up until they were forced to go to bed. Amber became a regular at Sultan's house, participating in their ways. Sometimes she even sat with them around a pot of flour paste, cutting and folding the newspapers Nuria's younger siblings had been gathering and glued them into cone-shaped paper bags, which the children later sold to the shops along the Promenade. Sultan pickled the green pine cones just before they reached maturity and sold them to the pickle shops near the boat landing, which attracted customers from far away.

Her oldest son was named Umit, which meant "Hope," but the kids called him Nivea. He floated, weightless and transparent, wandering from house to house, unexpectedly materializing at people's windows with his beatific smile and asking the women for "Nivea." These tender-hearted ladies had no trouble parting with their empty cream jars, uttering their blessings. Nivea's face would glow, a halo around his head, as he disappeared into his corner of the shack, carrying an armful of blue glass jars.

"What do you do with them?" Amber asked but could never get an answer. Nivea smiled a toothless smile and offered her one of his jars like a precious seashell.

That summer, Nivea's beard grew, covering his entire face, cheeks, forehead, even his nose—he had reached puberty—and in the mornings, Nuria shaved him with a razor while the neighborhood kids watched in fascination. But that was not his only change as other impulses stirred inside his body. During the full moon, Nivea marched to the middle of the field, raised his head toward the sky, and howled.

First the townspeople imagined him as the gray wolf of Ergenekon legends, the wolf of freedom, a sacred beast. But when this savage synchronization persisted, it startled them, who now suspected Nivea of being a werewolf. Especially when the entire canine population of Cordelio gathered around him in packs, honoring him as the alpha male, and howled in chorus. Neighbors with sticks and stones chased away the dogs, which they believed to be the children of the devil, but since their religion did not permit killing dogs, they exiled them instead to the

Bitch Island, where the packs wandered day and night, howled, and ate one another.

"*Nivea, Nivea, Nivea,*" the boy sang. *Nivea, Nivea, Nivea* (to the tune of *figaro, figaro, figaro* . . .).

"Stop howling and attracting the goddamn dogs or else we'll have to send you to the Bitch Island, too," Hamid Bey scolded the boy. Nivea smiled and nodded.

After that, every full moon Sultan tied Nivea's hands behind his back, kept him in the outhouse, which shook with tormented sounds until the sun rose. Then Nivea sat in front of the shack next to Sultan doing nothing but simply holding his blissful smile. When people looked at his face, their troubles melted; they had an enchanted day.

One day, when Amber went looking for Nuria, she found the shack empty. She tiptoed into Nuria's room where she had never been invited before, looking for the dresses that Camilla had given to Nuria. Instead, she stumbled into the barnacle where Nivea lay fast asleep. Next to his bed was a pyramid of Nivea jars, mathematically precise and neatly balanced, a cerulean radiance on Nivea's cherubic face. (As she piled up Campbell's soup cans at Warhol's studio many years later, Amber would remember this moment.)

She was still mesmerized watching him sleep when Nuria found her.

"What are you doing here?"

"I was looking for you."

"Come on, then. I'll take you to my secret place."

Instead of their usual walk through the pinion forest, they turned inland where the density of settlements gradually subsided and the houses disappeared completely.

In the small meadow by the winter creek, the ruins of an ancient Roman temple greeted them. Arches and columns still mysteriously suspended in the air. Capitals and broken pieces lying scattered about. Parched grass and thistles sprouted between the stones and turtles wandered among them. Nuria pointed at a patch of honey-colored soil where water flowed. "There," she said. "And I'm the only one who knows about it. Promise me, on your mother's dead body, you'll never tell anyone."

"Why should I?"

"Have you ever ate dirt before?"

Amber shook her head.

"I'll show you, then. We'll make dirt soup. All right?"

Nuria dug the pale soil and scooped it into the olive oil can she was carrying. Then added a little water from another part of the creek, mixing it into a thin mud. She offered some to Amber, who refused.

"It looks like diarrhea."

Nuria shrugged and dug in with her fingers; as if licking some scrumptious chocolate frosting, she made satisfied gurgles in her throat. "Try some," she said. "Really. It's delicious. I promise."

To Amber, it tasted like sand but gradually she could taste the salt.

"Now we take our pants down and make *kaka* under the tree because, like earthworms, when we eat the dirt and then shit, it fertilizes the soil," Nuria instructed Amber. "I return in the winter, gather it, and sell it for fuel."

That's how Nuria introduced Amber to *geophagy*—the practice of eating soil. Amber had read about it in *Life* magazine. People in Africa, especially pregnant women, did it because the dirt is what gave them minerals they couldn't get from another source. But some slaves died from eating too much of it.

It was a difficult taste at first, like halvah or olives, but soon,

Amber had developed such an intense craving for dirt soup that she'd often walk to the mound by herself without Nuria. Sometimes she rolled the dirt into marble-sized balls, brought the pellets back, and hid them in the old brick oven in the coop where Dudu and Scheherazade lived. But soon the mean goat, who had also developed a taste for dirt, managed to pry open the oven with its horns and devoured Amber's coveted pellets.

In their secret place Nuria asked Amber about "wadding."

"Do you want me to show you?"

"Alright."

"Take off your panties, then."

Amber reluctantly obeyed and watched Nuria do the same. She had often been curious when they peed together. Nuria kneeled down on the ground and stuck her head under Amber's skirt.

"I'm going to give you butterfly kisses there," Nuria said rolling her head between Amber's legs.

Amber giggled, feeling funny shivers and goose bumps through her body. Suddenly, Nuria stopped, pulled out her head, and said, "Now your turn."

Amber imitated, lifting Nuria's skirt and inhaling a musky world of scents and steam. She blinked her eyelashes and Nuria pressed herself against Amber's face.

"I'm not crazy about this," Amber announced abruptly, pulling her face out of her friend's skirt but Nuria smiled so sweetly that she couldn't just walk away.

"OK, then lie down. I'll show you something else." She pulled her skirt up to her waist, soldered her lower body on Amber's, glued her tiny sex to hers, and began to undulate vigorously. Amber sensed something forbidden with what they were doing but the pleasure she also felt was confusing.

"Where did you learn this?" she asked Nuria.

"The Grocer with Flies. He does it to me sometimes in the back of the shop and gives me free candy."

"Yuck. What if someone comes through the trees and sees us like this?"

But she drifted into the rhythms of pleasure, little seeds bursting inside her. She wanted her friend to do it again. They had a real secret now.

The girls returned several times to their spot for wadding. But after a while, Amber retreated. She even stopped going to Sultan's for pinion roasts or pickling. Nuria's weakness for this was much greater than hers. The neediness scared Amber.

Nuria whined when Amber no longer wanted to play in their secret place.

"Just once more."

"No."

"Why not?"

" 'Cause . . ."

"Please!"

"Only if you give me back my dresses in return."

Nuria made no objections. Her world was more immediate. She reimbursed Amber for each wadding. One by one, the empty steamer's trunk filled with her old dresses—polka dots, stripes, eyelet, silk, and organdy. Others did not fail to notice. Malika asked where they came from.

"From the well, of course."

Malika was startled, realizing that another being was part of her private world. How did this happen? Had the child seen her by the well?

The last time Nuria and Amber went to the mound, they took off their underwear and rolled on each other.

"I get my last dress today."

Nuria slapped Amber's face. "You're a stingy bitch."

"You're a slut."

"You're nothing. Zero. Your grandmother is a *gavour*. A *Rum*. A Greek. Her real name is not Malika. It's Maria. Everyone knows so!"

Amber snapped her dress and began to run but stopped dead in her tracks. Behind the shrubbery a man was pointing his thing at them, huge and red like amanita mushrooms and prickly. His eyes were bulging and fixed. The girls rustled off, terrified of being followed, but the only thing that followed them was the horrible and unforgettable groans of the man that sounded like a donkey braying. *Ahi, ahi, ahi.*

After the day they had seen the man expose himself, the girls mysteriously stopped talking to each other. Such things happen. Because Amber had retrieved her last dress? Hard to say. Or Nuria's sharp confessional.

Amber realized she was one-quarter Greek. A mongrel. A *gavour*. An infidel. A sense of separation from the familiar chilled her heart. It had never occurred to her to question why Malika spoke with an obvious lispy accent or she and Camilla spoke Greek to one another when they were alone. Children accepted such inexplicables. It was a no-no to ask questions that challenged adults. It wasn't fair. Nothing was fair. Nothing.

In no time, Nuria found a new best friend and Amber began accompanying Hamid Bey to his storefront office near the Promenade.

She'd sit on an overstuffed green armchair, watching her grandfather assemble minuscule axles, dials, with miniature screwdrivers and pinchers, his loupe projecting out as if an extension of his eye. With the tiniest of tweezers he would pick up the tiniest of rubies, diamonds, and emeralds and stick them into the tiniest holes holding together the tiniest wheels while in the background hundreds of cuckoos leapt out of their windows simultaneously, creating such an insane cacophony that people came every hour on the hour to hear them—especially at noon—accompanied by the municipal brass. It was magic.

Sometimes, Amber sat at Hamid Bey's desk and played with his sturdy Remington, quickly figuring out where the keys were, typing letters to her parents in America.

> *Dear anne and baba,*
>   *I learned to type. How are you? I'm fine. How is Ann Arbor? I miss you. When are you coming back? Do you love me?*
>   *Your faithful daughter,*
>   *Amber*

> *PS. I got all my dresses back!*

She became so adept at typing—not using only one finger as would be expected but all ten flying as if she had been trained in a secretarial course; in fact, every time she hit a key it seemed to play a musical note, creating uncanny songs. First the people of Cordelio watched the poor little rich girl at the keyboard but gradually, those who could not read or write came to her for letters. Ten *kurush* a page for normal letters. Fifteen for love letters and twenty-five for business letters—cheaper than all the other men with typewriters along the Promenade.

They told her the sentiments, the tears they shed, the hopes they had and Amber typed them into words in the same way that she had learned to write love letters for her nanny Gonca. Women preferred confiding in a little girl more than the men sitting with their portables along the quay.

Afterward, her grandfather notarized the letters with his golden seal. Hamid Bey's business soared that summer. Even though he never said anything and never showed explicit affection, it was clear that he enjoyed Amber's company. In the evening, after leaving the shop, they went to the waterfront and bought from the fisherman the catch freshly pulled in, still thrashing around in tin cans.

"Why does that fish have green blood?"

"Because it lived in the deep. The red turns green thirty meters below the sea," he explained.

At dinner, Hamid Bey sat on a divan, one leg bent, the other crossed, raised his only arm in the air—the other lost in the war—like a conductor preparing to lead a symphony; he brought his knife down onto his plate with a swooping motion, seemingly manipulated by a force larger than himself. Then he entered it smoothly into the torso of the *chipura* fish, where it was slit. A rivulet of blood trickled out of its side. It was green.

He separated the two halves with small sawing motions, careful not to disturb the bone. Then, with sleight of hand, his knife turned into a fork, which he slid right under the spine and separated it from the bottom, in one swift slide.

The way Hamid Bey's other empty sleeve sat in such silence, often stuck inside a vest pocket, had always brought on a sense of sorrow to Amber, while the fascination in wanting to see the place from where it had been severed continued to nag her.

The fish skeleton sprung out as perfect as in cartoons—freed from its flesh and all, the vertebrae, the tail, the head still attached. But before removing it to another plate, he probed into the cheek and pulled out a pinkish bead-like thing from right behind the eye.

"The pearl of the fish," he told Amber. "Here, you eat it. You'll have better vision. One of the most valuable things in life is to learn to eat fish properly. When you're finished, nothing should be left except the bare bones and those, sculpturally intact."

After dinner, Hamid Bey brought Scheherazade into the living room, closed all the doors and windows, and released the fox out of her cage. Scheherazade went slinking around the room, leaving her scent on every available surface. After the marking, Malika fed her a fresh mackerel and she curled up on a kilim next to Amber's feet and let the girl run her fingers in the luxurious blue fur. Sometimes she stuck her nose in the door and tried pushing it open with her paw but it was effectively bolted. Still, Scheherazade never gave up, until she lost her eyes.

It is hard to know how it all started but one thing is for sure, Dudu the goat didn't care much for Amber. She did not stop with eating the dirt soup pellets in the brick oven. She came charging after her aggressively, forging her head into the girl's bottom. It hurt as she fell on the ground, knocking down a terra-cotta jug, which broke into thousands of fragments. Her face fell into the shards and was covered with lesions. She swore revenge.

The day Amber let Scheherazade out of the cage, knowing she wasn't supposed to, Malika had gone to the market. Although the vixen was as docile as a tame puppy, her freedom would threaten Dudu. It freaked her all right. Dudu ran right out of the turquoise cottage, kicking and baaing, and scared the wits out of the chickens and the cats. Poor Scheherazade, bewildered by this pandemonium, began stalking one of the cats instead of going after Dudu. The cat bristled its back, mustering up all its viciousness, hissed, and snapped back, claws out all the way. An agonized howl and suddenly, Scheherazade's left eye spilled like a soft-boiled egg and the right was hanging from its socket. The fox was growling now, ready to attack anything in sight.

The goat wandered off, smug and free of guilt. Amber backed away and quickly shut the door to the cottage and latched it. She was out of breath, already confronting a moral dilemma, since her intention had been to torment the goat, not the fox. Poor, poor Scheherazade.

When Hamid Bey returned early from a funeral that afternoon, he found Dudu chewing the arugula patch in the neighbor's garden. "Stupid little girl," he yelled at Amber. "What prompted you to let her out?"

He captured the goat and brought her into the shed, then quickly came out. "Amber, where are you?"

Amber came out, her heart leaping out of its place.

"Tell me what happened here."

"I don't know."

"A blind fox is not worth its keep," Hamid Bey told her. "You knew that." With his single arm, he removed his pistol from the Liberation War mounted on the wall next to his picture and went back to the shed.

The gunshot was heard throughout Cordelio but people assumed it was coming from the vaudeville group who had just pitched their tent in the meadow behind Seven Whiskers Street, who must have been rehearsing an act.

Amber was grounded. In the morning, Malika served her breakfast inside. Amber sat alone at the table, putting feta and rose jam on her bread. Fat particles from the boiled milk floated to the surface, making the taste so nauseating that Amber squeezed a lemon into it. The milk curdled immediately and congealed.

"Look," she told Malika. "It's bad milk. I can't drink it."

"I don't understand why," Malika said in her lispy Greek accent of which Amber was now self-consciously aware. "I just milked Dudu early this morning. I don't understand how it could have curdled so quickly. Not particularly a hot day."

Amber was saved from drinking milk that day. The next day,

she repeated the same. Malika sensed something was fishy; her granddaughter was capable of great mischief but Malika could not put her finger on it.

"It must be Dudu," Amber insisted. "She's a mean goat, capable of only producing curdled milk."

"That's rubbish," Malika objected. "I've never had problems with her before. It wasn't curdled when I milked her this morning. Who's ever heard of a thing like that? A goat with curdled milk?"

But when the episode continued day after day, Malika began having her own doubts. She began scolding the goat while she expressed her udders. "Now you're not going to give me curdled milk, are you?"

Dudu kicked her, knocked down the bucket, wasting the milk. That was the last straw.

The following week, when a peddler passed through, collecting mollusks for mother-of-pearl to decorate string instruments, he left with Dudu.

Malika drew some water from the well, undid her bun, and began washing her cascading white hair. She let Amber comb it afterward and pick up the fallen silver strands stuck on her austere dark-colored dress.

"What is your real name?" Amber blurted out.

"What do you mean?"

"I mean, you don't have to hide it from me. I know you're a *Rum* and your real name is Maria."

Malika, timid as a deer, became stiff. She wiped her hands on her apron and went inside.

"You lied to me," Amber shouted after her.

When Amber came in later, she found Maria lying on a hammock in the verandah, her eyes shut but still racing rapidly under the lids.

She walked up to the hammock and climbed next to Maria. She cuddled up to her and ran her hands on the old woman's face. "I didn't mean to upset you," she said.

Maria bit her lips and hung on to her emotions. "We wanted to protect you. In case hate returns someday, we didn't want you to be vulnerable. We've been through things we don't want to remember. Remembering brings them back to life. It's best you don't know certain things."

They lay together, their arms entwined, and eventually fell asleep. These secrets obviously belonged here, she could not carry them to Istanbul where her parents planned to settle after Ann Arbor. But she had not yet discovered the secret in her backyard.

꿍

The vaudeville group had finished pitching their tent, suddenly transforming the meadow behind us into a festive carnival with dancing bears, cauldrons of boiled corn, pickle stands, cradle swings—ecstasy for children in the vicinity. People came from all over town seeking thrills in the clamoring crowd. The town perverts, too, lurked around every corner, brushing their vital parts on unsuspecting women as if by accident, seeking dark corners in crowded places to molest children.

The girls had been alerted to the prospect of a stranger's eager hands wandering into their place of shame down there. Their sacred *am*. Beware of those big bad hands. Never, ever let them creep into your secret parts. One of the kids said he'd seen a man rub himself against Nuria, then stick his hand under her skirt while watching the show in the fringes of the vaudeville tent, where the people stood who could not afford to pay.

All the kids went the opening night but Hamid Bey would not allow Amber, who still had to pay penance for releasing Scheherazade. So she lay in bed listening to the music from the tent blasting over a loudspeaker, then spreading like an omnipotent cloud. She listened to two women's voices in a duet:

Neredesin kizim?	*Where are you, daughter?*
Buradayim anne.	*I'm here, mother.*
Napiyorsun kizim?	*What are you doing, daughter?*
Dans ediyorum, anne	*I'm dancing, mother.*
Kiminle kizim?	*With whom, my daughter?*
Bir Rusla, anne.	*With a Russian, mother.*

Then, the thumping began that shook me like an earthquake. Rapid thumping of feet. The beating of a tambourine. It was a humid summer night, Malika asleep on a floor bed, slipping on to the cool tiles, and Hamid Bey snored in rhythm on his regal brass bed.

Rusun aski baska,	*A Russian's love is fiery,*
Rusun aski baska,	*A Russian's love is passionate,*
Hey kazaska.	*So, let's dance the Cossacka.*
Hey kazaska	*Hey, Cossackska.*

Russians were bad people, troublemakers throughout history, Hamid Bey had told her. Now someone in there was dancing with a Russian? Was she a bad girl herself? She was a bad girl. All her fault.

Scheherazade's ghost haunted her dreams. Every night the fox wandered into the bedroom and sniffed her hair while she slept. She could hear Nivea's howling in the distance. The thumping of feet intensified as if suddenly more of them were jumping around and kicking legs close to the ground. *Thump, thump. Kick, kick. Thump, thump.*

Amber could no longer endure the oppression of humidity. She tiptoed outside, crossed the field, glaring with spotlights. People, tall people, had gathered all around the tent making it difficult to peek. So she sneaked to the backside, crawled under the bleachers.

A fat man with a dark mustache, wearing a turban and two large hoop earrings, almost tripped over her. He darted into the center of the tent and boomed into his megaphone: "Now, ladies and gentlemen, here comes our most fabulous, most enchanting Dandy Girl, the magnificent *Bobstil girl!*"

A drum began to beat suspensefully as a fleshy woman dressed in skimpy satin shorts and net stockings and held by a harness was lowered from the top of the tent.

Bobstilim sendin	*You are my dandy,*
Yanima geldin	*You came to my side,*
Kalbimi deldin	*You punctured my heart,*
Aşkimi serdin	*And spread my love.*

How the mind rejects things out of context! She'd lost so much weight that Amber could not trust her eyes at first, but the voice, the voice was unmistakable. The voice of Lili Marlene. *When I'm calling you ooo-ooo-ooo-ooo-ooo-ooo . . .*

Bobstilin şapkasi	*The dandy's hat*
Ayni vapur bacasi	*Is just like a ship's chimney.*
Bobstilin kravati	*The dandy's necktie*
O da vapur halati	*Is the ship's rope.*

At one point the Bobstil girl's eyes fixed in Amber's direction, seemed to catch hers, lingered longer. How could she see anyone when the bright lights were shining right into her eyes, especially a small head poking in between people's feet?

Big applause. The Bobstil girl went backstage and the fat majordomo appeared again with a hatful of vulgar jokes to fill the time. Some sidekicks in sequined bathing suits came out and did a roll of cartwheels in the arena. Suddenly, a dramatic drumbeat. Cymbals. *Clash, bam.* The majordomo announced: "Ladies and gentleman, now Salome, the enchantress with seven veils. Here she comes."

Veiled in layers of diaphanous fabric, carrying a tray with a bearded man's head covered with blood, a woman rushed into the center of the tent. Was the head real? Whose head? So tiny, shriveled like a coconut, like the ones in cannibal movies.

Salome swirled and spun like a dervish, balancing the tray perfectly on her head, swirled and spun. Then placed it in front of the majordomo now sitting on a throne and began undulating. She swirled around, dancing slowly, very slowly, as if in a sufic trance that continued for what seemed like eternity. The veils unpeeled layer by layer. The colors of the rainbow floated in the air as the eager hands of the audience grabbed for them.

Amber recalled the day when Iskender had pulled out the silk scarves, in rainbow colors. Red, orange, yellow, green, blue, indigo, violet.

The dancer had achieved a sense of equilibrium that allowed effortless harmony. This was a dance of survival. A strip, a tease. Salome, a whore. Salome, the courageous, peeled off her defenses, making herself vulnerable to death.

"She is mourning for her lover whose head she offers on a tray, a macabre nightmare of betrayal," hissed the majordomo.

As Amber watched the blur of rainbow colors, she felt

dizzy. When Salome finally removed the last veil, the child's suspicion was confirmed. Salome and the Bobstil girl were one and the same—none other than her wayward aunt Papatya.

The intermission followed. Amber left immediately and began walking back, a blackbird in her chest. Even the ice-cream cart could not entice her. She passed through walls of familiar faces. In the dark, a voice pursued: "Amber, Amber, Amber." Amber began to run but Papatya caught up with her and cuddled the girl in her arms. The flood lights came on. The field pulsated with an eerie brilliance.

The neighborhood kids watched on the fringes. Amber wanted to pretend she did not know this woman but she could not free herself. Papatya squeezed and kissed her—her cheeks, her eyes, every part of her face.

"What on earth are you doing here, sugar plum?" she asked, tears rolling down her cheeks.

"My grandparents Taşpinar," pointing at me. "They live there, at the turquoise house."

Papatya withdrew for a moment, her eyes sunk inside. "They mustn't see me," she said. "You won't tell them, will you?"

Amber shook her head.

"Where are your parents?"

"In America."

"In America? Why? Why didn't they take you along?"

"Onions," Amber told her. "I told them I would eat them but they didn't want to take a chance."

"Onions? That can't be the real reason."

Amber began to whimper. Papatya rocked her in her arms. "Hush. Hush. Doesn't make any sense," she said, "but does anything? Don't be sad, my little Amber. You have a long life ahead of you. *Inşallah,* you'll find your way to America someday. Things have a way of coming a full circle. But hush now."

Amber began breathing normally and wiped her eyes. "How come you're with the carnival?"

"The only way I could dance," Papatya said. "God put me on this earth to sing and to dance. I'm only doing his will."

"Are you coming back?"

Long silence. "I don't think so. I am a different person now. They won't take me back. Besides, I wouldn't fit in anymore."

"They sold the Spinsters Apartment," Amber told her. "Everyone now scattered all over the place. My parents in America; Aida and the General moved to Istanbul. Aunt Mihriban and the matriarchs have gone back to whatever is left of the burnt plantation. Only Sibel's family stayed in Ankara."

"Not our doing," she said. "None of this. Kismet can't be dismissed. It was meant to be this way. No one's to blame."

"Everyone thought you ran off with Uncle Rodrigo."

"Oh, no. Wasn't meant to be. He ran off to Egypt with his coffee beans for bigger and better dreams. The fish that gets away is always big."

"But he stole our money. Scattered us all."

"Who knows? Maybe it was our own doing. You see, one must never precede a wise man or follow a fool. Our fortune had already taken its turn. Nothing we could do but lose. We were tired of the burden. I think the family wanted to lose the wealth so they didn't have to be responsible for it. Sometimes it's a curse to have more than enough."

Someone called out, "Salome! Next act. Get back here."

Papatya quickly kissed Amber, disappeared into the tent. The neighborhood kids had been watching them from a distance, Nuria and all. She came prancing toward Amber. "What did she tell you?"

"Nothing."

"You're so lucky," she told Amber with admiration and envy

in her voice. "Bobstil girl spoke to you. Why did she speak to you?"

"She thought I was someone else. Another girl."

"She kissed you!"

"I'm tired," Amber said. "Leave me alone."

"Tomorrow?"

Amber sneaked back, crawled in bed next to Malika. The old woman cradled her. Another duet wafted from the tent.

Ah, kizim kizim,	*Ah, daughter daughter,*
Edali kizim	*Capricious daughter,*
Çekilmiyor nazin	*Can't bear your whim,*
Seni de bir sarhoş istiyor	*A drunkard wants to marry you.*
Ne yapam kizim?	*What should I do?*

Amber was fast asleep before the final refrain.

Ah, ana ana,	*Ah, mother mother,*
Gözleri yana	*Weeping eyes,*
Üzülmuyor sakin	*Don't worry.*
İçer, içer sarhoş olur	*He would only get drunk,*
Sarilir bana	*And make love to me.*

～

The first thing in the morning, Amber returned to the tent looking for Papatya to give her a basket of figs from the orchard. The majordomo, sitting on a bleacher, was sewing sequins on his costume. He looked so old, so ordinary in the daylight without his flashy costume and makeup.

"I was looking for Salome."

"Salome is gone."

"Where?"

"Where, I don't know."

"Isn't she coming back?"

"I don't know."

It was the end of summer. A letter awaited Amber from Ann Arbor. Cadri and Camilla were on their way back.

II

The Prodigal Daughter's Return

You navigated with raging soul far from the paternal
home, passing beyond the seas' double rocks and now
you inhabit a foreign land.

AESCHYLUS, *Medea*

"So, how do they know a virgin?" she asked.

"The hymen. If it doesn't bleed, the girl's been defiled."

On her wedding night, when Esma didn't show blood, her husband had killed a rooster to save face, smeared the blood on their wedding sheets, and hung them up on the flag pole for all the neighborhood to see. She broke down, cried, told him she was innocent; she'd never been touched before. Deep down, he did not believe but, nevertheless, remained with her till his death. A rare thing. Set the tenor of their marriage. Maybe even his early departure.

In her adolescence, Amber had recurrent nightmares of pain and hemorrhage caused by piercing of the hymen—that thin mucous membrane rumored to veil the orifice of a virgin's vagina, the same way the veil itself protected a woman's face. Coital caress a terrifying curse; the wedding night, a kind of mutilation a woman had to endure. Confusing since the god of marriage, a handsome youth carrying a torch, was also called Hymen.

The fear of unbearable pain, not the morals, restrained her, so she laughed at Cadri's resonant words as he saw her off to America. "Honor your virtue." Honor virtue. Virtue. Honor your corner, and your partner, eight hands round we go.

Merely hours after her departure, she had disobeyed him, flown the coop of captivity. No pain or blood but the unbearable knowing that she could never return to live in the old country again was the greater pain. She had become an exile.

Twenty-five years passed before she first returned. And this last time, he had already passed away, a few months before.

Essence of Honey Street

ᔐ

(1997)

Homesickness transforms the objects of our memories into poetic ideals whose fine qualities grow in our eyes, while their defects always soften with time and absence and are almost erased by our imagination.

GEORGE SAND, *Horace*

೩

Once an easy street, quiet, with a row of pretty houses boasting fragrance gardens and ornate verandahs, where everyone knew everyone, over the years, Essence of Honey Street had become the nucleus of a bustling metropolis. Amber did not recognize it.

At the terminal across from the mosque, the one with the incomplete minaret, Camilla was running toward them, astonishingly more diminutive than imprinted in Amber's memory— a horizontal expansion that made her resemble some character out of *Alice in Wonderland*. She led a chorus of women, familiar faces with lost names, hands raised to the sky, singing the same lyrics. "Welcome home, sweet darling. Welcome home, at last."

With her two-packs-a-day voice, Camilla greeted them, as if time had done nothing to diminish intimacy. Who was she embracing? The eighteen-year-old voluptuary who had left on such a sweltering day as this twenty-five years ago or the forty-something woman of the world?

Then, she fixed on Nellie. Squeezed the young girl's cheek. "Love of my life you're so skinny."

"But graceful as a pheasant," Aida interjected, appearing behind Camilla, a brilliant debut as always, decked out in a metallic shantung coat with a matching turban. She drew Amber into her arms and felt the void of her aunt's missing left breast.

Amber had not recuperated from the arrogant welcome at the airport when the customs officials had confiscated the prosthesis, her gift for Aida. *Not listed in the tariff.* A hundred dollars would have remedied the situation but she refused to yield to corrupt afflictions of her countrymen that had once chased her away. Not a good welcome, face to face so soon with the reasons for her exile.

The women quickly fell into a sobbing mass, flesh on flesh, stayed heaped to prolong the taste of reunion. Sucking, licking, pinching.

In her absence the city had grown more than ten times its former size. Lured by the legend of pavements made of gold, peasants from remote villages swarmed in like locusts. What they found were garbage hills instead and houses of tin and cow pies. Some fled to Germany where cheap labor was desirable; others filled their souls and lungs with methane. The ones that returned formed a new class. To accommodate their uncultivated needs, the elegant houses collapsed overnight, stacks of boxes replaced them.

The Essence of Honey street, the refuge of Amber's adolescence, had mutated into one of those nondescript roads, eclipsing the city's glorious architectural past. Ancient arches, columns, soft-flowing arabesques clashed with straight-edged atrocities that spread across the skyline, haphazardly constructed out of the poorest supplies, attitude, and craftsmanship that made them serious earthquake hazards. Domes and cupolas of its

former silhouette crumbled into the earth for future excavations. Precious tiles buried under concrete as people turned
color blind, painting their city gray. The city was mourning,
unaware, the passing of glory—Byzance, Constantinople, and
Stamboul.

That's what Amber learned the day of her returning. Not
much left to hold on to. Maybe the sea.

She could not find her way home. How could she? To imagine that the charming villa of her youth, if I may say so, was replaced by a building of six, seven stories, surrounded by the
same straight-angled high-rises with bland windows and sharp
balconies, buildings that spread like gossip. Row after row.

"If you only knew what a nightmare it was to build this
place. No skilled workers left here," Camilla complained as she
led Amber and Nellie up the stairs. All gone to Germany,
Switzerland—places in Europe to make better money. Lots better. So, we end up suffering the leftovers."

The potent blending of sewer and mothballs attacked
Amber and Nellie instantly. The floors crackled with white
crystals—Camilla had sprinkled naphthalene on everything
produced on a loom with the same fervor she sprinkled salt on
her cooking.

Amber began to cough. The mothballs made her lungs
burn, her skin itch, her eyes water. A heat rose inside of her. She
went for the windows.

"Don't open them," Camilla shouted, "the draft will kill me.
I don't need pneumonia, you know? Besides the sun would
bleach the furniture."

What furniture, Amber wanted to say. Where my
grandma Esma's gorgeous carpets? The Shiraz, the Isphahan, the
Hereke? The furniture she once transported all the way from her
home in Macedonia on muleback? The textiles Iskender Bey had

brought back from his travels? The fabrics once woven at the
İpekçi silkworks?

"There is no draft. Even if there were, it wouldn't be half as
harmful as inhaling mothball dust," she said instead. "It's a hundred and fifteen degrees outside, mother. Not a whisper of a
breeze."

Camilla led them to the bedroom that she and Cadri had
shared. Amber recognized the twin beds her parents had custom
ordered with "harvest gold" upholstery, after returning from
America in the Fifties. His and hers. Just like in the movies of
that time.

"You and Nellie can sleep here."

Camilla went around shutting all the windows Amber had
been opening. Close, open. Open, close. She rushed from room
to room as if she'd swallowed a bottle of amphetamines, gathering things, speaking endlessly.

Amber's eyes were flooding, her throat scratchy. It was
hopeless. She threw herself on the bed but bounced back instantly. The bedding, too, embalmed in a snow of mothballs
that ground against her skin like particles of sand.

"Why, mother, why on earth do you put poison on the
sheets? Moths don't eat cotton pillowcases, you know?"

"These moths do. They'll even eat the fuzz off your ear."

"I don't want to lecture you, of course, but you've really
overdone it with naphthalene. Why don't you use cedar wood or
something? It's nontoxic; smells good."

"I loathe moths. They're greedy; they eat everything. They
always eat right in front where it shows—never sleeves and parts
you can mend. I had a favorite green cashmere sweater; they ate
it down to a piece of lace."

"Now instead, they will eat your lungs down to a piece of
lace," Amber mumbled.

Camilla left abruptly and Amber shut the door to take some space so she wouldn't explode. It had been a long journey. Nellie had already passed out on her bed. She had been nervous to take this trip with her daughter but Nellie seemed to be adjusting better than herself. She sprayed the room with Camilla's eau de cologne, which only made the smell more noxious, sort of like a lemon-scented pesticide. She opened the balcony door to air out the bedding.

The street noise boomed like thunder out of a loudspeaker, the narrow street below deeply groaning. The neglected roads crumbled for lack of maintenance. Mountains of debris blocked the streets, shades of gray and brown tinting the landscape like an old daguerreotype. This, once her city, now bewildered and detached.

A group of pedestrians was waiting for the light to change, standing by a gargantuan statue of Atatürk, with his index finger pointing ahead at a peasant woman cuddling a bouquet of wheat and a young soldier charging ahead with his bayonet.

A bevy of schoolgirls not much younger than Nellie, wearing head scarves, crossed the street. Atatürk stood in the background with the same intensity pointing his finger at them.

"I wonder what he'd think of all this," Amber told Camilla, who stuck her head out another window. "Girls wearing scarves. Women wearing long coats, their heads covered, moving about the streets like black bundles. It's an effort to remember they are human beings with minds and souls and bodies. And all these bearded men wearing beanies. I can't believe this reversal."

"You've seen nothing yet. They're everywhere now," Camilla pined. "How it breaks my heart to see such young girls covering themselves. Even at the University. Atatürk would stir in his grave if he knew what this country has come to after all his efforts to elevate women. But, what can we do? We're a poor country."

"What does it have to do with being poor?"

"Poor people need religion. Fundamentalism is an answer to industrialization."

"They need dreams."

Children in black uniforms with white piqué collars skipped, crossing the street, swinging their faux leather schoolbags as they ran through a red light. No one seemed to pay attention to the color of the light. Befuddled peasants struggled on foot, weighed down by enormous bundles containing their humble lives. Everything appeared in gradations of black, against the most emphatic surge of human movement, scintillating like capillary motion. The compulsive fatalism of the city screamed out in the confusion of horns, the intermittent voices of the drivers snarling at each other while honking like furious geese.

Only one house remained untouched in the entire neighborhood, a double-storied stone and stucco with a striped awning above its balcony. Colorful items of laundry strung across like a charm bracelet. Overgrown with potted crawlers and fuchsia vines now cascading down each side of the facade into a wild garden of stones, driftwood, animal skeletons.

Amber remembered the energetic old man who had built it, his daughter widowed seven times, and the plump Sultana figs from their orchard—now filled with a bunch of high-rises—he brought as a gift at early morning dew.

"That house is so unkempt and hideous, full of all those dead things—skulls and shells," Camilla complained. "Disgrace of the neighborhood. I wish they'd bulldoze it."

But a warm glow had filled Amber's face from the first moment it had caught her eyes. Dwarfed among the giant dwellings. It had a voice. Its heart was still beating. On an impulse, she took its picture with Nellie's camera (a ritual she'd continue to perform everyday after that, at different hours, in different lights, like Monet's cathedrals). She needed to invent a small obsession to maintain her grounding.

"Who lives there now?" she asked Camilla.

Judging from the manner in which Camilla twisted her lips and shook her head, she obviously had opinions. "They say he's an artist. No, an archaeologist or something. Rejects all offers to tear down the eyesore. His parents were immigrants to Germany. He was born there. Looks just like an Allemagne. Blond hair, blue eyes, tall. A *gavour*, if you ask me. Nobody really knows much about him. Except . . ."

"What?"

"Never mind."

"I like it," Amber told her. "The last survivor of the dreams of the Essence of Honey Street. Remember when all the other houses looked like that? Remember what this villa looked like?"

"Don't be so sentimental. Our villa was in shambles. I spent all my time trying to find repairmen. The time had come to tear it down. I'm too old to maintain such nonsense. Don't you understand? At my age I need modern comforts. I need people to look after me."

Amber could sense it coming and she took a breath to avoid biting the bait.

"Yes," she said a bit distracted. "Don't we all? But speaking of modern comforts, how do I light the *chauffe bain* for hot water?"

"You wouldn't know how. I'll do it."

The gas smell from the burner mingled with mothballs and toilet water. Amber went around opening the windows again when they heard a small explosion.

"Damn it," Camilla shouted. "The pilot went out. We never get enough gas pressure here."

"Never mind. I'll take a cold shower. In fact, I'd prefer it on a day like this. Much more refreshing."

"I don't want you to catch cold. Besides, terrible for your menstrual. You'd get unbearable cramps."

"I'm used to cold showers; they make me feel alive. Great for circulation and all sorts of other things."

"Well, you can't, anyway. Not enough water. Not on this side of the Baghdad Boulevard. Our water supply is reserved for the nouveau riche. Or Arabs. They bought our country. You should see how they've infested our beautiful Tarabia; we call it Arabia now. You should see their fountains flowing while we can't even flush our toilets."

So, instead, Camilla offered Amber the water in the bucket to wash her hair. She'd heat it over the stove. She gave her a monogrammed Turkish towel, crusted with mothballs, to dry her hair.

Amber sat on a stool inside the lavender tub ladling the water, pouring it over her head, recycling it, pouring it and again as if lost in a distant trance. In the hollowness of her mother's bathroom, she remembered the loneliness of the first time she took a bath by herself at the Spinsters Apartment.

۞

Sleep was playing hide and seek.

Amber lay awake waiting for the curfew, for the streets and for her mother to hush. She lay on her father's bed—Nellie on the matching twin—watching the hypnotic motion of a pair of not-too-distant searchlights cast from Leander's lighthouse through the lace curtains.

"What am I doing here?" she asked out loud.

Nellie woke out of her jet lag stupor. "What do you mean?"

"I don't know."

"I thought you wanted to see how she was surviving without your dad."

At midnight, a piercing siren resonated and the muezzin's voice came out of a loudspeaker; then the city died. The streets quickly became deserted and hollow, all sounds ceased, except the occasional beating of horse hooves on the pavement, an ominous siren of a patrol car, or intermittent barking of dog packs traveling through the barren streets in search of food. It was a synthetic silence as if the streets were populated with other invisible predators.

"This silence spooks me, Mom," Nellie stirred in bed. "It's too weird. I can't get to sleep and I hate this Martial Law curfew stuff."

"Let's get some air."

They tiptoed out to the balcony so as not to arouse Camilla. One by one the lights went off in the high-rise compounds across the way, except the little house of charm. The moon diffused through the clouds cast an artificial shadow like stage lighting, murky and jaundiced under the dim street lamps. Concrete monoliths, placed at obtuse angles, lurked above them like oversized constructivist robots—identical blocks, stacked-together Lego cities but in shades of gray. Two windows and a balcony. A canvas of muted and hard-edged half tones—the buildings, the sky, even the trees.

"Something almost living about these buildings, Mom, like some mechanical Japanese robots; you can almost see them marching, can't you? Marching to crush the city. It must have been tough to grow up here."

"It was different then, spacious and green. Practically countryside. Not that different than our place in California."

"How old were you?"

"In my teens. We built the house after my parents returned
from America. Early sixties, just when my hormones were going
berserk, my breasts budding. I remember one summer, I
bleached my hair with peroxide. Wore it like some bad imitation
of Brigitte Bardot, fluffed and teased, preparing to cruise the
streets arm in arm with girlfriends in ballerina shoes, looking
for adventure."

"And your parents didn't mind?"

"Sure they did. When Camilla saw my brassy mane, she
freaked, '*Eyvah*, what will the neighbors think? Cadri, you ought
to have a talk with her.' So, my father lunched in frowned silence, chewing his food so loud you could jump out of your
skin, then, wiped his mouth menacingly with his napkin and
asked me to follow him to his *pensatorio*."

"What's that?"

"His thinking room. He always had one. He closed the
door. 'You shamed us, Amber,' he said. 'How could you have
done that to your hair!' I said, all my friends are doing it. It's in.
Don't you like it?

"He snorted, trying to conceal what was inside him and had
to admit, yes, it did make me look attractive somewhat but I
shouldn't have done it anyway because girls from nice families
just don't do things like that. 'Makes them look like common
trash. Do you understand?' I told him that the matriarchs always
put indigo on their hair. And Aida and Sibel dye theirs blond.
'That's different,' he said. 'They are women. You are a girl. They
have it done professionally.' 'So next time I'll go to the hair-
dresser?' I'd gone too far. Well, he slapped me."

"He slapped you? How old were you?"

"Maybe sixteen—the only time he ever did such a thing. Surely couldn't have been just about my hair. Strangely, that was the moment I knew I'd leave, I'd go away, far away from here. The slap sent me much further than he could have imagined."

They each slipped into their silent worlds for a moment.

"What did you do, I mean, how did you have fun in those days?"

"Oh, we were just a bunch of teenagers like anywhere . . ."

Amber almost went into a trance and recreated the world of her youth for her daughter. She told Nellie how they were over-stimulated by the voices of Johnny Mathis, Domenico Modugno, Charles Aznavour, seeking role models in fan magazines and comic books and Hollywood musicals, of a world oceans away that existed in movies and pop songs. How they obsessively mimicked American teen trends, going broke on orlon twin sets, bobby sox, penny loafers, saddle shoes bought in the PX black market. How hot rods and hot dogs were as exotic to them as the harems and baklava elsewhere. How their mothers' handknit sweaters were no longer good enough because they represented a world they desired to outgrow, instead flaunting Bermuda shorts—that exclusively hideous American bad taste. But they loved anything American because it was American.

I still retain the memory of the languorous afternoons on Essence of Honey Street when Amber was an adolescent. While women snored in their siestas, while men played bezique in the club house, the young kids swooned with "Wild Is the Wind" and "Nada Per Me," smoking Salems and Kents, cartons scored on a whole month's allowance. But miraculously they managed somehow with a few phrases in English from rock 'n' roll and comics, befriending the GI connections and all, cute blond boys with combat boots and guns, chewing Bazooka, thrown into a desolate Anatolian wilderness. Give me. I love you. Want a date? Take me to the prom. Let's go to the hop. Jiminy Cricket. Holy macaroon. Hardy har har. See you later, alligator. After while, crocodile. I went digging ditches but now I dig it the most. While they pretended to be Bettys and Veronicas, seeking to pair off with Archies, Reggies, and Jugheads, their grandmothers, dressed in black babushkas and shabby dark clothes, sat on the terraces, carrying the sadness of all they'd ever lost as they counted their amber worry beads. Ah, what's the world coming to?

Romance entered their hearts through pirated *True Love* and *Photoplay*. They drooled over Ricky and Dave Nelson whom they knew only through secondhand fan magazines since TV had not yet arrived, chasing boys who resembled them—the summers on the beach bleached even the darkest mop of hair, especially with a little help from H_2O_2, hydrogen peroxide, the brassy sleaze. Girls and boys both.

Siesta hours spent in front of mirrors instead of in bed, carefully painting faces, ironing nylon underwear. Arm in arm, the girls strolled down the Essence of Honey Street to the Baghdad Boulevard to promenade their tits and tans. Sometimes headed for Suadiye Beach, or to the club Circle d'Orient, sipping sour-cherry Fruko, meals charged to their fathers' accounts. Their eyes searched for love, Frankie Laine's "Smoke Gets in Your Eyes" blending with Zeki Müren singing "My Beautiful Magnolia" over loudspeakers from here all the way over there to Bostanci, where the lights are.

They giggled and checked out the boys promenading in their skimpy bathing suits as they became aroused and took fast dives into the water to conceal their tumescence. At sunset, they watched the beach people rinsing the sand off their bodies in outdoor showers. Or dark men in dark sunglasses dressed in white, pushing ashore in Chris Craft boats—assembled from kits their relatives had sent them from America—to pick up

older girls in stylish bathing suits and drift off toward the
Prince Islands, shimmering like fish scales under the last rays of
the sun.

"Sounds just like American teens in fifties movies," Nellie
told Amber. "Totally weird."

"Totally. We even had discos."

How they'd sneak into the Atomic Discotheque, ordering
Cinzano sodas—no age restriction—DJs hard breathing "You
Mean Everything to Me" and "Wild Is the Wind," dancing
cheek to cheek with boys or doing the twist, later rubbing fig
milk on their necks to conceal the hickeys.

Just before dark, they returned arm in arm back to the
Essence of Honey Street, tousled and sheltering secrets the others shared but could not betray. Blooming lindens formed a
canopy of sweet pollen exuding a scent similar to sex, these
same trees now reaching the edge of the balcony.

This was all before we lost color. All the houses were
painted in candy colors with green shutters and quaint gardens
where tomatoes and roses grew intertwined. Single-family
dwellings, you know? Housing nuclear families. Ozzie and Har-
riets of Turkey.

But only on the surface. In their hearts the Turks were still
nomads who'd lived in tribes for thousands of years, pitching
their tents wherever the wind blew, sinking into the earth to
sleep unconcerned about rooting. Home was a part of their
body, an appendage ready to dismantle and abandon at a moment's notice. Permanence of home was an incomprehensible
notion. Home was transience. Home was the steppes, the desert,
the caves, the mountains. Home was you. Your body.

Their invasions stopped here—the farthest stretch to the
west. The indestructible doors closed and they would forever be
pounding on them, begging to be allowed in, desperately yearn-

ing to become part of the West while trying to destroy it. But in their obsession, they found themselves conquered by the need for sameness, imitating forms they did not understand, homes that did not belong to them. Their confidence gone, they became unfathomable. Like their houses and sacred spaces, they hid behind the emptiness in between the facades of a movie set or locked their women behind lattices, behind veils to cover their shame, which they couldn't contain. They had lost their souls.

When they arrived here, clustering in cloistered neighborhoods, they still coveted the country life. All they knew. Each settlement grew into a village with no center but itself—a nomadic European city where people sat on their verandahs and balconies, where everyone knew everyone. When drought threatened, the women gathered around fountains to fill their olive-oil cans with water and gossip. The men sat in cafés all day long, sipping *nargilehs*. They couldn't walk down the street without stopping at each house to make a connection.

But as the wild folk kept invading the city, looking for gold, it had to expand upward. Closer to God, they said, but closer to Satan as well. The houses disappeared. The boxes rose vertically and multiplied. People above, people below, and people on each side. Strangers from different tribes crossing. Look at us now.

Trees ruled while all of us houses disappeared one by one but finding themselves in our shadow, they too began losing their force, their branches. Cypresses kept company to the dead like willowy widows in mourning. Plane trees sprouted in the middle of a boulevard on small islands while cars raced full speed around them. The love of trees made it a taboo to cut them—especially the ancient ones. Here, trees are untouchables, sacred, ancestors to be worshipped, not cut down. Planting a tree is as sacred as a year's worship, their Prophet said. The earth was for digging to make dwellings but the trees were the dwellings of the spirits of ancestors, their abuse punishable by death. But in history, the heathen hordes riding through, not recognizing the tree spirits, set them afire. The forests blazed in the night, filled with the agony of the burning souls. Deserts formed.

Amber still seemed edgy and undone as she reminisced about her own past. "I'm sorry, I've gone off like that," she told Nellie. "Just that it stirs up so much in me to be here again."

"It's cool, Mom."

She continued looking at this landscape of gray sarcophagi, which had at first brought drought to her soul; an unexpected kindness overwhelmed her. As if her exposition had purged her of some pain. A tender reprieve. Her face opened, then turned dark.

"We mustn't stay here long," she told Nellie. "It's like quicksand. I feel this place devouring me already."

"Anytime you say then." Nellie kissed her goodnight, and returned to bed.

Amber lingered at the balcony until a pink faintness tinted the sky, highlighting the receding necropolis. A distant calling from the belly of the beast rose, the lips of the electronic muezzin welcomed the new dawn. *Allahuakbar.*

As soon as the sun appeared behind the unfinished minaret, the screeching of carts began as usual. The sonorous incantations of the peddlers, honking of the horns, megaphones advertising domestic movies playing at outdoor cinemas, political campaigns with horrendously addictive jingles. Essence of Honey Street once again became the main artery of their loud declarations, alarming the sleeper, with no forewarning into the syncopated whirlwind of a bustling survival.

The street was pulsating. Nellie jumped to her feet and ran

under the doorway as if suspecting an earthquake, an instinct acquired from living in San Francisco but aware of the same vulnerability here. Then, peeking out the balcony window, she smirked as she struggled to close the crack between the curtains.

"I've been awake almost all night with that creepy silence. Now this. What is going on, Mom?"

"Just people peddling their stuff—yogurt, watermelons, and spices. That's the way things are advertised."

"Do they have to bawl so loud?"

"It's a way of creating camaraderie and competition. Through their songs."

"I don't get it."

A green John Deere tractor approached between the row of haphazard trees; a father and son, perched on a pile of stacked leeks and onions, stopped in front. At the same moment someone tapped at the bedroom door; without waiting for a reply, Camilla walked in.

"Damn it," she said. "I knew this noise would wake you up. I knew it. Go back to sleep. Here, try these. One pair for you, the other for Nellie." She stuffed Amber's ears with a set of plugs made of wax. "You can't get this kind here, the very best. Molds into any shape you want. Now you know why I ask you to send me these every Christmas." Camilla looked out the window before she left the room. "I better run down and get a basket. And you get some more sleep."

"Remember, I'm allergic to onions," Amber reminded her.

"I'm getting them for myself."

"We go through this battle of onions every time I return," Amber complained to Nellie rolling her eyes.

"How can anyone cook without onions?" Camilla continued. "It's impossible."

"Look, I don't like being allergic myself. A real drag. Every time I eat out, I have to make a scene. But dammit, I'm allergic. And that's that."

"Psychosomatic."

"Whatever."

"You can't cook without onions. It's unheard of."

"Well, I've learned to."

From the fourth-floor balcony, Camilla lowered the basket. The son weighed them and filled the basket with leeks and onions. Camilla pulled it back up.

The morning air was cool when they got up. Amber slipped on a cardigan.

"Your sweater is reversed," Camilla laughed. "You know, if you put on your clothes inside out, then your whole day will turn inside out."

"It already is."

Later, the three of them sat on the balcony, at a table with a checkered plastic tablecloth. Camilla had slaved the entire week preparing food for their arrival. A colorful array of *dolmas*—stuffed peppers, eggplant, tomatoes, squash.

"No onions," she said. "Really. No onions in the *dolmas*."

Amber took a bite, rolling the food slowly in her mouth, felt the unmistakable crunchy texture. With great drama and ceremony, she spat her food on her fork and smeared it on the edge of her plate. Camilla and Nellie ate in silence. She, then, proceeded to pick at the stuffing, sorting out every morsel that had the potential of being an onion. She stared at Camilla, who didn't utter a word. Her mouth became tight and twisted. In turn Amber's did, as well. Camilla took a deep breath, looked undeservedly hurt. She stood up and began clearing the table.

"You were mean," Nellie told her mother when Camilla left the room.

"She knows I'm allergic. She's known all my life. I'm not going to eat onions and get sick just to please her."

"You're a guest in her house."

"I'm not sure now who is the mother and who is the child."

"Neither am I."

The next day Camilla served meatballs and *boerek* for lunch.

"Without onions," she said.

This time she was telling the truth.

Another peddler went by.

> *There are beans,*
> *There are peaches,*
> *There are grapes,*
> *Tomatoes,*
> *Hot peppers,*
> *Eggplant.*

The following night Amber was visited by a dream. It was so vivid that if it were possible to watch her while she slept, you could see the dream itself as if played on a movie screen.

> *Dressed in a sequined outfit with baggy harem pants and a veil over her face, she's flying on a magic carpet over the city constructed in Disney studios until a wind machine starts blowing with great intensity. She tumbles down, corkscrew fashion, landing inside bubbling lava. She burns all over but is still alive. She decides to peel her burned skin and shed it like a snake crawling out of its own. She emerges raw and jelly-like, painfully vulnerable, like the bird embryos at her grandparents' Turquoise house. The phone rings.*

Camilla was nudging Amber, handing her the receiver on a long chord. "For you."

"It's me, Amber my love. Can you come here please?" Aida's raspy voice uttered with a sense of emergency.

"What's the matter?

"Nothing," she said, "nothing. Just come here." And hung up.

Camilla raised the glass of night water by Amber's bedside, shook her head disapprovingly.

"You haven't covered your glass. That's what the doilies are for, the ones you make fun of. You never know what may fall into it when you're asleep. Moths, fleas, spiders. You know what I found one morning in your father's glass? A dead cockroach. But the worst, the worst thing happened to Gonca—God bless her soul."

Amber had heard this story many times before but she'd persevere for another round. She had just arrived. She was testing her ability to maintain her cool as long as possible. She was a grown woman. No intention of falling into an old pattern.

"Gonca always used to take water to bed and never bothered to cover it," Camilla continued. "So, one night, splash. A lizard fell into her glass."

"How did the lizard come into the house?" Nellie asked.

"Oh, her children must have brought them in from the sewers or something. And poor, poor Gonca, she drank it in her sleep, swallowed the lizard, and the lizard ate her from the inside."

"I was told she died of liver cancer."

"Yeah, well, it spread to her liver, too."

Amber did not like being reminded of Gonca's death. Camilla was grossly exaggerating the way it had happened. She had an uncanny way of dramatizing the way people died though she had not yet told Amber about Cadri's.

The TV was already chirping in the living room. Camilla
kept it on all hours of the day to fill her silence, even at night
when she slept, for the warmth of human voices, to see people
talking, touching each other. She talked back to the screen when
she was alone and received answers. Her interactive toy.

A documentary showed a torrent of rain. A hill destroyed
by erosion. Peasants in colorful clothes marched up the hill,
kneeled on the ground as though they were performing *namaz*,
going through the gestures of prayer while planting. The re-
porter held a handful of seeds. "From this you grow a tree, and
from a tree a whole forest," while time-lapse photography
showed the seedlings slowly curling into full-grown trees within
seconds. "Trees are your friends. Planting one counts more than
a year's prayer, *sevap*," he continued and offered free seedlings to
anyone who wanted to plant a tree and gave a toll-free number
to call. Right after that, a young Turkish man in a fancy suit
who looked like he had stepped out of Emporio Armani, carrying a briefcase, went into Istanbul Hilton and flashed a card.
The closeup read, "The Blue Card. Makes dreams a reality."
And showed a montage of a high-rise apartment, the latest
model domestic Renault, a microwave manufactured by Arcos,
Turkey's very own GE.

"Your old flame Erol is now the president of Arcos. If
you'd only stayed," Camilla never neglected to lament, "you
could have had some of the richest men in Turkey. So many
good families tell me they wanted you for their sons. You could
have had any one of them. You could have lived like a queen."

"Yeah? And become a society bimbo with a leather tan, gold
jewelry, and a bunch of dysfunctional children?"

"Musa Kurtman wanted you so badly. They say, he's going
to be the next president."

"I hear he's gone Fundamentalist."

"It's true. Maybe it's a good thing you didn't. He and his men pray five times a day, all have beards. But he's so successful. We see them on TV all the time. Then there's your classmate Tansu, the corrupt prime minister. What a bad egg she turned out to be. You could've been, you could've had everything you ever wanted, Amber. You could've been a star."

"But instead. Instead a struggling architect. At your age, still working," Amber imitated her voice sarcastically. "Kismet." She went for a cigarette. Her first in twenty years.

"I should never have allowed you to go to America."

"It wasn't your choice. I was eighteen."

Camilla lit a cigarette and escaped into the kitchen. She boiled the milk for Amber's coffee. Starbuck's, from California. The princess.

"The milk is already pasteurized, mother. You don't need to boil it."

"Pasteurized, fasterized. All the same. Who knows what microbes are floating in it. You don't understand those things. You're too American now."

Amber poured the coffee. "Would you like some?"

"No thanks."

"I've brought some decaf coffee, too."

Camilla clicked her tongue. "No, I prefer Nescafé."

Perhaps the sight of coffee beans evoked a bitterness in her, Amber thought. Perhaps, it brought back memories of the decaf plantation. Of Papatya and Rodrigo. Loss of their charmed lives. All the unexpected compromises. Strange, how the inhabitants of Spinsters Apartment were all gone now—except Camilla and Aida. The older generation dead, the children scattered all over the world under different names. They'd married foreigners—German, Spanish, Swedish, American, Australian, Argentine. Uncanny that the only ones who carried the family name had no sons of their own. No one to pass on the name. The İpekçis were about to expire.

"I wish you'd bought a bottle of whiskey at the Duty Free store," Camilla complained.

"Whiskey? You drink whiskey? That's new."

"Nice to have it around when company comes. I like serving it to my lady friends, other volunteers for the Red Crescent and the Cancer Society."

"I asked if you wanted me to bring anything and you said, earplugs, vitamins, and denture cleanser. That's all. It's not fair that you want me to second guess and get upset if I don't."

"I beg your pardon."

Camilla returned to her TV. Amber paced up and down the hall, sipping her coffee.

"What did Aida want?"

"I don't know. Sounded like she'd had a bad night. She asked me to come over."

"You've just arrived here, Amber. Don't get sucked into it. She always wags her tail like a bitch to get what she wants—the old *coquotte*. Unbelievable."

"What's a *coquotte*?"

"A coquette. Ah, she makes me so mad. She looks like a sausage oozing out of its sack, the way her boobs—what's left of them, mind you—spill out of her cleavage. And her hair hennaed that blazing harlot red. Not to mention those false eyelashes, always partly unglued, drooping down her lids. Or her silver lamé ankle straps with dainty Louis Quinze heels, she's not ashamed to wear even in the daytime. I can go on and on. A woman should behave her age. Who does she think she is, still the ingénue at the beauty pageant or what? Is that why she takes pleasure in seducing young boys less than half her age to remember what she has lost?"

"What boys?" Amber asked. "That sounds interesting."

"I will not gossip."

"Not fair. You started it. You made me curious. Talk now, will you?"

"Well, promise over my dead body, you won't tell her or anyone else, especially her. Promise?"

"Touch my heart."

"Well, she took up with a neighbor a few months ago, the one who lives in that hideous old house you like so much, the one with the bones and things—the one you keep taking pictures of."

"Really? Who is he? What do you know of him?"

"People say his parents went to Germany as workers and made a lot of money manufacturing shish-kebab skewers, *cezves*, samovars, coffee mills, that sort of thing. When they returned, bought that house from the old man's daughter, and became respectable."

"Where are they now?"

"Ah, such an awful story. They were driving to Ankara when a truck full of nitroglycerin crashed into them. They melted like candles immediately, both husband and wife disappeared into thin air. Not even a trace of their skeletons," Camilla told with the authority of someone who had been there. "God rest their soul. Then, Teoman, that's the boy's name, came back from Germany—he was learning archaeology or ornithology or something—and moved into that house. He had many offers to turn it into an apartment building like we all did but he refused to conform. He said he liked it the way it was when he lived there with his parents. Imbecile. What progress would there ever be if everyone thought like that? Stubborn as a goat, too. Not a drop of Turkishness left in him—a *gavour* like you. Blue eyes, tall— must have Albanian blood, maybe Macedonian—even speaks with a phony accent."

"You seem to know quite a lot about him. How did he hook up with Aida?"

"Aida is shameless. Almost old enough to be his grandmother but people saw them walking down the Baghdad Boulevard, holding hands and sharing a peach melba at the Divan Café. Would you believe? And the neighbors—you know the old-maid sisters—they say he goes into her house at night. This kind of thing just doesn't happen here. Shame. *Çok ayip. Çok. Çok.*"

"Come on, mother. She's a widow. She's lonely," Amber told her as she discreetly squeezed a bit of lemon into the milk—the old trick. "She just had a mastectomy. Can a little companionship hurt? If it makes her feel good, why shouldn't she have some fun? Life is short."

"We're all widows," Camilla snapped. "But we're naked without our customs."

"So?"

"It's not the done thing."

The boiled milk had curdled from the lemon. Amber poured herself a new cup of coffee and the fresh pasteurized milk. She retired to the bathroom for solitude, the singular place to retreat, the only place she'd be allowed to close the door, be alone to get to herself.

⌁

Aida's apartment faces the east corner of the Essence of Honey Street, like a Siamese twin. When she opened the door, she looked frog-eyed as if she'd been up all night wrestling with aimless insomnia, her eyebrows not yet penciled, her lashes not yet glued, her face unformed like some kind of an alien creature, her chest lopsided—not yet given her new breast—the one for which Amber would begrudgingly have to bribe a Turkish customs official in the end.

In her quilted fuchsia robe, she struggled across the hall into the bedroom, threw herself on the bed, flashing the pose of an exhausted odalisque past her prime.

"Have you ever been in love, Amber?" she asked.

"You woke me up at seven in the morning to ask me this?"

"I woke you up because my heart feels dark."

Amber touched Aida's cheek. "I'm so sorry," she said. "Sure, I have fallen in love."

"With Nellie's father?"

"Oh, it's a complicated story."

"Do we have anything better to do to pass the day?"

"I don't want to get all stirred up."

"Would you like another cup of tea?

"No thanks."

"I'd bet you'd like some *salep*. Don't get up."

Amber's eyes scanned the room in distraction, fixing on the glass case containing the handkerchief monogrammed "KA," the coronet of the beauty queen. A dried bouquet of faded roses emanated a vinegary scent. Inside the case was Aida's wedding picture with the lieutenant, noticeable under her shimmering satin gown, her ripe belly. Camilla had told her that yes, Aida was pregnant when they got married but she miscarried when they went to Germany where the lieutenant was sent as the military attaché.

Above the mirror, two uniformed men trapped in frames, her husband, the General, and Atatürk—granted the great man's pictures adorned every good home in the country, and every office but rarely a bedroom.

"Such intense eyes. Don't you feel invaded with those guys staring at you day and night?" Amber asked as she sipped her cinnamon *salep*.

"Not at all. Women reserve intimacy for mirrors. We talk to ourselves in our reflections. Maybe the only place where we tell the truth. But those men can't see my reflection, how can they invade me? The consolation is they're watching as I groom myself. Do you understand?"

Amber nodded although she clearly was not sure what Aida meant.

"You were young when you lost Nellie's father. How come you never remarried, Amber?" Aida pursued. "We know so little of your life."

"You were pretty young yourself when the General died. How come you never did either?"

"I couldn't have. They'd stone widows who even dared smile at a man in those days—not like where you live where you can marry a hundred times if you want. Right? Look at Elizabeth Taylor."

The moiré skirts wrapped around the chair and the table of her vanity, a great assortment of old bottles of rancid perfume crowding the lacquered surface. Amber picked a blue glass one with a black cat. "*Chat Noir*. Genies in perfume bottles," she smiled.

"What do you mean?"

"My first vanity lesson. Remember?"

"Vaguely. Remind me."

"We were visiting Uncle Iskender's plantation. Just before the fire. I was only seven. You found me in front of your vanity doused with perfume and makeup."

The instance had faded from Aida's memory. She had no recollection. "Oh yes, I remember," she lied.

Amber reached inside her bag. "I never forgot," she said as she slowly pulled out a box wrapped in used gift paper and ribboned. Aida's eyes shifted from Amber's hand to her eyes, and from eyes to hand; her smile stayed constant betraying her heart, pounding vigorously underneath her scarred cleavage—the crescent and the star vanished along with her right breast.

"Just a little gift."

Aida ceremoniously placed the box on top of a tray, made up of iridescent butterfly wings of blue, green, and gold that the General had brought back from the Korean War. As she unwrapped the paper like a curious child opening a Christmas present, tiny vials of transparent liquids rolled onto the tray.

She plucked each little bottle, holding them at an arm's length from her eyes to read the labels. (Aida would never consider wearing reading-glasses): "Poison, Joy, Opium, Obsession, Shocking, Temptation," she chanted. "And Shalimar!"

"And this, Elizabeth Taylor's perfume. Black Pearls."

"I'm not crazy about the smell but Shalimar was always my favorite. The General used to bring me huge bottles from Paris when he was a military adviser there. Used to be my perfume. Everyone knew I was coming before they saw me. Haven't had a dab for eons though. Not available here, you know? Oh, Amber, you're such an angel."

She dipped the tip of her index finger in the perfume and dabbed it behind her ears, on her inner wrists, then aimed at her Y-shaped vein. "This is where a man should always kiss a woman, where these two veins meet. This is where we like to be kissed, don't we?"

"Yes, don't we?" Amber laughed. "Yes, I've heard that story many times, many versions. But never from you."

"That's how the General seduced me—just a lieutenant, then. By kissing this very vein."

Laced porcelain ballerinas pirouetted around a revolving tray. A box of bird's-eye maple, inlaid with vermilion and ebony flowers, played "Twinkle, Twinkle Little Star." Another box of Thai silk played "La Marseillaise."

Atatürk and the lesser General looked on under their bushy eyebrows—another thing they had in common. Amber picked up a picture of Aida, with Papatya and Sibel all in pubescent prime, dressed identically in sailor suits, lined up like chorus girls. Another, in classical folk costumes, harem pants, vests, scarves, the ever-unresolved duality.

"The lovely silk princesses," Amber mused. "And the gorgeous beauty queen . . ."

"Yes. The glorious moment of the family. I'm sure you've heard it all. Come here and sit next to me. Tell me your version."

"*Bir varmış, bir yokmuş,*" Amber began. "Once was a silkmaker with three daughters. One daughter was cold but cunning, the second could sing as lovely as a nightingale, and the third daughter was of such great beauty that not even the *houris* in the garden of Paradise could hold a candle to her. Lovelier even than the moon; that's why they'd named her Aida, the Queen of the Moon. So exquisite was Aida as she came into womanhood that the family, enslaved by her beauty, devoted all their being to creating magnificent garments to display her.

"The world and everything it promised was at Aida's fingertips. Suitors came for her from all over the kingdom. She possessed the kind of magic that made people want to build palaces for her. To climb Mount Ararat. To kill a giant. Vanquish a dragon. To start a war. To go to the moon. Always the unattainable. She could have been a queen—not only a beauty queen but a real one. Many Arab princes and emirs left gifts at her doorstep. Many generals brought trophies. In fact, even the great leader Atatürk was so bewitched by her beauty that he himself offered her the crown."

Aida's eyes were fixed on the two portraits as she listened, her pupils reduced to a pinpoint through which only her own memories could filter their way. "Our family was so insecure of their past without which they felt faceless, Amber. So they invented a good story to shine. To have something to pass on. So no one would know our mediocrity."

"So, you're saying it never happened?"

"Not the way everyone imagines."

"You never met Atatürk?"

"Of course, I did. When he came to the beauty contest—I've never seen a man more powerful, more commanding, charismatic, handsome. I would have given anything to be his slave. But all he could do was to crown me. That's all. Simple as that."

"That's all? I don't believe it."

"Believe what you will."

"You never went out with him?"

She clicked her tongue, meaning "no."

"You never cruised in his Daimler?" (Amber had seen it in the museum in Anit Kabir, Atatürk's mausoleum now completed, fantasized Atatürk and Aida tussling in the backseat.) "You never made love to him?"

Aida clicked her tongue again.

"I don't believe it."

"Until I die, the only truth remains as is."

Amber pointed at the picture of Atatürk and the General. "You know, they're listening and they know the truth."

"Yes, and I'm getting tired of performing for them. So, I'll tell you as it happened. Sure, I danced with him. And went out in his Daimler lots of times but never with him. Always with your uncle, the General, since he drove Atatürk around in those days, he had the use of his car."

"Well, this is really something. I just don't know what to believe."

"Does it matter? No, it doesn't. Everyone sees things with different eyes. Just make up any old story. Doesn't have to match mine or theirs, does it? Anyway, forget all this nonsense, continue on with your story. Alright?"

"So the years passed and kismet carried Aida to old age where her beauty was irretrievable. She lost her hair; she lost her skin; she even lost one of her breasts. She became obsessed about returning to her youth, seeking potions to smooth out her flesh, concoctions to get rid of her wrinkles, even handsome youths, young enough to be her grandsons, to flatter her charms."

"*Aman, aman!* What did you hear?"

"That you have a lover."

This really set Aida off. She began to fire. "Those whores just can't endure seeing light in people's eyes; they delight in misery, resent another's good fortune. May Allah choke them with their judgments. May Satan curse their tongues so they can never speak again." Then, she broke into tears. "If they knew. If they only knew how much I suffered," she cried. "Amber, my dream, you don't know what we're living through here. Happiness is a source of envy. Misfortune is cause for celebration. People behave as if they are put in this world to make others' lives miserable, as if life itself is easy to begin with. Tell me. How can we survive without compassion? With the evil eye cast out of every window, we're to wear these stupid charms. But they don't seem to do much good, do they? You're lucky you didn't stay here to rot and stink like linen seed, like the rest of us. Allah was on your side. I wish I could've done what you did. I wish I too could've escaped."

This sudden Allah talk made Amber nervous. "Every place has its own challenges," she said.

"Not like this. Where you live, a woman my age and a young man are still allowed friendship. Aren't they?"

"Yeah, but people still think it's a little . . . unusual."

"So? Who minds being unusual? Haven't I always been unusual but wasted all my resources pretending otherwise? Haven't
you? Isn't that why you left this place? To find somewhere where
you can be unusual? You can't really hide that kind of thing for
very long, you know? Somehow, the truth leaks. Like it's leaking
now and I'm getting devastated trying to keep it all in. I don't
care anymore what they think—spider-brained people, their
mouths should be stuffed with cayenne and sewn up. Their eyes
poked for seeing evil in everything. Their cunts circumcised . . ."

"Who is he, anyway?" Amber interrupted.

"The sweetest boy in the world."

"Are you in love?"

"In love? In love? People just wouldn't understand this kind
of thing. What do they know of love? You know those two old
maids on the first floor? The sisters—I think they're queer that
way or something. I think their father fucked them and they did
it to each other. Those evil bitches hide behind the shutters all
day long, spying on everyone who goes by. Seeing but not being
seen. They watch the young girls and boys flirting innocently,
the same way they did when you were growing up. They set
traps, make gossip. They ruin lives. I've heard they've been going
around saying I'm running a rendezvous house here or something. That they've seen men come and go. All I want is some
privacy. Hags. Allah's going to rain stones from the sky to punish them. You'll see. May their tongues have a stroke. May crows
scoop out their eyes."

"Tell me what really is going on."

Aida sat at her vanity and began brushing her hair vigorously with the carved ivory set Iskender had brought back for
her from the Silk Road.

"People began to talk so we were forced to stop seeing each
other—wrote letters instead, talked in whispers on the phone

but out of the window, I could still see his place. I'd see him put things on his verandah, a different flower everyday to communicate. Flowers have a language, you know—pansies mean fond thoughts; purple columbine, resolution; red poppies, consolation; lilies of the valley, return of happiness; angelica, inspiration. But how long can one go on like this?"

"Why do you care if they gossip. So what? You're a grown woman for God's sake."

"So we made a date for last Tuesday night. He refused to come in the front door to avoid the old-maid sisters, so what does he do? He climbs up the wisteria vine to my balcony like Romeo or something. He could have fallen off, broken his head, be paralyzed, you know? But instead, he risked his life, dear boy.

"But the old maids saw him anyway. The next thing, I hear the police knocking at the door. I tell him to go hide in the wardrobe. And I ask the police what they want. They say they had a complaint that there was a man in here. So I tell them to help themselves, real nonchalant-like so they won't suspect. It works like a dream. I think that wardrobe has some sort of a spell—used to belong to your grandmother Esma. How she would have adored you! Life is cruel. Anyway, without really checking around, they leave but I know they haven't given up and will keep an eye on the house all night. How am I going to get him out?"

"Can they search without a warrant?"

"They can do whatever they damn please. So I keep him in the famous wardrobe all night and all next day, afraid to utter a word, to walk around so the floors creak, making the sisters suspicious. We sit with fear all this time, the fear of being shamed. The next day, just before dawn, he climbs down the vine again and this time gets away unseen." She wiped her eyes. "After that, we had to swear not to see each other. What choice did we have?"

"Maybe I can arrange something. Maybe you and I could go somewhere together and he could meet us."

"*Yok.* No point in playing with fire and getting you involved in all this. He's in my heart and I'm in his. All that matters. I've lost so much already." She pointed at her missing breast. "Sometimes I still feel its ghost. What's left to nurture? Light me a cigarette, will you? I usually don't smoke—not to avoid cancer but because the stuff makes you smell disgusting. But I want one now and don't give a damn about the smell because no one's coming close enough to smell me anyway."

Amber picked out a gold-filtered cigarette from a crystal container, lit it with a matching table lighter, and gave it to Aida.

"Have you ever had plastic surgery, Amber?" Obviously she was trying to change the subject, jumping around like a butterfly.

"What are you talking about?"

"Have you ever had your face done?"

"No, why should I?"

"There must be something about your looks that irritates you. We all have those features we cannot tolerate about ourselves."

"Well, I probably could use a straighter nose, a sharper chin. Maybe bigger boobs and thinner thighs, smaller ass. Sure, lots of things. But so what? We were talking about you and . . ."

"You change them. If you don't like something about yourself and can do something about it, you should. Otherwise, you make yourself miserable each morning you catch your reflection in the damn mirror as you wash your face. Some women think they have to persevere through life burdened by their imperfections, flaws, impediments. But why, why suffer? We are victims of our chemistry, after all, every day aging cell by cell. A woman past her prime has nothing left. Her glow gone, her scent, her desire."

"Old age can be the best time in your life if you accept it and do it gracefully," Amber told her aunt.

"Maybe so where you come from. Can't say that about here, though. You're either a young woman or an old hag. Nothing in-between. Anyway, I've made up my mind. Once, I used to cast spells to keep away Azrael, the death angel. He's come around a few times, you know? Now, I wish sometimes he'd do it more often. Someone to bump against, you know? Anyway, I have some money saved up and I'm going to have a face lift and also one of those things where they suck the fat out of your arms and thighs. They say they can even take the lard from your ass and shoot it into your breasts." Aida pushed up her sleeve, flashed at Amber the sagging flesh under her upper arms. She exaggerated. "And this! Must be jelly 'cause jam don't shake like this. This bag of mutton fat. This elephant skin. The sign of a crone."

"Where are you having this done?" Amber pursued.

"In Bursa. This doctor has a house and he does you and you can stay there until you're done. Very, very private. Zeki Müren the singer had his face stretched there. Tansu goes for her colla-gen shots or whatever. And the former president's wife. Remem-ber, how her legs used to look like an elephant's? He tapered them and gave her ankles."

"But from what I hear, it doesn't always work," Amber ar-gued. "Lots of horror stories. And once you do it, you have to do it again. And there comes a time when you are stretched to the max and can't any more, you know?"

"Who cares?" Aida shrugged. "By then, most likely I'll be compost anyway. Who cares?"

"I do and he must."

Aida's eyes watered again. Amber stood up to get her a tissue. She was distracted by a sepia photograph of Iskender taken in Isphahan, his arm resting on the shoulder of a small dark man. In the back, in her father Cadri's handwriting, it said, Iskender with Pierre Loti. Loti? The famous French author. Next to it was Iskender as a young man with his sisters Esma and Mihriban sitting in a field somewhere, smiling so innocently. How young their skin . . .

Across from Aida's bed stood the famous wardrobe in which Süleyman had arrived one night to court Esma, the night Aida was conceived. It also watched.

"Did you know my grandmother Esma very well?" Amber asked.

"I knew her well and I loved her. I loved her more than my own parents."

"Surely you must have sensed something."

Aida gave her a look to see if they were talking about the same thing. "Yes," she said, "every child dreams that her parents are not her real parents. But mine turned out to be true . . . Cadri told me everything before he died."

"Did he tell you about your father?"

"He said my father was their tutor. Killed in the war."

"That's what they all thought," Amber said.

"Are you trying to tell me something?"

"You asked me earlier if I had ever been in love. It seems the only men I seem to be capable of loving are old men, as you seem to prefer young men. Iskender, Süleyman . . ."

"Who's Süleyman?"

"Your father."

"You talk as if you know him." She looked confused.

"I did. In the late seventies, Sam and I were living in a

Greenwich Village apartment. One day a guy showed up at the door, the old-world type like so many of the old guys around who came to the newsstand across the street for egg creams.

"He was holding a clipping in his hand with my picture—I'd been interviewed for an architectural magazine, you see? I'd won an award. He asked if I were related to the İpekçi family who'd been in the silk business and I told him yes. He told me he was an old friend of my grandmother's and that I reminded him of her. He had also known my father as a boy. I invited him inside.

"It was a July day like this, despite the laboring water fan, the heat was hellish. I offered him some lemonade that I'd freshly squeezed and in order to show his gratitude, he took a small can of Secret out of his vest pocket and sprayed the air. That's how our friendship began. With Secret.

"He was a strikingly handsome man, although the wrinkles revealed a lot of wear and tear and he had a noticeable limp. He wore his long hair in a ponytail, and his clothes were kind of shabby but the shabbiness that comes with the wearing-out of something finely made—like patina, vintage, or *shibui*.

"He said his name was Süleyman. His eyes slowly scanned our studio, strips of film that hung from the ceiling, heaped into a garbage can, a table cluttered with reels and mounted handwheels, maquettes for dream communities and blueprints. He checked out the photographs on the walls, Sam's hard-edged, high-contrast, shockingly stark *kodaliths* of New York City next to the sepia ghosts of our forgotten ancestors. His eyes stopped on the picture of my grandmother, dressed in a black *charshaf* and veil.

" 'Esma was about your age in that picture. Did you know her?' he asked.

"I was startled by the matter-of-fact tone in his question. 'She died the night I was born,' I told him.

" 'I've always loved her,' he said, his voice cracking. 'Even after she betrayed me.'

"Then, he told me of their secret love, his nocturnal visits to the house in Smyrna, the poems through which they spoke, hiding in your wardrobe, the night of the double moons. He had wanted so much to marry her but she would not break the sanctity of her widowhood. Then Uncle Iskender had gotten wind of their liaison and had interfered to protect the family honor."

Amber paused for a moment and looked at Aida, vigorously cracking pumpkin seeds with her teeth.

"Go on."

"About that time, the war had broken out and despite his good judgment, Süleyman enlisted. He was captured and tortured like many. He spent a whole year by himself in total darkness, except for the singular ray that leaked when someone brought him bread and water. That's all he had. Bread and water, once in a while a couple of olives.

" 'When I returned to Izmir, I immediately went to visit your grandmother, determined to take a chance even if I'd be punished. I'd already been punished too many times,' he continued. 'Just as I was about to knock at the door, I met a man on the street who had some dealings with your uncle Iskender. Loathsome character; looked like a ferret. In fact, they called him Ferret.

" 'He told me that he was now happily married to Esma. I did not believe him so I followed him. He stopped at the *boza* stand and bought a pitcher, went around the obsidian and knocked at the door. I saw a woman open the door and knew he must have been telling me the truth.'

" 'But he wasn't,' I objected. 'My grandmother never remarried. I do remember a guy they called Ferret, though, who stank so bad that he was chased out of town.'

"The old man suddenly grew silent. He excused himself and left abruptly. I realized why as he stumbled down the corridor leading to the stairs when I heard him grunt like a tormented lion. The entire block trembled from his rage until the sirens came.

"But he had left his calling card and I knew where he lived. That night I told Sam about the visit. 'How on earth did he end up in New York City?' Sam wanted to know. I didn't know.

"The following week my uncle Aladdin, his wife Sophie, and my two cousins Kitty and Gypsy invited us to their place in Massachusetts for Thanksgiving. I asked Süleyman to come along but did not tell him where. I wanted the whole thing to be a surprise.

"I cannot tell you how moving it was when Aladdin and Süleyman encountered each other, that instant recognition of something clicked that had no memory.

"'Columbus did not discover America,' Süleyman told Aladdin.

"'Already other people were living here,' Aladdin replied. They embraced while the rest of us stared, dumbfounded.

"After that, Süleyman visited me regularly every Wednesday afternoon; when Sam worked in the stockyards to support us, Süleyman and I sat across from each other on one of the Louis Quinze twin couches, one that had belonged to my grandmother, the other to Uncle Iskender—the only pieces of furniture I took with me to America. We had tea. I told him how Esma had given me the middle name of Süleyman. I told him of the time I visited Iskender in the silk plantation shortly before his death.

"He told me how after assuming Esma was married to the Ferret, he had given in to the snow, rescued by the night watchman, and after filling his blood with a warm brew, sauntered down aimlessly to the waterfront, jumped a freighter that took him to New York. Once there, he decided to stay and got a job as a typesetter, invented a special form of typography that brought him wealth but he had never, never found another love.

"I told him stories of our family, the fire at the plantation, the beauty contest, the Spinsters Apartment, the years of the family the poor guy had missed out on—whatever I could think of. With each story our lives became more deeply entwined. Sam and I began calling him grandpa. Then, one day, we were taking a walk in Central Park. An early spring day, daffodils in bloom. Birds and butterflies everywhere. Suddenly, a nightingale landed on Süleyman's shoulder, then flew away. Süleyman went running after the bird like a boy. I tried stopping him but he ran infinitely faster than I ever could. By the time I reached him, it was too late. His heart had already stopped. But pink roses were blooming out of his fingertips.

"Uncle Aladdin and I had him cremated. I brought his ashes with me. I thought I might go to Izmir where the old house used to be—I'm sure they must have demolished it long ago but still—and scatter them under the Adonis tree, if it still exists. Let me know if you want to feel them. After all he was your father."

꒰

Aida asked Amber to accompany her to Bursa for the ordeal while she told everyone else, including Camilla, she was going in for a hysterectomy but Camilla, keen as a fox, smelled something fishy.

"Why go all the way to Bursa for a hysterectomy," she probed, "when we have the best doctors here? Doctor Eliksir has sloshed around in her private parts for half a century, for God's sake. He surely knows his way in."

"Doctor Eliksir must be a cadaver by now. I mean, last time I saw him he was quaking like he had Parkinson's and that was some years ago. Besides, she's not really going for a hysterectomy; she's getting her face done. And you're not going to tell a soul!"

"I'll be damned. *Se faire peau neuve*," Camilla shook her head. "*Tsk, tsk, tsk.* How can the new hide conceal the real scars?"

"Yeah, but it will lift her spirits. She's been awfully depressed lately, you know? She needs a perk."

"I know. Not the same since they scraped out her breast. Poor thing. She no longer goes around saying, 'I was never born and I'll never die.' Go, go with her. She needs someone, Amber. Osman, that criminal son of hers, still in Bakirkoy asylum. No use to anyone. She's got no one else. Go, go hold her hand."

Amber wanted them to cross to Bursa on the ferry as in her childhood; but Aida said, "Don't be an imbecile. Those boats now carry only the *kurban*, the sacrificial lambs. Only the livestock takes the ferry now. You want to lead us to the slaughterhouse?" A bucket full of laughter. Aida's laughter even more infectious than her face. Lingers on one's skin.

They took a bus instead—supposed to be air-conditioned but wasn't—that let them off in downtown Bursa, spewing with confusion and panic. What a rude baptism into Asia! Amber thought as the clouds of pollution darkened her heart. No sign of silk at the Koza Han, the silk market, though it was just about harvesting time, no cocoon baskets. Instead, strings of kebab shops lined the main street, mustached man with menacing scimitars spinning animal carcasses oozing with grease, slicing paper-thin pieces of meat. Swords strung with tomatoes, peppers, slices of onion, piled into perfectly balanced pyramids decorated each window. Smell of freshly baked pita. Songs wafted from loudspeakers out of the open windows in waves. And flies, flies stuck to everything.

The facemaker's house was in an area called Grasshopper near the thermal baths. "Looked like the kind of place one would go to for an illegal abortion in Cleveland," Amber told Camilla later. A concrete and stone building with Astroturf flooring, partially boarded up to make it seem uninhabited. An air of illicitness stifled the entryway and the rancid smell of meat. Amber had strong misgivings from the beginning. She wondered if the knives were clean, if they knew how to apply anesthesia properly. If they had medical training. Emergency procedures. Insurance.

"So this is where you'll spend the next couple of weeks?"

"I know what you are thinking but it's all a front to avoid the sinister taxes. They say it's pretty nice inside. When I'm finished," Aida smiled coquettishly, "you'll be jealous because I'll look like I'm your sister."

"You don't have to try that hard. You already do."

A woman wearing a white babushka parted the door. Aida gave her name.

"What about her?" the woman asked, meaning Amber.

"She's my niece. Just accompanied me here."

"You're sure you don't want me to stay for the operation?" Amber asked. "I'd gladly, you know."

"I'm sure."

"Call if you need anything on my cell phone, then. If you want me to come and get you at any time, I will. I'll miss you madly. Good luck, OK?"

Aida lifted her sweater, flashed her evil-eye charms. "Don't worry," she said. "I'm well protected, as you can see."

Amber put her arms around her aunt, feeling the abundance of flesh around the love handles, the flat absence of a breast. I've got to get the prosthesis back from the customs she thought, even if it means yielding to their corruption. The door closed behind her with an eerie hollowness.

Since her bus was not leaving until late that night, Amber wanted to escape the madness of human chaos downtown. Yes, there was the Emerald Mosque and the Emerald Mausoleum but a glimpse at the snowy peaks of Mount Olympus, the peach orchards, and the scent of wild hyacinth infinitely more enticing.

She told the taxi driver to take her to the İpekçi plantation. He looked at her a bit puzzled but didn't say a thing. He drove on the paved road like a kamikaze and smoked like a fiend. Turkish rap blasted out of the speakers—a barking chorus of canines. Amber tried putting on the seat belt. There was none.

"Where are you from?" he asked.

"America."

"Dallas (pronouncing it dull-us)?"

"No, I'm from California."

"Too bad for you. Dallas very beautiful."

"You've been there?"

"Every Friday at eight. Every Friday night," he said. "I never miss."

"How long will it take to get up there?"

"Fifteen, twenty minutes."

"Used to take five hours on a buggy up Mount Olympus."

"You've been before?"

"Yes, I have."

She was thirsty. They stopped at a café shaded by an ancient plane tree. Amber ordered some *Gaseuse*.

"Big sister, *Gaseuse* disappeared way before I was even conceived," the waiter told her impatiently. "But we have good Pepsi and Seven-up. We have Diet Coke. Even Snapple."

A stork stirred on the roof of an old school. In the vast panorama stretching before them, the tip of a minaret encrusted with emerald tiles rose out of a cloud of smog. A small bird-of-prey swept down the mountain and landed on a cypress tree nearby. It was a merlin.

Cadri's voice came to Amber, slowly enunciating his catechisms as if he were sitting across from her. "Do you know what it's called?"

"The Emerald Minaret."

"And next to it?"

"I can't see."

"The Emerald Mouseleum. And the city below?"

The city below cluttered and rambling and gray, an opaque, brownish smoke rising out of the silk factories; the city, warped by earthquakes and the sadistic rule of its sultans, was still called the emerald city, but nothing was green, except the tip of the minaret. The mosque and the mausoleum, no longer visible from the mountain, blocked by an accordion of apartment houses.

The driver, jazzed up after consuming a large bottle of warm Coke, took fast turns, sweeping between trucks, brimmed with crates of peaches, goats, and chickens, whizzing from both directions, more ruthless, rude, and dangerously competitive than in Istanbul. An ancient tractor transporting a family with many children had stalled the flow of traffic. Amber shrank, squeezed between wagons on both sides, the tires almost rubbing against each other, the awful smell of burning rubber. A truck passed out of turn, sideswiping the taxi.

The taxi driver stopped the car dead. Gave the arm. "*Ayi,*" he screamed at the truck driver. "Retarded bear." "Bear" was the worst possible insult.

"Son of a whore," the truck driver shouted back.

"Donkey's son donkey."

"Animal."

"Fuck your mom."

The sounds of angry horns. Drivers creeping out of their vehicles. Taking sides.

"Please, let's go," Amber pleaded.

They continued farther up the mountain. The traffic thinned. The taxi turned off a dirt road and came to a halt. "Here we are, *abla*," the driver said, pointing at a cinderblock shack. "The İpekçi plantation."

"Where's the rest?"

He shook his head. "I don't know what you're talking about. This *is* the old İpekçi plantation. Isn't that where you wanted me to take you?"

No trace of the white oleander hedges, no pavilions with colossal arches and columns shaded by cedars of Lebanon, surrounded by reflection ponds and fountains. Not even traces of charcoal from the fire, hidden underneath thistle and wild hyacinth. Only a modest cinderblock dwelling remained, unkempt, smothered with weeds. An overgrown, untended vegetable garden. Giant eggplants and squash. Neglected mulberry trees scattered here and there, their leaves all but gone; they bore fruit now—long white berries. The silkworms, too, gone.

The fire had razed the plantation right after their visit. Cadri and Camilla had lied to Amber but she had sensed it, all that running about, all those whispers. She had sensed something unspeakable. Then, Cadri's sudden return to the plantation. She kept asking about Iskender. Cadri said he was fine, just a bit ailing. He's a very old man after all.

She had discovered Iskender's obituary in a newspaper, a stack used for toilet paper at a public bathroom. She had recognized his picture and used her rudimentary knowledge of reading to decipher what it said. Even that had not convinced her entirely. Iskender was bigger than life. He was mythical, immortal.

But afterward she had gone into a flurry of a painting spell and painted all the walls in her room and the curtains and the furniture in red. Every night she lay in bed, her eyes open, imagining the curtain parting and Iskender coming in through a cloud of fireflies.

But now standing along the ravine, looking at this empty wilderness that surrounded them, it struck her with disturbing certainty that Iskender, the silkworks, the plantation had only existed to paint her childhood, to introduce the colors of love and pain, short-lived but held long. *The dreams of a seven-year-old are so vast they could encompass her whole future and determine her journey through life.* Iskender's words came to her. Who would've really known?

Shards of clay where she stood, broken pieces of old glass sparkled iridescently. Rotting old rags, rusty pieces of metal, a hole in the ground. Follow the white rabbit. A caterpillar smoking a hookah. *Do caterpillars have dreams? The most amazing kind.* She stirred the junk with her feet, made a semicircle. It seemed like the lid of a brown bottle at first but so perfectly shaped that she picked it up and brushed off the dirt. She spat on it to make it clearer. The amber egg! Inside, the silkworm trying to escape. *Bombyx mori.* The night of the fireflies it was lost. She clutched the egg and held it close to her heart. She was not going to let anyone take it away from her now.

Aida returned to the Essence of Honey Street two weeks later, confining herself to her apartment, refusing to see or speak to anyone. When Amber came to bring the prosthesis that she had finally been able to clear from the customs, acquiesced to the bribe, no answer.

The TV was blabbing inside the apartment. Amber rang the bell again. Still no response. She banged on the door. She yelled out. No response.

"Let me in or I'll call the fire department and climb up to your balcony. I mean it. If I break my neck, it will be all your fault and I'll sue you for all your billions! Come on, be a sport. Please!"

Mickey Mouse shades, her hair wrapped in a gold turban, dressed in a yellow terry robe, looking as if she had stepped out of a bad Hollywood movie, Aida parted the door. She didn't say a word but led Amber into the living room. Pursing her lips like the elephant man, she talked in a babyish voice—all that was available to her now. "I know you're dying to see it," she said, "so that you can tell me you were right. You'd warned me so."

"I just came to see how you are, Aunt Aida, for god's sake."

"Well, see it, then." She dramatically removed her shades. An experiment gone awry, a reflection on the distorting mirror of a fun house, her skin creased like a premature baby's stewed in the maternal liquids. The exaggerated lines around her eyes made her resemble the bride of Fu Manchu and the corners of her mouth curled up in a clownish smile—Jack Nicholson in *Batman*. She couldn't really move her jaw very well, except to part her lips ever so slightly—barely wide enough to make smoke rings and blow words. The place under her arms, drained of fat now, scarred like a badly performed cesarean.

Amber could not imagine a greater tragedy for her aunt who, even in her aging, even after losing her family and her breast, had still retained an innocent grace. "You have to sue the bastard," she told Aida.

"Do you think I'd want people to know I had my face lifted and they screwed up? They'd think I was an idiot. They'd chew it like gum and pass it from mouth to mouth. What good is money now that I don't have my face anymore?"

"You're not planning to hide here the rest of your life?"

Aida dropped her head, didn't say anything at first. "No one will see me like this, Amber," she said, wiping her tears. "I will not leave my house. I will not. I will not."

"It's all right," Amber said. "You don't have to." She held her aunt in her arms like a child. "I brought you a gift." It seemed odd to be presenting the prosthesis at a moment like this. But she had intended to give it to Aida and there it was.

Aida opened the case and in a breast-shaped mold was the artificial breast. She took it out, squeezed it, and burst into laughter. She laughed harsh and throaty.

༄

"Poor Aida," Camilla said when later she heard. "I must go visit her often. I'll get a big box of pistachio delight from the Divan Café, her favorite. That should cheer her up a bit, don't you think?"

But Aida refused seeing Camilla or anyone else, except Amber and the concierge's wife, who did her shopping and cleaned the house. Confining herself to her apartment, she shut out the world. Or so everyone thought.

"What about your young man? Are you still in touch?" Amber could not resist asking her. She had been watching the quaint little house every day in hopes of getting a glimpse of someone. But she never saw anyone, even though she was certain somebody lived there. The lights went on every evening, and every morning she saw a different kind of flower on the balcony and looked in her book of flowers, trying to identify the message.

"I can't bear the thought of him ever seeing me like this." Aida drifted back into watching a Turkish sitcom and eating pumpkin seeds. "I wanted to be beautiful for him."

"Poor Aida," Camilla shook her head, listening to Amber, as they fed on takeout kebabs and Nellie watched TV in the living room. "What a grotesque misadventure. Satan talked her into changing her face. I'm sure of it but why did she have to listen? It's always been Aida's great weakness. Her vanity, her doom."

It was a salubrious summer evening. Amber was beginning to feel stir-crazy.

"Do you guys want to walk to the Baghdad Boulevard? I'll treat you to some ice cream," Amber offered, eager to break out of the claustrophobia.

Camilla said she was too tired. Nellie wanted to watch Turkish MTV instead.

"Then, I'm going to the grocer's to get some chocolate."

"You're eating too much chocolate, Amber. You'll get acne. Bad for your liver, too. Makes it grow hot. Gives you migraines."

"But it makes me feel good," Amber smiled and walked out.

"Mom, get me one of those chocolate pistachio bars, would you?" Nellie yelled out over a Madonna look-alike singing to the tune of "Material Girl" in Turkish.

Essence of Honey Street was unusually empty and sullen for such an evening. Windows strobed with phosphorescent colors emanating from TV sets in every building. The muezzin sang through the loudspeaker on top of the unfinished minaret.

Someone was following Amber. The street was well lit. People still lingered at their balconies—some having dinner. She had nothing except a few liras and her keys.

The steps quickened and caught up with her. Amber turned

around flushed, her heart racing, and stopped. She flashed a mean look, ready to shout obscenities when she caught his eyes. There was no malice in them. He bowed apologetically.

"I didn't mean to be rude," he said, talking with a slight accent. "I'm sorry if I frightened you. But I had no other choice. You see, I've been trying to contact your aunt. Unsuccessfully. I'd be grateful if you'd deliver this note to her personally."

He possessed the composure, the clarity of a Victorian gentleman almost. Nothing seemed further removed from Camilla's description of him as a gigolo. He was a tall man and not so young. Sea blue eyes. Intense forehead. Grounded, with a warm gentle voice.

Amber took the note and walked away without a word. She sensed the shadows of the old-maid sisters fidgeting behind their jealousy shades. As she walked up the stairs, she could hear noise and chatter rising out of Aida's. It had to be the TV but the uneven levels made it sound like real people.

Instead of Aida, another woman who looked as though she was from an alien distance answered the door. When she saw Amber, she shrank like a vampire confronted with a cross. Her hairline had a deep scar framing her face. "Someone's here, Aida?"

"My niece. The only one who's seen me besides you all. Come inside, Amber, join the circle. Come. Don't be timid."

In Aida's dimly lit living room, seven other women with damaged faces sat solemnly, dressed in colorless rags, heads covered like devout Moslems—unusual sort of company for Aida.

"I have to call mother first, you know how nervous she gets when I'm late," Amber made an excuse.

"Go, you go call her then."

"I'm at Aida's," Amber told Camilla on the phone.

"You said you were going to the store to get chocolate."

"I did but on the way I stopped by to see Aida."

"You promised Nellie a pistachio bar."

"You told me yourself Aida needs me. I'll be back soon."

"Don't be too late. You don't want to get caught breaking the Martial Law. Besides, I want to go to bed early tonight."

"Don't worry. I have a key."

The women drank their coffee from Aida's fine Sevres demitasse cups. Aida took her last sip. She turned the cup upside down, placed it on the saucer, then spun it three times before setting it on the end table. For a while, she joined the chatter, occasionally checking to see if the bottom of the saucer had cooled down. Convinced at last, she handed the cup to the woman who'd opened the door. The woman lifted the cup and lingered inside.

"A lot of darkness," she told Aida. "Your heart is blackened. You're worried about someone. A young man. Not a lover. A relative. A son maybe? I see this black bird hovering above him. But look at this, look at this cloud lifting above your head. It's going to lift, puff, just like that and you'll be flying in the air, carefree. Look at the wings. See how you're flying?"

Amber had a sudden flash of realization. *Your son maybe?* Not Osman, not the demented psychopath and pedophile who's restrained in some institution but . . . not a lover but a son? Whose son? Maybe she did not have a miscarriage. Maybe she had the child in Germany and had to give him up. But why? Suddenly, the pieces of the puzzle seemed to fit.

Aida was still lost in her coffee sludge while a woman with a wispy voice read from a newspaper as the rest listened. At first, it sounded like poetry—the tone suggested that—but the words disintegrated into the story of a man who had cooked and eaten his three wives. When the woman finished, the others sighed, shook their heads. Another began to read: "Epileptic Deaf

Mute Drowns in Primitive Toilet." They read horrible stories and they laughed at the saddest and cruelest things.

"What kind of a party is this?" Amber asked the woman who had answered the door.

"A depression party," the woman replied. "Can't you tell? We try to think of the most depressing things. It cancels our own suffering, makes us feel better about what happened to us."

Another woman sitting next to her whispered, "We prefer the dark. We are the shadow women. This is the shadow women's society. We're all survivors, always ending on our four feet like cats."

This was a Walpurgis night. Amber felt the pull of the subterranean realm of human imperfection and misery, inviting her to its catacombs. She had a great urge to find the door.

Aida ran after her. "Are you leaving?"

"Camilla needs me."

"She always needs you," Aida said. "So, give her what she wants. She's your only mother. What have you got to lose?"

Then Amber handed her the note. Aida recognized the handwriting at once. She faked a courageous smile. "What comes from fate should be returned to fate. Tell him, hearts are made of crystal, once broken they can't be mended," she chirped in her elephant man's voice.

Everything happened that night with an element of predetermined synchronicity. The entire world seemed choreographed like a magnetic energy field of attractions and repulsions. No gravity. One will, only.

As Amber walked down the Essence of Honey Street, under the canopy of sweet-smelling linden blossoms, she felt an urge to let the fermented air fill her body with all its colors and spread into everything surrounding her. Her pain. Aida's. Camilla's. Maria's. Nellie, too, already nurturing her own, inherited from the rest.

"If I fall apart, who'll catch me?" she said aloud. "No one to catch me. No mother or father. No lover. No close friend. No therapist. No spiritual teacher. Nothing. No one."

"It's all here," a voice responded inside her. "All here." She looked up at the apartment building with its many units, barbecues smelling of mutton and fish, wisps of Oriental music. Out of Camilla's living room window, flashes of color from the TV blinked like signals from an alien spaceship.

"Neither one would notice me come in anyway," she thought. "They're already lost in their worlds. I could quietly slip into the bedroom, pretend to be asleep. But they'd feel me and I couldn't bear being in their proximity now. Besides, no pistachio delight." The grocery was closed.

She circled around the block a couple of times before heading toward the Baghdad Boulevard. Something surely would be open there. She'd walk down. See the young kids cruising. Look in the shop windows. A cappuccino at the Divan Café. But first, she had to make another stop.

꒜

The closeup view of the house with the green awning surpassed the spell of its distant charm. A light was on. Amber rang the doorbell after making sure no one was watching. There was no answer. She rang again. The entrance was so dimly lit that when the door opened, she could not make out his features.

"I delivered the note," she told him.

"Did she read it?"

"Yes. 'What comes from fate should be returned to fate,' she told me to tell you. And, 'a heart is like a crystal, once broken it cannot be mended.'"

"I didn't mean to hurt her," he said.

"Look. I think I figured out who you must be. Your relationship to Aida and all that. We don't have to play games."

He nodded as if he was expecting this. "Sooner or later someone would put the pieces together. If there were true secrets, they wouldn't be alive. In fact, I'm glad someone knows. Someone like you. Would you like a glass of *çay*?"

"No, thank you. I'm walking down to the Baghdad Boulevard to get some things. It's getting late."

"Wait for me."

When he went inside to get his jacket, Amber noticed the miniature paintings all over the walls. Little jewels, highly detailed watercolors of perfect shapes, perfect light. A dim dreaminess in their tones. A certain melancholy.

"Are they yours?"

He nodded.

"I thought you were an archaeologist."

"I am."

"They're really beautiful. I think it's best we walk separately to the end of Essence of Honey Street. They'll gossip if they see us together. Can we meet in front of Kenan's kebab shop?"

They walked separately on parallel streets in the same direction toward the minibus road where *dolmuş* vans packed with people whizzed through at murderous speed. *Dolmuş* meant stuffed, a van stuffed to the brim with people.

They met by the kebab shop, continued walking in silence until he saw an opening, took her arm, and together they darted across the road trying to dodge the fanatic motorists. They turned left on the Chicken Does Not Run street for three blocks down to the Cyber Café, winding down streets with enormous holes dug up for constructions now abandoned like empty graves. Left again on Abraham from Black Hell street, to the produce market with empty stalls. Then, right up to the tunnel under the railroad station. Suddenly, the purring hum of the elegant Baghdad Boulevard with its boutiques, Italian-style interior-design stores, open-air cafés, clubs and discos, where well-dressed people strolled day and night, as always, through streets lined with vacation houses, down to the waterfront.

They had not exchanged any words but were arm in arm and she could feel her breast leaning into his arm. It felt unusually natural as if a lifelong bond existed between them.

"What happened to the beach that used to be here?" she asked looking at a long stretch of landfill.

"They closed all the beaches along the Marmara. The oil leaks from tankers coming from the Black Sea. There's no marine life left in the Marmara or the Aegean. Not safe to swim anymore."

She took him to the site of the old İpekçi home along the water's edge, which had had its own beach. The iron gate leading up to it still remained, as did the alley of tall palm trees since they were invulnerable. But instead of the waterfront houses, an expressway, the scenic driving route. Instead of the crashing of the waves, the ebb and flow of traffic.

"Have you ever been here before? Did she bring you here?" she asked him.

"No. Where are we?"

"This used to be the family summer house, belonged to my grandmother's family. We came here every summer when I was little. All of us İpekçis. We had several other houses too, and plantations."

Weary of walking, they sat on a tide breaker, facing Marmara. The wind was slightly sharp. He moved closer to her and put his arm around her shoulder to keep her warm. She snuggled up to him. They held each other like survivors of a shipwreck, witnesses of something unspoken. Knots loosened up bit by bit until the holding became undone. Fear, like rain clouds, came and went, leaving them weightless, purged of malice.

No fear, no doubt, no concern for the consequences. His kindness flowed into her body, every touch unlocking her twisted chain of pain. He didn't invade her privacy. Maybe why she trusted him so easily. He didn't impose his will. He was her familiar. Her cousin.

She was afraid to let him touch her secrets, her breath, her voice, eyes empty of lies. She was afraid the touch might evoke all the ways she'd been betrayed. She was afraid to touch him. That night they weren't human but the greater ones who had known no suffering, who had no memory of this life.

Then the train stopped at the station across the way, unloaded. People came and went but no one seemed to notice their cocooned presence. Like the way it had been with Iskender. They could have stayed like this as long as they could but the sounds of the curfew sirens reminded them of their situation.

When they returned to the streets, the veil had lifted, Essence of Honey Street, lost in the world of interpretations. Teoman was leaving the following day for the Aegean, to join an archaeological team in Aphrodisias. They promised to stay in touch and parted.

～

Amber did not want to sleep that night, fearing that she might lose this day, remembering all the times that sleep had led her to the realm of forgetfulness.

"What will happen to us, what with our need to repeat, to prolong, to resolve?"

As she tiptoed toward her bedroom she shared with Nellie, she noticed Camilla's light, which every night stayed on for a long time after they all turned in. Camilla had insomnia, had to stay up for long hours reading. Sometimes all night. She said old people don't need sleep as they did when they were young.

Her door was slightly parted so Amber could see the inside without being seen. Camilla was getting undressed and talking to herself. She can't stop talking, Amber thought. Her compulsion. She talks over everyone else's voices and in her solitude she's talking over her own. Poor lonesome woman.

She listened. It was a murmur, she couldn't hear all the words but made out her name, and Nellie's, her father's, and Maria's, and Aida's, before she realized that her mother was praying aloud, to a god of her invention—had to be a god, she had forgotten her goddesses long ago even though she was from the Aegean—making up the conventions as she went. She called him Allah, but it was not the Allah of the Moslems but her own. An Allah, part Catholic, part Sunni, and mostly pagan.

That night Amber watched Camilla as she thanked her god for things, as she asked for his help and talked about having the strength to accomplish the things she needed to accomplish before reuniting with her partner, Cadri. She prayed for all. When finished, she rubbed her face with her hands like a child and whispered, "Amen."

She was in her underwear, waist-high loose cotton briefs and a thermal tank top. She liked keeping warm. Her back to Amber, who was amazed at how remarkably young Camilla's body looked—no cellulite, no flabs, no curvature of the spine. She had a perfect posture, a large head and a short torso but everything flat and sexless like a naked doll. She pulled a faded flannel gown over her head and turned off the lights.

This is my mother. My mother Camilla. This is the woman. This woman alone. This alone woman. Not the one in my pictures. Not the one in my stories. This is my mother. Not my

Dolores Del Rio mother but this poor woman. This gnome-like woman. Not my beautiful mother. My mother in crepe de chine. Not my pistachio mother. Not the one who spoke the language of the flowers. Not the one reading *Forever Amber.*

This is my mother, she had to remind herself, the woman who gave birth to me, who brought me up. The woman who opened her legs and pushed me out. The young bride who battled the Red Woman. Whose breasts I sucked. Her skin has lost its flex irrevocably, and her teeth, all made of plastic and movable. She smells like an old woman despite the eau de cologne— maybe because of the cologne. Lemon blossoms, always. Looking at Camilla's miniature figure, her squished-up face with the same characteristics as mine, I see my own cronehood in the mirror. I forgive her everything. Even her endless chatter. I forgive.

The burden had suddenly been lifted and Amber felt the relief of holding nothing, no gravity, no inertia, alive again. Distilled.

The Turquoise Cottage

❧

(1997)

"When I was a child, my grandmother had an altar in the attic decorated with icons of Jesus, Mary, and other saints, and I played with them because I had no dolls," Camilla told Amber as they sat on a divan drinking caravan tea. "My father lived in a trunk near the saints. Once in a while, I opened the trunk, took out the picture of the man dressed in a royal aide's uniform with jeweled epaulets and a fancy fez, so dashingly handsome, so infinitely much more charismatic than any of the soldiers marching down the streets of Bornova in their rhythmic swish of soles and clump of heels. *Swish, clump, swish, clump. Swish, clump.* Day and night.

"When other children talked of their fathers and asked about mine, I'd just lead them to the attic, open the trunk, and pull out the photograph with certain pride. In my lonelier moments I'd talk to him. Kiss him. I'd imagine a warmth other than the women's, the only kind I'd ever known so far."

Nellie returned with some raisin cake Camilla had baked that morning and joined them. Until now Camilla had never made a reference to her childhood. But that morning, as if she had intuited her daughter's softening and forgiveness, she revealed her secret in a matter-of-fact voice.

"I was merely a baby when my father disappeared into the Liberation War, leaving nothing to his wife except a gold watch. My mother, Maria, who'd changed her name to Malika and converted from Greek Orthodoxy to Islam to please her husband, sought refuge at her mother's in Bornova, the lovely tree-lined suburb of Smyrna, an oasis for the European aristocracy—Girauds, Whitalls, Pattersons, La Fontaines, Bealhommes, de Hochpieds, Burkards, Grimanis—all the wealthy Rums."

The lore of silk and spice, brought on caravans of camels through the silk road to the port of Smyrna, had lured these expatriates to Bornova since the sixteenth century. Some settled there to build the Smyrna railroad, a thin, umbilicus of Europe. (Train stations in the area are still reminiscent of the Victorian country stations in England.) Europeans owned the tracks, the cars, the bulking bins full of figs, raisins, currants, licorice, olive oil, and later carpets and minerals. They insulated their possessions with a colony of Christians at every station. Bornova became a refuge for every persecuted European aristocrat, even exiles from the French revolution. No wonder they had named the central avenue shaded by ancient plane trees Champs des Exilées. The boulevard of exiles.

It rained profusely in Bornova, cascading madly down from Lake Tantalus, breaking through its banks, sending torrential red waters and giant boulders through the village. Behind it, the Tantalus mountains displayed their wooded slopes and the snowy peaks of the Nymph Mountain hovered across the Smyrna plain.

The people of Bornova lived in a kind of enchanted microcosm surrounded by manicured gardens, cultivated mainly by the British and French gardeners, where water poured from the mouths of ancient Byzantine and Roman lions, where Grecian urns and terra-cotta pots lined stone walkways, where lemon trees and Basra palms shaded the gazebos. From the ornate balconies with crumbling balustrades, reminiscent of Provence, bowers of Banksian roses tumbled down and among groves of *Smilax officinalis*, Asian roses bloomed. Wisteria climbed the pergolas and the walls of the houses; plumbago trailed along wooden balconies and crimson sage and thyme scattered on the gravel walks. Everywhere, fountains played into the pools of spring water while Venetian blackamoors contemplated the ponds full of ancient carp.

The Grimani coat of arms carved in an oval over the white garden gate showed an olive branch, a testament to the source of the family's prosperity whose olive trees spread in great silver waves along the Aegean.

"We weren't Greeks. We were Rums, Christian subjects of the Ottoman Empire. All the Rums adopted Greek as their language but my grandparents were Venetians, Grimani or Armani, that's what they were called."

"Armani! There is a very famous fashion designer by that name," Nellie exclaimed, finding a point of reference to her own world. "You think we're related?"

"Maybe," Camilla shrugged. "Who knows? We've got relatives in every crevice of the world. Anyway. The war was at its peak. We'd lost our country to the Allies who were dissecting it as if it were some laboratory animal, dividing up the sections, devouring us. So Atatürk and the rebels had begun a war against them, you know, the Liberation War, Gallipoli and all that? That's when my mother and I had to flee from Izmir to Bornova where she had been disowned.

"My grandmother was a widow with two unmarried daughters. Her two sons were off fighting in the war. No men around. She had not talked to my mother since her marriage to a Turk but there we were, no other place to go, and she accepted us with open arms. It was the first time she had seen me. She called me Lulu.

"Day and night, all you could hear was the creaking of the carriages, the sounds of horse hooves. I was always curious. Once, through the garden gate, I caught a glimpse of a convoy of carriages full of men in Greek uniform, piled on top of each other, bleeding and bandaged, filthy and fatigued, driving listlessly toward the Champs des Exilées. I ran inside, afraid of being kidnapped—not uncommon for little girls to disappear in those times—and threw myself in my mother's arms.

"The next morning, we woke up to the gunshots and cannons exploding. The heyday for the deserters and looters as the defeated Greek army wedged its way toward the Aegean. They tramped boldly through the streets, firing rifles in the air as they shattered shop windows. By late afternoon, they had advanced toward the residential section.

" 'They're here,' I heard my grandmother scream. My aunt Anna and my mother quickly bundled me up, we hurried to the French hospital trying to dodge the flying bullets. On the way, in a puddle of blood, lay a dead horse with its mouth and eyes open like that horrid Picasso mural *Guernica*. Another horse was on fire as it flew, raging through the streets like a nightmare. These images permanently tattooed on my vision.

"The garden of the French hospital was full of wailing people, dead, injured, molested, robbed. The gunshots persisted all night long. In the morning, a lead silence. They were gone.

"We returned home only to discover the doors, the windows of the beautiful house shattered; the whole estate robbed and vandalized. Everything inside smashed. Defecated. An odious smell in the air. Smell of hatred. The sounds of humans wailing to recover from this inhuman assault. A chorus of tears.

"Our English neighbors, the Whithalls, sheltered us. The diplomatic corps would hang their flags in front of their houses that gave them immunity. But we were not the only ones with damaged homes and souls. Though their hearts were big, it wasn't easy to feed so many people in those times, you know? But they were good, generous people even though the British were the enemy.

"We huddled together in a large salon sharing a cauldron of bulgur until an enormous cloud of crimson and black smoke appeared beyond the snowy peaks of the rugged Nymph mountain. Someone said, 'Look! Smyrna is burning.' Over the garden, through a sea of olive trees I saw three lofty pinnacles of smoke rising, flecked with bursts of orange flame, tilting like banners in the wind, melting and distending into the slopes. That's how I saw the great Smyrna conflagration. The Greeks' revenge, they told us, although the Greeks claimed the Turks had burnt the Armenian and Rum segments of their own city. They had poured gasoline into the Bay, set all the boats on fire, in the process destroying most of the fish and the dolphins. The four-thousand-year-old city lost just like that. Above and below."

Camilla seemed exhausted by the story she was telling but her eyes were intense. She didn't appear ready to quit. Amber and Nellie were all ears.

"After we were convinced that the soldiers and the looters had evacuated Bornova, we returned to our house; the women went to work with hammer, nail, and saw, carpentry a trade they knew nothing of, pampered women with pampered hands. But they all had the instinct for making a nest and we were able to move back into the house.

261

"Things quieted down for a while. One day, I was playing alone in the garden when I became aware of a man, dressed in a dirty khaki uniform, watching me through the gate. A man with sunken cheeks, worn-out eyes, and a missing arm. When he met my eyes, he opened the latch and came through.

" 'What's your name?' he asked.

"Afraid he'd hurt me if I didn't respond, 'Lulu,' I told him timidly. That's what they called me then. Lulu was my real name."

"Why did they change it?"

"Because they didn't want me to have problems. He grabbed me with his only arm; I screamed. He said, 'I'm your father, Lulu. Don't be afraid.' I looked at his empty sleeve. I told him that my father lived in a trunk, he has no beard, he has nice clothes, and two arms.

"Hearing my scream, my mother had come out running and saw the man. 'Hamid Bey!' she shouted, turned away, and wiped her eyes. Couples didn't embrace each other in public in those days, you know? So they stood away from each other with great restraint, while the rest of the family gathered around this man masquerading as my father.

"After cleaning up, he wanted me to sit on his lap. I ran away. 'Come back, my little girl, I'm your father,' he yelled out. I ran up to the attic, pulled my father's picture out of the trunk, and flaunted it. 'You are a liar,' I said. 'This is my father. This handsome man. Not a bum like you. Go away and leave us alone.'

"He shaved and put on an elegant house robe. When I saw his face, I did see the resemblance to the picture but for months I still couldn't let him near me. I felt betrayed by everyone and only found comfort in escaping to talk to my father in the trunk. But I was curious about the one-armed stranger, so accustomed to sleeping in the rugged hills, that the sense of a soft bed only brought pain. For months, he slept directly on the hardwood floor, with merely his army coat covering him. The war had hardened him, everyone said.

"It took more than a year to warm up to my father, to call him *baba*. I watched him at dawn, watched him walk out to the patio and turn East as the sun rose. I saw him bend down and touch the Earth with his forehead. Before long, without knowing what it was, I was doing the same. Only this way could I make a connection to him. But afterward, still sneaking up to the attic to play with my Mary and Jesus icons.

"Both of my mother's brothers were killed in the war but because the family were Rums, her two unmarried sisters, Anna and Elpida, were among those deported to Greece. Ethnic exchange, they called it. My grandmother soon died of grief. They left all their property, land, a fleet of *phaeton* carriages, everything to my mother but my father wouldn't have anything to do with all that. 'Bad money,' he said, 'we cannot profit from another's misfortune.'

"My mother and I took care packages to the dock in Smyrna. Meatballs, hard-boiled eggs, *börek*, things like that. I could still see Aunt Anna and Aunt Elpida waving, my mother choking with emotion. They must have been in their late teens then. Never heard from them after that. Who knows what happened? The letters never got through I suppose. I wonder how they survived. For all I know, we must have relatives in Greece. There, I told you everything. Are you satisfied now?"

"I don't understand why you kept all this inside yourself for so many years," Amber replied. "It's such a devastating story. I don't understand why you never wanted to tell me, wanted me to know. It would have given me so much insight into things."

"Because we could not endure living through it all over

again. Don't you see? We wanted to hide our ethnicity in case of another crisis. Every time there's hostility in Cyprus, every time the Greeks and Turks started posturing, they'd turn against the Rums. Besides, I didn't want to expose you to meanness at school, discrimination and all that. I didn't want to disgrace your father's family. If you didn't know the truth, you wouldn't have to lie. You understand?"

"You can't stop protecting me," Amber said.

"I try. I'm your mother."

"You think it's better that I live in a world of denial?"

"Don't be ungrateful."

"I just want to make my own decisions about how I feel."

Camilla pursed her lips and walked out of the room. Amber rolled her eyes.

"You've hurt her feelings. Right after she told you that sad story. You always tell me to be compassionate yet you were . . . it wasn't cool," Nellie scolded her. "Do you smell something burning?"

They ran into the kitchen.

"The mousakka is done. Go sit down at the table. What would you like to drink, Coca-Cola or beer?" Camilla had switched to the practical mood as if nothing had happened. Amber and Nellie exchanged glances.

Camilla heaped the eggplant on their plates. "You've got my stubborn streak in you, Amber," she whispered, trying to hold back her tears. "Just like my mother. Runs in our blood, I guess. But it catches up with you later. You'll see." She reached inside her apron pocket, handed Amber an official-looking letter. "You asked to know the truth. Here is the truth."

The letter in Turkish was full of legal jargon Amber did not comprehend but she understood this much: the government was going to tear down Maria's house in Cordelio to widen the street. They were repossessing her property and evicting her.

"The compensation wouldn't even feed a family of gypsies for a week," Camilla said.

"Can they just do that?"

"The government can do whatever it wants. But my poor mother, she has nothing left except her tiny cottage. Where she used to keep the chickens. Remember? Nowhere else to go."

"She's a hundred years old, for God's sake! Shouldn't she be living with someone anyway?"

"There's no one. All dead. My father. My brothers. No one to share the responsibility of taking care of her except me. She'll have to come and live with me now. She won't want to do that. We tried before but she and your father, God bless his soul, didn't get along. Besides, she's too attached to her home. She won't let go. It will break her heart."

"What will you do then?"

"I can't do anything. I can't get myself to give her the news. It's the only thing she has left. A tiny shack. As if it weren't torture enough that they took away her house to build that wretched power station. Our family is unlucky, I tell you. How will I take care of her? I'm an old woman myself."

"Can't you put her into a nursing home or something. Don't they have places like that here?"

"Sure, we have a few houses of repose. We have them. But they won't accept anyone that old. Even if they are healthy."

"What about getting a girl from a village? A caregiver."

"*Yok*. That's a thing of the past. No such girls anymore. Not the way it used to be with Gonca, her sisters, all the others we had. They were family. Nowadays village girls are floozies. They flirt with boys on the streets. You even see them sitting on park benches and kissing in public. They won't take on work like that.

Besides, you know, I can't stand having strangers in the house. They snoop in your drawers. They eavesdrop behind closed doors. They steal things and whoosh, they're gone. You know how I've always disliked having servants. Thank you very much, my daughter, but no thank you."

"There must be something you can do," Amber insisted. "What do others do who are incapable of taking care of their old?"

"Nothing I can do," Camilla said. "I've thought of everything. I've taken care of people all my life, now just as I am about to take a breath . . . I can't leave her now. It's my lottery. You're not here to help me out. No one is. I'm all alone."

"What do you want from me?"

"I want you to visit your grandmother and break the news. She'll listen to you more than she'd ever listen to me, I don't know why. I've always been a good daughter. Besides, you may never see her again. Who knows when you'll come back—if ever . . ."

"When I wanted to visit her before, you told me she wouldn't even recognize me."

"I take it back. Her memory is better than yours and mine put together. She remembers everything that happened in the past. Maybe even too much."

"You told me she couldn't talk."

"True."

"What was that all about? What do you mean she can't talk? Is she incapable of speech or she just refuses to?"

"Well, one day, she just stopped talking. We'd gone to the *bostan*, the local farm, to get some eggplants and hot peppers. Suddenly I saw her heading toward the well that the government was going to close because, they said, there was malaria in it, but the *bostanci* wouldn't let them because he believed a spirit lived inside and needed the sun. If you ask me, adders and other snakes were what lived in that well. Millions of them, still sacred to the Great Mother in those parts so they don't kill them.

"They let him put some mesh covering on the well but all the neighbors condemned it just the same. Nobody dared go near it anymore. Nobody. So, I see her walking up to the well and I shout, 'Stop mother, where are you going?' She charges ahead as if she doesn't hear me. Nothing's wrong with her hearing, you know? She even hears things far away, faint whispers in other people's rooms. But she doesn't hear me and keeps going up to the well. I say stop again, that well is condemned, but she pays no attention. So, I drop the sack of eggplants, run after her, and grab her arm. She looks at me and she doesn't say anything but there's this kind of wild eyes on her face. I say, 'What's the matter, mother? Why are you scowling like that?' She still doesn't say anything, like she's got her tongue paralyzed.

"Since that day, she hasn't said a word to me. More than a year ago. She hears and understands things when you talk to her but never talks back. Your father used to say that she doesn't talk because I talk too much. I say she doesn't talk because she's a stubborn mule. Anyway, that's the way it goes. I'm warning you. Don't expect to have a conversation with her. She's like a seashell with a withdrawn bug inside. But what could you do? If you break the shell, the bug would die."

Amber and Nellie agreed to go to Cordelio to break the news about her house and bring Maria back. Camilla was worried that Maria might refuse to leave and she would have to be evicted by force. She wasn't optimistic. She said they needed a miracle. She warned Amber of Maria's other strange habits.

"My mother carries a Singapore Airlines bag strapped over her shoulder wherever she goes. No one knows where she found it but it's become the sanctuary of her soul. She carries in it money that's no longer any good, money her relatives must have buried before fleeing long ago. The grocer told me, she comes in with the old money and gives it to him. He doesn't want to tell her it is no good, so he takes it and gives her things. Later, I send him money to make up for what she spends."

"What else is in the bag?" Amber asked.

"My father's pocket watch. She gets panicked every few minutes and winds it. Then, she gets frustrated because she keeps going back in time. So I have to wind it back to the normal time but she messes it up again. So many times I've seen her dump the contents of the bag all over the place when she couldn't find the watch. I'm telling you all this so that you know what to expect."

꒰꜀

Amber opened the wooden gate into a garden entrance with an energetic riot of plants. The creepers strangled the sunlight; the bell-shaped blossoms of trumpet vines, morning glory, and hibiscus dangled from their limp stems. Nellie followed her mother down the stone walk, each dragging carry-ons with wheels.

At the entrance, they noticed freshly picked crisp white gardenias, unblemished yet voluptuous in their amorous prime, floating in a clay bowl. Amber touched her nose, locking the scent in her nostrils so the intoxication would linger. She reveled in her gratitude to the deities for creating such whiteness, the nobility of the soul who placed beauty at the entrance of this humble sanctuary. She thanked her for the chance to smell them, for having such a fine moment in her life.

Then she sensed it. The silent, almost subliminal movement under the petals, drawing tiny ripples in the water. Not the air, nor the breeze. Another life stirred underneath, forcing itself out, as the unconscious, black, spindly locomotion of the mosquito larvae struggled to become parasites. The water served the insect and the flower.

"Deceptive facade of beauty," Nellie said proud of her observation and choice of words. "But you're not going to let this ruin our day, mom, are you?"

Amber snapped out of her indulgence and smiled. "Not when you're with me to set things straight."

The door, the windows were open but no one was home. Inside, life reduced to its minimum simplicity—a faded kilim worn to a mud color, a mattress covered with a white piqué spread, a small table and a chair in a corner, a coal-burning stove painted blue. Herbs bunched together hung from the low ceiling, a basket of ripe figs graced the table.

The picture of Hamid Bey, wearing a magnificent tasseled fez and military regalia, in an oval frame—painfully young, already stern, handsome as can be. Not the old man she remembered who had once sat opposite from her and fixed watches.

"The one Camilla discovered in the trunk," Amber told Nellie. "Her real father."

What did not appear in the picture was Hamid Bey's vacant sleeve, stuck permanently inside his coat pocket. He had not yet lost it.

They went out the back door. Nellie seized Amber's hand and pointed at the exterior wall, painted ochre on one side, winding around and merging with the turquoise color as if someone had run out of paint in the middle. Cool. She quickly snapped a Polaroid.

They followed the antediluvian grapevine climbing the arbor into the small courtyard, dodging the shriveled dark buttons that lay scattered on the ground, bleeding burgundy stains. Leaves of tobacco stretched across the low clothes lines, drying.

Even in her long black dress and scarf, Maria blended into the landscape, imitating its colors like a chameleon. By the lichen-and-moss-covered old well with an ancient herringbone pattern of the stones, she stood with her back to them, the Singapore Airlines bag slung over her shoulder. She stood staring into the well.

Now, she'll pick up a stone. She'll make a wish. She'll throw it in the well, we'll hear its hollow echo, Amber anticipated, but Maria just stood still. Just the way she had seen her by this well when she was little, before she made her wish.

Despite her hundred years, osteoporosis had not entered Maria's bones. She stood straight as a ruler, transfixed, elsewhere, focused on some link inside the well, some link to her existence. And whatever it was, Amber herself was dying to discover.

She inched closer but Maria, still oblivious to their presence, continued her meditation. Her face, an ancient map of life lines on her turtle skin and, on her right cheek, a huge mole resembling a chocolate chip. Amber imagined that the map of lines was some sort of a key to deciphering her life.

She was about to leave quietly, out of respect for privacy, and wait for Maria in the cottage when Maria riveted her head in slow motion and fixed her eyes on Amber. She gazed for a long time, focusing precisely, adjusting to the presence of another being, then its link to her own life. She took her time, the image dissolving so smoothly that the transition was unnoticeable. For Amber the moment had become unbearable; someone had to say something quickly. Since Maria no longer spoke, the burden of breaking the silence was Amber's. To say what? Hello, grandma. Do you recognize me? To say, hi, how are you? Isn't it a nice day? To say lasting, profound words. Unforgettable lines. To say what?

Instead came her own silence. Amber and her grandmother Maria cleansed each other with their eyes until the air around them became so light that it made them weightless. A bluish aura surrounded Maria's body. Her features began to quiver, subtle changes of skin-deep colors flashed a thousand faces at Amber. Ape women, witches, demented old hags, voluptuous sirens, female Buddhas, antediluvian crones, queens, baby girls, virgins, strange animals, prehistoric female deities, and all else in between.

Amber was assimilating every persona she reflected, crumbling at times with the uncertainty of not knowing how far she might fall, flashing a smile to avoid confronting ugliness or, by turning away, breaking the connection. At times, she felt like laughing to quell her nervousness. Tears filled their eyes not of their own wanting but because of so many layers of transparence, which created a kind of opaqueness. All she could do was to sigh as if gasping for breath. At times it seemed as though Maria's feet were leaving the ground; she was about to levitate like a Chagall woman.

Amber was seeing a secret. She had no idea where the old woman's vitality was emanating from but she watched the heaving of the waves. She imagined Maria was a saint. If she was, then what about Camilla and herself? What if sainthood was hereditary? Could she inherit this gift and pass it on to her daughter?

Just as her ego separated from the rare moment, the waves began to subside, Maria's face came into full focus and remained there. She looked ordinary—a hundred-year-old woman, an ancient artifact full of moments of joy and horror, with the most intricate web of wrinkles and a chocolate-chip mole.

"Do you know me?" Amber spoke softly, trying with her voice not to agitate the rhythm of Maria's awareness. Maria acted as if she hadn't heard Amber's words and turned to Nellie instead, scanning her as she had Amber, then returned to the moment.

"Baby chicken yellow," she said.

"What?" Amber asked alarmed by her talking.

"Her hair. Baby-chicken-yellow," Maria repeated.

"She is talking!" Nellie exclaimed.

"So, there was nothing wrong with your tongue," Amber teased as she put her arms around Maria's frail body, this tiny woman like herself, shrunken even tinier with age. She absorbed her not with a clutching, suffocating grasp but almost blending with each inhalation and exhalation. As Maria entered into her field of energy, Amber saw the impeccable motion of her skin, the tiny tremor of her cells like some small animal, a squirrel or a rabbit. Her whiskers, her deep sniffling, her short breathing, the agitation of her heart.

Nellie was standing a few paces behind them, perfectly silent. An intense sound like wings slapping distracted all three. Maria and Amber separated.

"Look!" Nellie shouted, with boundless exuberance, pointing at the profusion of magenta flowers growing on the bougainvillea, covering the stone wall. A flock of hummingbirds, hundreds maybe, were ravaging the flowers in a flutter of erotic madness as if in an esoteric mating dance—now chasing each other, now competing for the orifice of a flower, now swooping so low that they almost got tangled in the women's hair.

"*Tweet, tweet, what a sweet bird am I.*" Nellie laughed. "I've never seen them so tiny. Almost like moths."

". . . but the same paisley eyes," Maria said.

"The birds?"

"The girl."

"Hello, *Anne-Anne-Anne*," Nellie flirted. *Anne* is mother. Two *Annes* grandmother, three great-grandmother. That she knew from her "Turkish for Travelers" guide. She took a Polaroid of the birds, gave it to Maria. Maria looked at the picture, trying to make sense of this strange sortilege.

"Take one of the two of us," Amber said while putting her arm around Maria, and her cheek against hers.

"Say cheese," Nellie said as she snapped.

Maria cringed when she heard the shutter click, afraid of having her soul stolen. And it was.

That picture of the two is on Amber's dresser now, among her perfume bottles, sitting on a tray made of thousands of brightly colored butterfly wings she inherited from Aida, the one that the General had brought back from Korea, along with all the other family relics she's inherited. She looks at Maria's face, complex like a walnut, more and more seeing the resemblance between them, wondering whether she will live long enough to have as many wrinkles as Maria, wondering whether she'll ever develop a chocolate-chip mole.

"Women always have late menopause in our family. I was almost sixty. Men die. Women always live a very long time," Camilla had told her once. "But we have to earn our wrinkles. Maria has earned enough for a hundred lifetimes."

꒰꒱

That night, they slept on the same narrow mattress from Amber's childhood on the vaporous tile floor, but the sheets and pillowcases were of the finest, crispest linen, edged with handmade shadow lace. Before nightfall Maria's fragile silhouette slithered into the garden, returning with a basket full of night-blooming jasmine petals, which she stuffed inside each pillow-case.

Maria had insisted on giving them her only mosquito net-ting and Nellie lit some foul-smelling green coil incense. Amber and Nellie lay on their sides without covers, their breath precip-itated from humidity that had absorbed the jasmine. Struggling to leave some emptiness between their bodies, every so often, they slid onto the tiles to cool off.

It was calm at first since mosquitoes fear the daylight. At sundown, emerging from their hiding places, they had begun rummaging for flesh. Around midnight, when the incense had burnt down to a filigree of ash, they were swarming in spirals like tiny tornadoes. All night, the nervous humming on the other side of the netting continued. Outside, the air was alive with the stirring of other insects and nocturnal beings, the whistling of tiny frogs, spool after spool, millions of them rolling.

The mean prospect of something kept Amber awake. She had not said anything about it, given even the slightest hint, but it seemed that she had not simply come here to visit Maria. She had a mission of some sort, difficult and disturbing. She was Camilla's emissary. She drifted in and out of sleep, drenched from the humidness, images and words from her dreams min-gled in a wild mélange of horny insects, verbose and histrionic.

At some point, she got up, dashing out before the mosqui-toes could assault her. But they found their way, going for her face first, then breasts as she ran out to the garden, warding them off as best she could.

Outside, cicadas were furiously rubbing their wings together in their mating madness. All at once, they'd start chanting, then just as mysteriously stop, leading on the frogs. Then, the silent insects insinuated themselves, tiptoeing spiders, enormous and fantastic, tiger-striped, dancing on invisible threads. Confusion of webs spread a canopy over the outhouse, the trickling of her water against spider's skids as Amber gingerly crouched over the hole to avoid getting bit.

Faint rays of light filtered in from a gas lamp crowded with moths, spotlighting the pistons of crimson hibiscus in explosion. Strange inverted lilies were opening their caves—everything fertile, flaunting its sex.

A bright object next to the clay bowl with the gardenias and mosquito larvae caught her attention. A hundred-*kuruş* coin. The edges of the petals now curling and blemished, the movement of the water more turbulent, the black limbs more persistent. She removed the gardenias and dumped the water on the ground, determined to destroy the parasites before they could hatch. The earth absorbed the water swiftly. She stumped on what she could not see, then filled the bowl again with fresh water from the terra-cotta jug on the patio and floated the gardenias.

Inside, an army of adult mosquitoes was buzzing now around Maria's head. Amber lit some more incense, which spread its noxious smoke; they scattered for a moment but in no time at all they would return.

Then, Maria screamed. She was whimpering, Amber thought she was speaking in tongues at first but sorted out words that were a mixture of Greek, Italian, and French. Incoherent incantations, the poor woman obviously trapped in a terrifying dream.

"Shouldn't we wake her up?" Nellie asked.

"It's not good to wake up a person having a nightmare or it never disappears."

They watched until Maria calmed down, until her breathing

became normal again. Then, it was Nellie's turn to go outside. Almost immediately, she came back breathless, snuggled up to her mother. Amber pushed her away.

"It's too hot, sweetie."

"There's a man outside," Nellie whispered.

"No one could come in through the gate. It's bolted."

"There *is*, Mom."

Amber seemed annoyed but she consoled her daughter. "Hush. Lie still, then, and pretend to be asleep. If he thinks you're unaware of his presence, he might leave you alone. If your eyes meet, it's dangerous."

So, the mother and daughter lay side by side, eyes shut, holding their breath, listening until another coil of incense expired and the mosquitoes returned. But no sign of any man.

"What sort of a man was it?"

"A tall man, standing right outside near the gardenia bowl; he had only one arm. Really scary. I almost bumped into him, he was so close. But something strange happened. Real strange. Like I did bump into him but felt nothing. Like there was no one there but just this hollow nothingness. He'd disappeared. I looked around, he wasn't anywhere in the garden. Then, I ran inside, afraid he might come back. But he didn't."

"He had only one arm?"

"Yes, I'm sure of that."

Perhaps hearing the stories about her one-armed grandfather from Camilla with an arm missing had put those visions in Nellie's head. No, she wasn't going to say anything. Not yet.

※

When the sound of things that live in the night ceased and they woke up, it had considerably cooled down. In the courtyard, two

Andalusian chickens were pecking seeds. Hard-shelled insects lay on the ground on their backs, kicking their legs. A tiger cat rolled around in the gravel, scratching himself.

Maria was in the patio, squeezing something milky out of a cheesecloth hanging from the arbor, draining the whey from the yogurt to prevent its souring from the heat.

"You know something?" Nellie asked.

"What?"

"You know who she looks like?"

"Who?"

"Yoda. You know, like in *Star Wars*."

"Yeah." She stared at the panoply of power lines behind the stone wall where her grandparents' old house used to be. The curiosity of Maria's fate, to be reduced to living in her old chicken shed, preoccupied her, a life full of dramatic twists and turns not unlike her own. How am I going to break the news? How will I tell her that in a couple of weeks they will bulldoze her home, her garden, her well?

Maria poured the tea into tiny glass cups with remarkably steady hands for an old person. Molasses, tahini, and rose-petal preserves had mysteriously materialized on the table. And figs, of course.

"Good dreams?" she asked.

"Nellie dreamed of a one-armed man."

"Bless her soul. He enters my dreams too, all the time," Maria said matter-of-factly. She placed a bowl of sour cherries on the table, then took a hairpin and, using it as a tool, began scooping out the pits. Juice spouting from the cherries left splashes of color on her white apron. She continued pulling the stems off with her withered fingers and dug in like a fiend with the hairpins. Amber began helping her. The chickens pecked at the pits. Nellie took pictures of everything.

"Aren't you too isolated here all by yourself?" she asked Maria.

"I have my own company."

"Why don't you go live with mother in Istanbul? She's so lonely."

"Maybe she wants to go back with you?"

"I didn't say that. I said she was lonely. She'd like you to come live with her in Istanbul. She's not used to being alone. You're her only blood left."

"She'd go back with you if it wasn't for me. I know."

"She wouldn't leave you, *Anne-Anne*. She wouldn't think of it. She wants to stay in her house. She wants you to come live with her."

"I did that once already."

"That was before my father died. It's different now. Just the two of you, mother and daughter . . ."

Maria sank into her chair. Some darkness curtained her eyes. "I'm an old woman," she said. "This is my home. (Bless her soul.) I'm not going anywhere. I won't leave even if they give me my weight in gold. Even if they build me a seraglio. Never mind me. Camilla can go back with you if that's what she wants."

"That's unfair. She'd never do that."

"Camilla always does what she wants. She's a stubborn mule. A chatterbox."

"She's not going to leave you!"

Maria covered the sour cherries with sugar, which released a sanguine syrup. "Camilla could go back with you if she wants. I don't care. Tell her, tell her I said that. I can't leave! I can't leave this place. How can I? Just think, who would feed him if I left?"

"You can bring the cat along if you want."

"No, not the cat," Maria continued in frustration, "but Hamid Bey."

"I knew it was him!" Nellie said. "That's who I saw last night."

"Yes, he comes out in the night, when everyone's asleep. He comes out, eats the food I leave for him, then puts a hundred-*kuruş* piece next to the gardenia bowl, and disappears. Every night this happens. I wonder where he gets the money—I never thought ghosts would use currency—but for sure he seems to care that I have enough to live on. I've never really seen him, you know? Well, except for once. Even then I can't say I saw him but I smelled him—barn hay smell, the way he smelled when he first came back from the war.

"It was pouring the day the Greeks came. A cyclone appeared in the Smyrna Bay. If it wasn't for the cyclone, they would have killed more people. But the cyclone destroyed many of their ships. They came with the cyclone, left with the fire.

"When he wouldn't cooperate, they arrested Hamid Bey and tortured him because he was working for the Intelligence. They kept him in a dark basement and starved him for weeks. He lived on cockroaches and ants, drinking his own blood to satisfy his thirst. But somehow he managed to escape one day just long enough to see me and Camilla for a few minutes, to give me his only remaining possession—his gold pocket watch which he had hidden between the rafters.

"He went on to Anatolia, leaving me alone in an infernal city. They'd taken everything from him; his hat, even his shoes. He had to travel through a long chain of Anatolian towns. First he went to Alaşehir and Salihli, weaving through mountains full of gangs, some of which were Nationalists, and other rebels. He joined the Liberation War as a civilian, continuing to work for the secret service to support Atatürk's national campaign. For three years, he walked barefoot through Nazilli, Mula, Antalya, Adana, and Mersin, which earned him a purple medal of distinction. Big sacrifice for a lousy piece of metal.

"Camilla was a baby, barely a year old. The Turks kicked us

out of our home because I was a Rum. We couldn't go out on the street. The Greeks walked around with rifles and bayonets ready to attack any moment. We had nothing, except his watch I had to pawn.

"So Camilla and I had to move in with my family in Bornova—my two sisters, Anna and Elpida, my mother trying to raise the children all by herself. My father was deceased. They'd drafted my two teenage brothers, Stefano only fourteen. Giorgio, sixteen. With no one left to manage the family business, I began taking work as a seamstress to help support the family, sewing for people who had formerly been family friends, even ones who had worked for us. But, because Hamid Bey was in the Intelligence, I was under constant surveillance, which made it difficult to get work. We couldn't even correspond with each other. I had to hide his photograph in a trunk.

"The way he smelled when he came back wasn't at all the way he'd smelled before. He was full of earth, blood, and hay. The smell he kept till the very end. The same smell rising from the well. That's how I knew. First that, then a phantom hovering over the well. I watched, standing still at the threshold, wanting so much to go outside to see him like he was, touch him to see if he was real, to ask if he could talk, but I knew somehow that this sort of thing would upset him and he'd punish me. So, I restrained myself. I stood still until he lowered himself into the well and disappeared out of sight.

"The next morning, I looked inside the well. I looked when the sun was brightest and you could see into the water clearly. Nothing, not even a speck of dust. The water still as a mirror. I knew the well was much deeper than you could see below the surface but if he went down that deep he was not human, otherwise his weight would make him float. Nothing was floating above that water, not even a mosquito.

"So, I look for him every night since. When the moon is brightest I don't sleep. I sit under the grape arbor, waiting for him to come back but you know, he never comes when I wait. I sit in the dark, warding off sleep with all my will but it always sneaks up on me. When I can no longer keep my head balanced on my neck I shuffle back into the cottage and fall on the mattress. Once or twice I even drifted away sitting on this bench and felt like a twisted roll of Easter bread when I opened my eyes but it was already dawn and he was gone. Sometimes, I think, I must have dreamed I saw him. I must have been seeing things. It was the shadow of a tree or something enlarged because the moon hit from a strange angle and I dreamed the rest. But I could swear I was awake. Still, I don't tell anyone about this, not even Camilla, because they may think I'm seeing things and I'm too old to take care of myself and they'd send me away somewhere, with crazy old people incapable of putting a spoon in their mouths. I'm happy living here by myself."

"Did you tell this to anyone?"

"Yes, I couldn't contain it any longer, so one day, I told Gülistan Hanum. You know, my next-door neighbor—the one with the stuttering son? Well, I couldn't keep my mouth shut. She said, nothing strange about it, her mother also had a spirit inside her well. Every night, she'd leave food for the spirit man while everyone slept. In the night, the spirit came and ate the food. Suddenly, everything in her mother's garden began to grow so big that the people from the newspaper came and took pictures of her vegetables and fruit. She had apples as large as watermelons. Tomatoes as enormous as pumpkins. Forget-me-nots like peonies.

"So, I left some food for him that night. Next to the magnolia bowl, so no other creatures could steal. I lay awake but did not stir. I did not want him to sense that I was waiting for him to come. The next morning, the food was gone but there was something else in the bowl—a hundred-*kuruş* coin. I did the same again that night, left food for him, and in the morning found another hundred-*kurush*.

"He never misses a day now, and neither do I. I take the hundred-*kuruş* to the grocer and buy Hamid Bey things to eat. He likes chocolate but he likes roasted chickpeas with white raisins even better, and dried fat Smyrna figs. Sultana grapes. And Kalamatas, too. Sometimes, I split the figs open, put hazelnuts inside, and he loves that. He also makes my garden grow. Look, look at that jasmine bush, look at the bougainvillea. Remember, they used to be nothing but spindly weeds when we lived in the big house. Look at them now! Tell me the truth, do you see them like this anywhere else? No, child. I'm not going to leave my home and go live with my daughter."

Maria grabbed the bowl of sour cherries and left the room in a hurry, making sure her Singapore Airlines bag was still slung on her shoulder. She went back to the well and reclaimed her silence like the day before. Amber hoped she'd forget, that she could return to her place inside the well that gave her dreams.

She took Nellie for a walk looking for clues of the past. The meadow behind where the vaudeville had once pitched their tent, where she had last seen her unfortunate Aunt Papatya. Nobody had ever heard from her again.

It was now crowded with midincome housing, the shack where Nuria's family lived long gone. Still, the pinion trees thrived, lining both sides of the street leading to the Cordone, the nuts scattered about everywhere, unpicked. Amber showed Nellie how to crack them and eat the nuts.

"Have you ever eaten dirt?"

"What do you mean?"

"I mean when you were little, taste the earth."

"Why would I want to?"

"Never mind."

In the afternoon, they left for Izmir, "for sightseeing," they told Maria. As Amber hugged Maria good-bye, the old woman was vacant, a grayness emanating out of her body, the color of resignation. She smelled of decay. Amber held her, trying to pay back some vitality, but the old woman had withdrawn, unable to receive.

The clouds obscured the sky as if it were going to rain. From a distance Maria looked like a cadaver now, the crone in a Munch painting, in her long black dress and scarf. A terra-cotta water jug in her hand. As is the custom, she poured the water after her guests, divining a smooth journey, fluid as a stream without any impediments. But the water meandered along the cracks of the cobbles, forming tiny rivulets, and evaporated with a hiss almost instantly.

Maria waved her head and arms like a puppet on a string. Amber and Nellie turned the corner toward the ferry landing. They walked a little, then stopped to wet their handkerchiefs at an old street fountain, dripping with sweat.

"Did you hear that?" Amber asked Nellie.

"Yeah, sounded like her, all right."

"I'm going back. It's not right to hold off any longer. I have to tell her."

Maria was still standing where they had left her.

"She'll leave me anyway," Maria said. "I know. If she doesn't go with you, she'll put me in one of those places with decrepit old folks."

"You're imagining things."

"I don't want to be left behind."

"You don't have to worry about that *Anne-Anne.*"

"It's all dirt at the end, anyway. What does it matter? No. I don't want to be left behind. Tell her, tell Camilla, I'll come live with her. He can find me there if he wants to. If he's a spirit, he can go anywhere. My life is spent waiting for him."

So Amber and Nellie stayed on a few more days to help her pack. One of the things Maria said she wanted to do before leaving was to dress the well. She'd never done it but she knew how from watching her mother and the other women in Bornova many times at midsummer.

"We must pick every petal from every flowering plant in the garden. The jasmine, the magnolia, the pomegranates, every single blossom of bougainvillea. Pick all the blossoms until all colors disappeared but green. Pick all and mix them so that you can't tell the scent of gardenia from rose. Jasmine from honeysuckle. Pick them and press them together so their shapes are homogenized and you couldn't tell iris from carnation. This way we make a picture of an offering."

They worked all day long. Longest when the sun was at its zenith. Maria wanted them to pick with their hands instead of clipping with scissors. "That way, they'd break naturally." Some plants disconnected easily but others resisted tearing from their branches, leaving them no choice but to twist and pull, mangling the break. It was violent. Each time, they could hear the flowers cry, they could sense the breaking of their own heart. They tore everything, until all disappeared but the green, and put it in the Singapore Airlines bag for pressing.

"The garden's never been this empty," Maria exclaimed. "Even when I was ill and could no longer tend to the plants that grew wild. Even the last time I picked the flowers, I still left a few so that something would remain for the birds and the bees to make more flowers. Seeds need colors to sprout. Without colors, we die."

"I know."

By late afternoon, they could already smell the fermentation of the blossoms, a sweet vinegar. At sundown, hummingbirds came flocking in, darting into the bougainvillea, not drawn by the magenta blossoms, but from force of habit. They twittered, buzzed, and hummed in the vine, seeking with their sensors the source of honey, which had fed generations of their species. They dared dive blindly into nonexistent floral orifices. They cried out like angry mice first, the whole flock, crescendoing into a lamentful symphony. They were sensing that the plant would no longer bear flowers, and nothing else of sweetness was left in the garden. They were sensing that they had lost their fountain of life and could never return. Their livelihood was gone. By dusk, all the birds were dead from exhaustion.

The House in Izmir

࿐

(1997)

Wherever the changes of my life may lead me in the future, it will remain my spiritual home until I die, a house to which one returns not with the certainty of welcoming human beings, nor familiarity in which every lichen-covered rock and rowan tree show known and reassuring faces.

Gavin Maxwell, *A Ring of Bright Water*

*I*n a sad state of dilapidation and disrepair, the wooden facade rotten with age, the delicate gingerbread pitifully bug-eaten, I had been on my deathbed for a long, long time. Pallid and peeling, worn out by the elements. The latticed balcony dangled in the air at a dangerous incline from the main facade and the rust had eaten the gutters. Some windows were broken; others boarded up just as it had been during the Great War. Without attention and respect for so long, fragile and brittle, not much hope to be resurrected.

The government official who came to inspect a few months ago declared me unsafe and condemned, but the latest owner, a sleazeball in the black-market trade, bribed him into keeping his mouth shut so that he could sell me and cash in.

The afternoon that the FOR SALE sign was plastered all over me, pedestrians shook their heads in disbelief or laughed at my condition. But then the unexpected wand of change. Once-in-a-lifetime kind of thing. As vivid as the day Esma had first arrived here.

Two women stood across the street and stared at me for a long time—one was fortyish, I'd say, the other less than half her age. Something seemed familiar about the older one, something about the way she tilted her head slightly to the right and those strange paisley eyes. If it weren't for her modern clothes and short hair, she was the spitting image of Esma about the time when she passed on.

They stood there, gazing at me, squinting their eyes, in deep contemplation. I could read their lips.

"That's the house, Nellie. Can you believe it, I was born there," she told the younger one, which made me almost jump out of my skin. I'm older than a century but during all these years and numerous occupations, only one child was born inside me—odd since so many women of child-rearing age had passed through. Amber was her name. Intense little girl. This would explain the uncanny resemblance. But why had she come back?

"How sad," Nellie replied. "It looks so unloved now."

"The poor thing. It looks totally abandoned. I don't think anyone's lived here for a long time."

They walked around to the side, passed through the wobbly gate, followed the small path leading to the water landing.

"I was only five when we left but I still dream about this house," Amber explained.

"I can relate to that. I still dream about the house where we lived in Vermont."

Suddenly, inside me, an anxious stirring and something parting the jalousie shutters upstairs, peering out.

The Adonis tree still stood firm. Amber had told Nellie about the old legend. They saw the nightingale perched on the branches, singing a cheerful, welcoming song. It was a tender day.

They sat at the dock all afternoon, looking out at the promenade across the Bay in Cordelio, watching the water traffic. For hours neither of them uttered a word. They watched the last sliver of the sun sink into the Aegean when Nellie reached out and touched her mother's shoulder. "We must go," she said. "It's getting dark. Your grandmother will worry."

Amber stood up and followed Nellie through the side portal but she had that sense of not wanting to part. They crossed the street, heading in the direction of the boat landing.

The nightingale thrashed around in the garden, jumping from branch to branch, singing a beckoning song. *Come back. Come back, the heart of my delight.* Of course, no one could understand the words other than me, except maybe the *jinns* who themselves were beginning to stir with restrained curiosity.

The nightingale leapt out of the Adonis tree and flew across the street—a taboo since the fuses of spirits are connected to their domicile where a strict treaty exists on the boundaries of their territories. Dangerous to cross, dangerous for the house spirits and the outdoor spirits to mingle. War among the spirits, the worst hazard.

She landed on Amber's shoulder.

"What a sweet bird," Nellie said enchanted. "Look, it's as if it's trying to communicate with us."

Then, the bird flew back and perched on the portico and began to sing.

"Sounds just like an old lullaby I used to hear when we lived here. *Dandini, dandini, danali bebek,*" she began humming.

"It's totally weird."

With instant determination, Amber ran across the street. She stopped in front of the sign on the front door.

"Where are you going, mother?" Nellie called back. She caught up with her mother. "What does it say? Condemned?"

"It says, FOR SALE."

Nellie, in a flicker, read her mother's mind. "God," she said, "who'd ever want to buy a dump like this?"

"I'd like to see what shape it's in. The frame looks strong and beautiful."

They sneaked in through the side door, which hung by a single hinge, as the people on the street peered at them suspiciously but refrained from eye contact, making no effort to acknowledge their presence, as if a ghostly secret had veiled their sight.

The back windows were effectively boarded up but one of the doors opening into the cellar gave way. Inside, the walls bulged, the floorboards broken, the windows shattered. Smelled of cat piss, a refuge for the neighborhood strays—skinny toms with enormous balls dangling from side to side, pregnant females rubbing their scent on the posts. A fresh litter of blind devilish black kittens shrieking.

"It's odd," Amber said. "This culture that once castrated men, that made eunuchs would not consider doing the same to their cats. All those litters of poor kittens we see at street corners, huddled together at busy intersections. Makes me so sad."

They opened the doors to various storage rooms. "And here is the little dungeon where they'd send me when I didn't eat my food, where parents' will dominated children's desires. There's no such thing as an empty room, you know?"

They began climbing up the uneven steps but the door leading up was bolted shut. So they returned to the street.

Amber's hands were unsteady like an old woman's as she jutted down the phone number on the "For Sale" sign.

"When are we going back to San Francisco?" Nellie asked.

"When the time is right," Amber replied. "Tomorrow, I want to come back with the realtor and look inside."

"You're not thinking what I'm afraid you're thinking, are you?"

"Maybe I am. I don't know what I'm going to do now that you'll be off to college. I can't continue living the same old life, trying to fill the missing gap. Anyway, did I ever tell you that my grandmother Esma had paid for this house with a twenty-five-carat sapphire?"

"You might be able to get it for a pair of Adidas now."

"Come on. Be a good sport."

⌇

That night is indescribable. The *jinns* came out of every crack, every crevice that still existed. The ghosts, the sirens, the imaginary people, all of them, even the Red Woman cracking her bones. Every broom and mop became alive. In a mad flurry they washed and scrubbed, dusted and polished, repaired and restored everything. Infused me with life juice, all was sparkling clean by sunrise.

They arrived at ten past ten, Amber, Nellie, and the last owner—a man named Firuzi. He unbolted the boards on the front entrance and led them in.

"Strange. It feels different than the way I remember leaving it," he told them. "Maybe the *jinns* have been awake all night long, cleaning and tidying it up." Demonic laughter.

"Looks different inside than the way I remember," Amber told Nellie. "The house that appeared in my recurrent dreams was much smaller. Much paler."

"You always said, a house is not a home until you've lived in it."

Amber shuffled from room to room like an apparition. She was wearing a cracked-cotton dress, easy for traveling. Nellie followed her in long strides. She was a tall young woman, slim, with long blond hair. She did not resemble any of the other İpekçi women. Except for the trademark paisley eyes.

"The ceilings seem much lower; the rooms much smaller," Amber continued. "Memory plays weird tricks. But I've been right about the light. Absolutely. Look at the way it funnels in between the tall facade and the obsidian, hitting those dented white marble slabs on the kitchen floor. As if it's bouncing back shadows of memory."

In the *hamam*, a pool of rain water had collected that leaked from the cracked skylight. For a fleeting moment Amber caught the reflection of Esma's face in the puddle, which she recognized from the photographs she'd seen of her. When she blinked, the face was gone. She recalled the sensation the previous day that had compelled her to return. The nightingale singing the tune to the old lullaby.

"Are there ghosts in the house?" she asked the man.

"Nah. I lived here for years, and nothing. It's a normal house."

"It needs a lot of work. It hasn't been maintained."

"It's an old house, lady. You can't expect much. Here we don't build houses to last more than a decade. This one's been around more than a century. What does that tell you?"

"What happened to the fourth and fifth floors? " Amber asked.

"It has never had any more than three floors."

How was it then that my parents had the fifth floor with a roof terrace from where I'd throw things on the street just to see where they would land? Amber wondered. She did not argue with the man. She did not want him to know her history.

A few hours later, it was a done deal. There were no real estate agents. No title companies, mortgage brokers. The balding man with the pot belly took the notarized papers. Amber counted ten billion liras in thousand-lira pieces—roughly seven thousand dollars—the amount she had won from the design competition. Heaps of banknotes delivered in a suitcase as in the movies. They shook hands. He left.

"You're crazy, mom," Nellie told her. "Think of all we could have done with so much money."

"Cheap price, for a good story," Amber smiled. "So many good stories here. It's my past, Nellie. Don't be disrespectful."

When they were alone, she took out her cell phone and dialed a number. Camilla's hello stretched like taffy on the other end, her unforgettable voice hardened with age and cigarettes.

"Hi, Mom."

"Why haven't you called me before!"

"We've been real busy."

"You were supposed to come back yesterday."

"I know but you'll never guess what happened."

"What? Is my mother all right?"

"She's fine. It's me. Well, I bought a house."

"What are you talking about?"

"The house in Izmir, the one we lived in, where I was born. You know the one in Karataş. Well, I bought it with my award money."

"You what?"

"I bought the house in Smyrna."

Camilla drooled a chain of incomprehensible nuggets. "Are you an imbecile? If you want to have a place in this country buy a nice new condo, not a ruin. God knows, we have plenty of those. You should come to your senses before it's too late, Amber."

"It is too late. I've already paid for it, signed the papers. I don't want a nice new condo. I want the house I was born in. In time, I'll restore it. After all, I didn't become an architect for nothing."

"You want a headache? You got one. It will collapse and crush you between its floors. You'll become a corpse in its cistern. Not to mention the ghosts . . ."

"What ghosts? There are no ghosts, you always told me when I was a child, when I saw things. I thought you didn't believe in the invisibles."

"Maybe I didn't but strange things in that house. Everyone said there were ghosts."

"I'm dying to meet them, then."

A long silence followed, then Camilla asked, "Did you talk to my mother about the eviction?"

"She's miserable but she's agreed to come and live with you."

"She talked to you?"

"Yes, she talks just fine."

"I can't believe it! She never said a word to me for more than a whole year!"

"Well, you said it would take a miracle. I guess it did. I didn't even have to tell her the truth after all. She decided on her own to come and live with you."

Camilla was sobbing at the other end.

"It's all right, mother. I'm sure she'll talk to you now."

"That's not why I'm crying. Something else. Something terrible, Amber."

"What? What happened?"

"Aida."

"What? Tell me."

"We're telling everyone that she had a heart attack but she really threw herself off her balcony. Seven stories."

"Oh my God. She jumped?"

"She jumped. She fell on the neon sign above the boutique and was electrocuted."

They were silent for a long time. Outside, perched on the Adonis tree, the nightingale was singing a mourning song.

"Was she sober?" Amber asked.

"We don't know. Maybe something in her medication pushed her over the edge. They found all kinds of pills at her bedside. She was preparing for it, no doubt. Notes all over her house about what to do in the event of her death, what to do with her things, who should get what. Obvious, she'd been plotting for some time, unable to cope with the agony of aging. She couldn't endure ugliness. Not Aida. No, she didn't die of the fall. She died of *chagrin d'amour*. Like your grandma Esma."

"I don't think so. That's not the way she'd choose to go. Not Aida. They're sure there was no foul play or anything?"

"Positive. A horrible mess though. She was unrecognizable."

"The Aida I know would have taken sugar-coated pink pills or drunk hemlock tea. She'd dress in something sexy and lay herself down pretty on a bed with flowers and other lovely things. Not smash her cartilage on a ton of concrete."

"That was before she lost her face. You know how she hated the way she looked. You know that. You know that better than anyone else. You saw her and you told me yourself. In fact, she hated her face so much, she must have poured vitriol on it before jumping off. Her face was already gone when they found her. It's a blessing they don't display the dead here like you do in America. No beautician could put her back together."

Camilla continued sobbing. Amber felt a soothing touch on her shoulder. She couldn't cry. No tears came. "When is her funeral?" she asked.

"We buried her yesterday," Camilla sighed. "The head of

the armed forces sent an enormous wreath of gladiolas. And all the other big generals. The prime minister. Foreign military attachés. They all came. I've never seen so many wreaths. You'd think royalty had died or something. We buried her in the new cemetery, all by herself. You know, the General is buried in the old one, the one where your father is, in the family plot but Aida was mugged there once when she went to visit him. She said, if they mug a live person think of what they can do to the dead. I won't allow them to dig me out to steal my teeth. So she bought a new lot at the new cemetery in a nice, clean part of the city, where the lawn is like astroturf, forever green. There are always guards looking after people, watering the flowers, and lots of room between the graves."

"Has anyone told Teoman?"

"No, he'd gone to Aphrodisias for an archaeological dig. We couldn't get hold of him."

"I have to find him. He'll be devastated. Why didn't you call me right away? When it happened?"

"What's the point? We bury our dead immediately, as you may remember. Besides, I didn't want to spoil your trip. You had enough problems dealing with my mother. Anyway, you're in Aida's will. She left you seven billion liras and some belongings."

⸙

A week later, as Amber and Nellie lay exhausted from cleaning and scrubbing, Aida's goods had arrived in a large crate. It took four men to carry it into the room that had once belonged to Esma and later had become Amber's nursery.

Inside the crate was Süleyman's wardrobe—once again finding its way back to this room. It was loaded with shoe boxes, the contents carefully marked. One contained a long hairpiece. Another, Esma's medallion with Süleyman's picture; then Iskender's ivory cane in which he had smuggled the *Bombyx mori,* the silk moth; the butterfly tray the General had brought back from Korea. One was marked for Nellie; inside, Aida's *crepe d'amour* dress with the famous stain.

Amber sorted through the contents, reliving the history of her family. Pictures of Cadri and Aladdin during circumcision, gorgeous Aida in her famous costumes—most in the municipal museum now—always posing. The days of the İpekçi family's glory came alive with a fine cast of characters. Pictures of their many homes—the plantation on Mount Olympus. The house in Moda. The Spinster's Apartment. Country outings with servants, mules, camels, water buffaloes. Hunting parties. Lambs on spits. Dancing bears. Engagements, weddings, circumcisions. Fragments.

One of the shoe boxes contained pictures of Aida and the General. Another was marked Atatürk. His monogrammed handkerchief—the one he had given Aida to wipe her tears of excitement—kept in a silk sachet. Photos of the beauty contest, the crowning. The wand and the coronet. The finalists with Atatürk. Aida in an astrakhan coat, sitting on the hood of the Daimler. Aida in a riding outfit next to Atatürk's racehorse. A little girl giving a bouquet of flowers to Aida while Atatürk stands behind her. Aida and Atatürk dancing. A buxom, plump, luscious Aida, with flawless skin and apple face, encased in a slinky satin gown, sleeveless, droopy shoulders, narrow hips, a flared skirt, just like the kind Jean Harlow would wear, which suggested a peach color although the photograph was black and white. His hair was slicked back, his classic profile focused singularly on Aida, who was beaming at the camera. (Barely discernible in the background, the lieutenant, the barber's son, his already bushy eyebrows pointed like number eight of the Arabic alphabet, behind a veil of cigarette smoke—obsessed with the woman and forever loyal to his general.)

Many faces of Aida flashed in Amber's memory—laughing and flirting coquettishly. Her voice flowing like a brook. But most vividly, the way she looked the last time Amber saw her on Essence of Honey Street. Camilla had said that you only remember people's dead faces. Not the way before, not the way they looked when they were young and attractive. It's best not to look at dead people.

The sweet kiss of Azrael had landed on Aida's Y-shaped vein. No matter what, the end of an iris is not pretty.

Amber opened another envelope. Her heart raced at a speed her body could not withstand. She tried breathing slowly.

Nellie found her distressed like that. "What's the matter? All you all right, Mom?"

"Nellie," she said, "draw me a bath. Please."

"There's no hot water."

"I'll take a cold bath. In fact that's exactly what I need. To chill out."

What Amber had discovered inside the box was a stack of letters on fine vellum, now slightly gone to seed, carrying an important signature—the handwriting of the man who had saved the country. The hero of heroes. The handsome man with the blond mustache. Letters no one knew existed. National treasures.

She looked out the window, seeing her first vision. The Aegean alive with history. The Adonis tree with her initials carved on it. ASI. She reached inside her pocket and pulled out the amber egg. A hand came out of the rock, holding a golden cocoon. The silk moth. *Bombyx mori.* She wondered whether the same ghosts still haunted the place, existing in another dimension still as children or, like herself, grown into maturity. She wondered if babies were still hidden in stork's nests. She heard the nightingale chirping the same old lullaby. *Dandini, dandini, danali bebek.*

She looked at the sea and recalled her first memory of its ebb and flow and how, after that, she could not exist unless she found the same motion again. The importance of the color blue in healing the soul and vastness of the blue. She thought how strange it was that she was sitting here, in her first room. The room where Esma and Süleyman had made love. Where babies were conceived. Where Esma had died. Where Cadri and Camilla cajoled with her. Ayşe and Gonca. The room that had been her nursery. Right here, with the faded and torn wallpaper with camellias on a teal background, so old that it was impossible anymore to identify the flowers.

The doors opened on the walls, blank canvases with no pictures, only faces of invisible people, whispering, laughing, cursing, reflecting dreams within dreams within dreams. Apparitions, sirenic lullabies, characters out of books and movies seemed to joust. In the dim hallways, the cellar, the attic, an endless shadow play parading from room to room, mingling and materializing everywhere. Her senses were full of this populus and all she had to do was to reach; she could touch them.

Why had she bought me? What was she going to do with me as an architect? She had to have a vision in her head. She had to have plans. Would she tear me down and replace me? Would she remodel the interior in a modern style? Or try to restore me to the way I was when I was first built? Could she become part of my life once again? I didn't yet know any of these things. But felt a strange sense of fate. Maybe it was written on her forehead, as they say here.

"No matter how hard we try, we cannot escape when change calls on us," Amber muttered to herself. Everything seemed to be changing now to accommodate her destiny. She decided to leap, not knowing whether she could fly.

"I own the house I was born in," she said out loud as if that would make it more real. "A dilapidated mess that could not be saved but I'll try to restore it anyway. I wonder what would happen to my life if I stayed here? I mean the life it took me more than twenty years to conjure up in another country. The stories I made up. All my other houses, friends, lovers. My curriculum vitae. My drawings—the tangible evidence of my existence. The language?

"What would it feel like to abandon one's existence, one's place, and go into another—in the middle of things, like this, not by mitigating circumstances but by one's own choice? I remember once, going through a dark night of the soul when Süleyman had talked to me of transubstantiation. He described it as completely leaving this life behind, waking up in another one. It seemed like a good solution until he told me that the only catch was, you had no recollection of the life you came from. You started over in total oblivion."

Of course, Nellie would be a reminder as she had always been. She'd accompanied Amber all the way back, kept her company, reminding her of her identity, the one that had taken years to forge, preventing her straying off. She felt grounded now, had her bearings. The past of her own choosing. Nellie could leave now if she wanted to, Amber could manage on her own.

"I'd always love your company but it may be time for your own walkabout. Besides, my real home is also in California now. This is just my spiritual home."

And Camilla, after what happened to Aida, Camilla would never want to leave Essence of Honey Street.

"My plants, my plants," she'd say. "I just cannot leave them behind. You understand, don't you, Amber?"

"Yes, I understand, mother."

"I cannot leave Maria behind either."

"Yes, of course."

"She'll live with me full time now. It's my duty. I must abide by it."

And Maria? It didn't matter to her all that much whether she went to Istanbul to live with her daughter, to America, or the moon. Amber had invited her to live here but Maria had refused—too full of associations. "It's an İpekçi house, not a Taşpinar," she'd said. Nothing could replace the turquoise cottage, her well, and the ghost of her husband who left her a hundred *kuruş* every night by the gardenias. Maria, who lived in a lost century with her spirits and entered that realm every day, who had never really crossed into this age. Who kept returning to a time that existed only in her memory.

She'd asked Amber what it was like to fly in an airplane. "Is it turbulent? Does it shake? Does it shake violently in the air?"

"No," Amber had told her, "it doesn't shake at all. You don't even know you're moving. It's a very smooth ride. Like floating in a *cayique* on a calm day but instead you are moving in the sky. You look out the window and see the clouds below you. Then, the door opens and you're in a different place far away."

"The way death must feel."

"Your bath is ready," Nellie called out. "You sure you want to do this? You may get pneumonia."

"You sound like my mother," Amber smiled.

"Well, we're kinda related, you know."

Amber sat in front of the worn marble sink and poured a pitcher of cold water over her shoulders. Goosebumps spread all over her flesh. How lucky am I to have choices, she thought. How lucky.

The muezzin's voice rose in the air. The nightingale sang a song of acceptance. A bus went by.

ACKNOWLEDGMENTS

In parts of Turkey, where I spent my childhood, the birds were believed to be spirits. My parents told me that my grandmother had become a nightingale after she died.

A few years ago, on a Christmas morning, I went into my study to write something new. I stared at the emptiness of the white paper for a long time. My mind was blank. I had nothing to say, as if a "bird had eaten my tongue." I was looking out of the enormous picture window at the rolling hills with ancient oaks, when from out of nowhere, a bird came flying directly toward me, crashed with an enormous thud, and died instantly.

It was still warm when I found it, a small falcon that I identified as a merlin, not a bird indigenous to Northern California where I live. Neither was this place on its migratory pattern.

The bird's death had aroused a great deal of emotion and I cried. I looked again at the emptiness of the white paper and suddenly words and tales came to life, flowing with unusual ease. I stayed in the room for a week and wrote ceaselessly. When I came out on the first day of the New Year, I had several pads full of words, the first draft of a novel.

Among the letters awaiting me was one from my mother who lives in Ankara. She said this was the most difficult letter of her life. My father had died unexpectedly of a heart attack in the late afternoon on Christmas day. He was sitting at his desk, drafting a letter to me. My mother had preferred to write than to call me to break the news, in order to retard the grief.

My father had died when the merlin had crashed itself against my window. Who is to know if this was merely a coincidence, or for that matter what coincidences really are?

The pads were put in a drawer to remain there untouched for seven years. When I finally had the courage to read them, they grew into *Seven Houses.*

I wish I'd been able to share this book with him. But then, perhaps, it might never have been written. Every book is a great collaboration and for this one I credit my grandmothers Maria and Zehra, Grandpapa Hamid, Uncle Aladdin, Aunt Ayhan, and, of course, my parents, Sadri and Yümniye, for giving me the yarns to spin.

For other writers and friends who encouraged me— Suzanne Lipsett, Vicky Doubleday, Nancy Van Norman Baer, Joan Baribault, Isabel Allende, Alice Walker, Susan Griffin, Kathryn Neville, Fatema Mernissi, Angie Thieriot, Carol Tarlow, Tracy Bernstein, my agents Bonnie Nadell and Jane Judd, my publisher Judith Curr and editor Rosemary Ahern, and many other kind people who remain behind the scenes, whose names remain unknown.

Thanks to Josh and Patty for being in my life and, as always, to Robert who is still stoking the fire, writing the love notes, and making the coffee.